Also by Antti Tuomainen and available from Orenda Books:
The Mine
The Man Who Died
Palm Beach, Finland
Little Siberia
The Rabbit Factor

ABOUT THE AUTHOR

Finnish Antti Tuomainen was an award-winning copywriter when he made his literary debut in 2007 as a suspense author. In 2011, Tuomainen's third novel, *The Healer*, was awarded the Clue Award for Best Finnish Crime Novel and was shortlisted for the Glass Key Award. In 2013, the Finnish press crowned Tuomainen the 'King of Helsinki Noir' when *Dark as My Heart* was published. With a piercing and evocative style, Tuomainen was one of the first to challenge the Scandinavian crime-genre formula, and his poignant, dark and hilarious *The Man Who Died* became an international bestseller, shortlisting for the Petrona and Last Laugh Awards. *Palm Beach, Finland* (2018) was an immense success, with *The Times* calling Tuomainen 'the funniest writer in Europe', and *Little Siberia* (2019) was shortlisted for the Capital Crime/Amazon Publishing Readers Awards, the Last Laugh Award and the CWA International Dagger, and won the Petrona Award for Best Scandinavian Crime Novel.

The Rabbit Factor, the prequel to *The Moose Paradox*, will soon be a major motion picture starring Steve Carell for Amazon Studios.

Follow Antti on Twitter @antti_tuomainen, or on Facebook: facebook.com/AnttiTuomainen.

ABOUT THE TRANSLATOR

David Hackston is a British translator of Finnish and Swedish literature and drama. Notable recent publications include Kati Hiekkapelto's Anna Fekete series (published by Orenda Books), Katja Kettu's wartime epic *The Midwife*, Pajtim Statovci's enigmatic debut *My Cat Yugoslavia* and its follow-up, *Crossing*, and Maria Peura's coming-of-age novel *At the Edge of Light*. He has also translated Antti Tuomainen's *The Mine*, *The Man Who Died*, *Palm Beach*, *Finland*, *Little Siberia* and *The Rabbit Factor* (all published by Orenda Books). In 2007 he was awarded the Finnish State Prize for Translation. David is also a professional countertenor and a founding member of the English Vocal Consort of Helsinki. Follow David on Twitter @Countertenorist.

The Moose Paradox

ANTTI TUOMAINEN

Translated from the Finnish by David Hackston

ORENDA
BOOKS

Orenda Books
16 Carson Road
West Dulwich
London SE21 8HU
www.orendabooks.co.uk

First published in the United Kingdom by Orenda Books, 2022
Originally published in Finland as *Hirvikaava* by Otava, 2021
Copyright © Antti Tuomainen, 2021
English language translation copyright © David Hackston, 2022

A catalogue record for this book is available from the British Library.

Hardback ISBN 978-1-914585-34-0
B-Format Paperback ISBN 978-1-914585-35-7
eISBN 978-1-914585-36-4

Typeset in Garamond by typesetter.org.uk
Printed and bound by CPI Group (UK) Ltd, Croydon CR0 4YY

Orenda Books is grateful for the financial support of FILI, who provided a
translation grant for this project.

For sales and distribution, please contact *info@orendabooks.co.uk*

For Anu

NOW

The new budget forecast is ready by half past ten. Because of the rapidly changing circumstances, I've had to cut our expenditure even more radically and cancel a number of investments that we had previously agreed upon; but I have tightened the belt equally, spreading the burden across all our departments. I have lowered my own salary to zero. Separately, I have drawn up a plan to create a financial buffer in case of an emergency, so that a situation like the current one – not to mention the recent threat of wholesale bankruptcy – will never happen again. Building up a buffer like this requires patience and frugality over many years, but the chances of it paying off one day will be greatly increased. The numbers speak for themselves: if we work systematically and trust in the facts, we will survive. This I know from personal experience.

Mathematics has saved my life, both figuratively and literally. This is what mathematics does: it saves us. It brings balance, clarity and peace of mind; it helps us see how things really are, it tells us what we should do in order to reach our goals. Though the current situation at the adventure park is challenging, I still believe that the future is bright, and it's all thanks to mathematics – and a little bit of effort. Of course, my views and feelings about this have re-configured slightly, mostly because I've been able to dedicate myself to the data and have been left to calculate things in peace.

The last customers left the park a while ago, and, according to the rota, today Kristian has locked everything up. During the daytime, the background noise in the park is like the rush of crashing waves. Now the sea has calmed, and everything is perfectly still.

I go through the Excel file one more time. The rows flow beautifully, complement one another, and the sums are correct. I notice I'm not so much checking things as going through them one more time, simply for my own pleasure. Perhaps this is just what I need after all the recent twists and turns and surprises: good old-fashioned arithmetic, clarifying and illuminating matters and the relationships between them. I have to remind myself that Schopenhauer needs his supper and maybe even someone to talk to (which, while not entirely unprecedented, is, statistically speaking, a much rarer occurrence), and I click the file shut. I stand up from my chair and blink my dry eyes; I can almost feel how red they are.

The door into the corridor is open, and I can't hear anything coming from Minttu K's room either: neither her rough, ratchety voice on the phone nor the radio, let alone a low-pitched snore infused with cigarettes and gin *lonkero*. My back feels stiff, and again I am reminded that I really ought to take up some kind of exercise, though I have no idea when I would find the time. I'm coming to realise there's no rest for the director of a successful adventure park.

I stare out of the window for a moment and see nothing but the empty, November-grey car park in front of me. Suddenly my attention is drawn to the furthest left-hand edge of the car park. It takes a few seconds for my brain to process what I see. The spot is right between two streetlamps, each pool of light barely touching the metal and the rubber, and this is why it takes a little while to put the shapes and contours together.

A bicycle.

It is propped on its kickstand, and in every respect it looks like a very average bicycle, parked and waiting for its owner. What seems somewhat out of the ordinary, however, is the bike's location, which cannot be considered remotely sensible: it is far away both from the road and from the main entrance to the park. In fact, it is far away from everything. I look at it a moment longer, unsure what I'm expecting to see. The bicycle is parked in the half-light. Eventually, I come to the obvious conclusion: someone has simply left it there.

I switch off my computer, take my scarf and coat from the stand and pull them on. I switch off the lights in my office and walk across the dusky main hall to the back door. I don't want to use the front door because opening and closing it again would require a complex series of checks and double-checks. The back door is quicker and handier.

I step out onto the loading bay, take the metallic steps down to ground level and set off around the building. I can hear the roar of traffic in the distance, and my own steps sound almost amplified.

The night air has that crisp, late-autumn note to it, and the earth is wet even without the rain. I arrive at the corner of the building, where I have a view of the full length of its left-hand wall, and the left side of the car park. This is the narrowest strip of the park's grounds. From the outer wall, it is only about five metres before the asphalt comes to an end and the terrain dips steeply down into a ditch, then rises up just as steeply at the edge of a small stretch of tangled woodland on the other side. I walk alongside the wall, and the strip feels more narrow and corridor-like with every step, as though the adjoining woodland were a united front, growing in strength and tightening its grip on the building with small, inexorable steps. Of course, this isn't literally true. What is true, however – though at first I think my eyes must be playing tricks on me – is that the bicycle has now disappeared.

Perhaps someone simply had a spot of acute, late-night business to attend to in the woods. We're all different, as I've come to appreciate on many occasions. If you have something to take care of, something you might not necessarily do elsewhere, then here, in a spruce forest in the middle of Vantaa, you can do it to your heart's content – spend a moment of time in your thicket of choice, before continuing on your way, the richer for it. But these thoughts are like matchsticks that won't quite light; they flare up only to go out right away. I'm indulging in wishful thinking, and I know it.

Then I see him.

A man running right towards me.

Like a bowling ball with legs, I think to myself.

And, in fact, it is in a bowling alley of sorts that we find ourselves. The strip of tarmac is long and narrow, and the bowling ball is hurtling towards me at a ferocious pace, right in the middle of the alley – and I am standing at the end. On top of this, the ball seems to be speeding up. I turn as soon as I realise what's happening. I set off running, and at the same moment I see that the corner of the building and the back yard are much further away than I had estimated.

I'm still stiff from all the hours sitting at my desk. The bowling ball's speed is quite simply greater than mine, I realise this from the very first step. But I have to run.

I quickly glance over my shoulder. The bowling ball is wearing a dark-blue tracksuit, a black or blue hoodie and a black woolly hat pulled almost right down over its face. Its short little legs look like something out of a cartoon, where the legs are replaced with a wildly spinning tornado. Arms punctuate its frantic run like a pair of pistons on overdrive. If this were any other situation, I would stand there watching the bowling ball's acceleration out of sheer fascination. Instead, I run as fast as I possibly can, and still I can hear the whirring machine gaining on me.

The corner is just up ahead.

The loading bay is right around the corner. At the other end of the loading bay is a ladder leading up to the roof. I can't think of anything else. If I can just reach the foot of the ladder and start climbing, I'll be able to kick at the fingers of anyone trying to climb up behind me. Naturally, this is a far from optimal solution. It's hard to think of many alternative scenarios, let alone consider which of them is the best choice, because the ball is rolling ever closer, and I am the tenpin.

I'm nearing the corner, it's only fifteen metres away. I reach the corner and change course.

I run towards the loading bay, only a few more steps until the steel stairs. I reach the foot of the stairs and start climbing up to the loading bay, one rattling rung at a time. I see the ladder in front of me and think I might just reach the lowest rung and make it up to the roof when...

The bowling ball slams into my back.

The impact knocks me forwards, as though someone has flung me up into the air. I slump face first to the latticed floor of the loading bay. I try to stand up, but I can't. Instead, a horse appears on my back. At least, that's what it feels like, as though rider and ridee have suddenly changed place.

The bowling ball presses down on my back, gripping my head in its hands – its cold fingers, stubby but strong, against my temples – then it lifts my head up ... and slams it right down again.

My forehead strikes the steel grille once, twice, thrice. I hear a dull metallic sound ringing in my ears and vibrating through my body. I grip the man's wrists, but they are thick and sturdy as pipes buried in the ground, which means I can't stop their movement. My forehead is battered against the grille over and over. When my head rises again, or, rather, when it is yanked upwards, ahead and to the left I see some wooden planks that I've been using to mend the Strawberry Maze.

I stretch out my arm, elongating my entire upper body, and

manage to grab hold of an L-shaped length of wood. I pull it closer, inch by inch, and eventually clasp my fingers tightly around it. At the same time, my forehead is still being thwacked against the steel floor, and I get the distinct impression that the steel will soon give way under the force of the blows. There isn't much time. I grip the plank as firmly as I can, make a quick assessment of the length of the bowling ball's back and the position of its head, and fling my arm backwards with all the strength I can muster.

As it lands, the sound the plank makes is surprising. It's soft and wet.

The ball's fingers release their grip and the horse on my back wobbles. I push myself up, and the horse staggers again, a little more violently this time, and I manage to crawl out from underneath it. I move my legs, stand up, and my first thought is that I ought to start running again. But that's not what happens. The beating my head has taken causes me considerable dizziness, and I have to move in careful, fumbling steps. I glance over my shoulder. The bowling ball is staring at something in his fingers, then he looks at me and holds up the focus of his attention for me to see. A tooth. It quickly dawns on me exactly where my wooden hammer struck him.

Square in the mouth.

The bowling ball throws the tooth from his hand. It arches through the air and disappears into the darkness. He wipes his bloody mouth on the back of his sleeve. Then he lunges at me again. I turn and dash into a sprint. Another mismatched bout of wrestling will be too much for me, I know that. But I run all the same, and it's only ten or so metres to the foot of the ladder. Every step requires the utmost concentration. Maybe that's why I haven't noticed that a third person has appeared on the loading bay too.

This new arrival is wearing a balaclava and is approaching me from the dark end of the loading bay. The balaclava first runs towards me then changes tack, and I can see he is trying to pass me.

A lot happens in the next two and a half seconds.

The bowling ball is about to catch up with me again; now he is only an arm's length away. The balaclava is approaching from the opposite direction, out of the darkness behind me, so it's likely that the bowling ball hasn't seen him.

As he runs forwards, the balaclava crouches down, snatches up the strawberry, and finally reaches me.

The strawberry in the balaclava's hands is part of the Strawberry Maze. It's a decoration, the same one I brought out here earlier this afternoon to take apart and put the pieces in two separate recycling bins, the plastic with the plastic and the metallic parts with the metal. It has a diameter of around sixty centimetres, and I've removed it from the park because it is broken and its cracked edges might injure the children.

I try to change direction, but this only makes me stumble and partially turn around. And then I see what happens next.

The balaclava and the bowling ball collide at full pelt. It might be more correct to say that the balaclava strikes the bowling ball with the strawberry, bringing it crashing down on his head. Or, to be even more precise, I should say that the bowling ball slams into the strawberry. The plastic cracks even further, and the bowling ball's head disappears inside the strawberry.

The strawberry becomes lodged around the man's shoulders, and the whole thing looks like a giant cochineal crown with a tuft of green hair on top. At the same time, the sharp straggles of steel wire cut into the man's neck, specifically his jugular. Which tears open. And the result of all this is...

...a strawberry-headed man staggering to regain his balance on the loading bay with a fountain of blood gushing from his neck.

I feel dizzy, my ears are rushing, and the only way I can remain upright is by gripping my knees for support. I assume there are several reasons for the dizziness: lack of oxygen, the sustained pummelling of my forehead against the steel grille and the gruesome sight in front of me. It's as though I'm watching a complex magic trick that has gone wrong somewhere along the line, or perhaps even an attempt at some kind of world record.

The man is clearly bewildered, a little discombobulated – who wouldn't be, after getting lodged inside a plastic strawberry and sustaining a deep laceration to the neck? And his subsequent actions aren't at all sensible. His arms are flailing here and there, and he seems to jump up and down on the spot, though what he really should do is...

The balaclava takes a few steps towards him, says something I can't hear, then approaches the man, his hands outstretched in what I assume is an attempt to help him. Perhaps the man hears the approaching footsteps and fatally misreads the situation. Either that, or something else makes him panic, and he suddenly spins round 180 degrees and bursts into a run.

My strawberry-headed assailant dashes across the loading bay, sputtering blood as he goes, his legs moving like little propellers.

The balaclava runs after him and shouts something again. It looks as though the man is speeding up. Then, only a few steps later, the strawberry starts to sway, and the orbit of the swaying motion increases with every step. The balaclava is about to catch up with him when the final sway makes any kind of assistance virtually impossible. The man dives from the bay into the night.

For a brief moment he flies through the glare of the streetlamps, the strawberry gleams, the blood spurts a red rainbow through the air, his legs paddle hard...

Then all the variables change at once.

Gravity has the last word.

The adventure park could be seen from afar. It was a brightly coloured, red-yellow-and-orange box, in size somewhere between Stockmann's department store and an average airport terminal. It was almost two hundred metres in length, stood fifteen metres tall, and on its roof in giant lettering was the park's name: YouMeFun. Right now, the wistful, beautiful November sunlight struck the sign, bathing the car park the size of three football pitches in gold and lending a soft sheen to the great mass of tin and steel standing proudly behind it.

I stopped at the traffic lights, looked up at the adventure park across the road and thought once again that something really was different.

Something had changed and changed for good.

This was my park, I thought to myself. The thought gave me strength. I had almost died trying to save this park. I had steered it out from under a mountain of debt, and though it might not be profitable yet, at least, in all probability, it would be a survivor.

Only six months ago I'd been forced to resign from my job as an actuary at a leading insurance company. I was faced with choosing between a change in my job description that would have seen me moving into a broom cupboard to conduct an endless stream of meaningless pseudo-calculations or taking part in an emotion-oriented, time-dynamic training programme, not to mention group yoga sessions. But only a moment after handing in my resignation, I learnt that my brother had passed away and

that I had inherited his adventure park. Upon arrival at said
adventure park, I learnt that I had inherited my brother's considerable debts too, debts that he had taken out with an assortment of
hard-boiled criminals. One thing led to another, and to save my
own life, the jobs of the staff, and the park itself, I had to resort to
some radical acts of self-defence, and as a result of this one of the
gangsters died after finding himself on the receiving end of the
kinetic intersection between me and a giant plastic rabbit's ear, I
ended up opening a payday-loan operation, then quickly running
it down again, I met an artist who aroused feelings I had hitherto
never experienced, I had to avoid both the crooks and the police
and witness an event that still makes me nervously fumble with
my neck.

After all this, the park's financial situation was still tough. There
was no other word for it.

I'd already resorted to numerous money-saving measures, and
I suspected there would be more of them down the line. I'd tried
to lead by example in every respect. My salary was already lower
than anybody else's, and I paid for my lunch and snacks myself at
the park's main eatery, the Curly Cake Café. I didn't want to cut
the other employees' salaries, but obviously I'd been forced to take
a closer look at budget allocations for each department. This
initially met with some resistance, but I defended my solutions
with a series of carefully compiled spreadsheets and stressed to the
staff at every turn that we had to look at things over a five- to ten-
year timeframe. This was greeted with silence. Which, in turn,
gave me the chance to outline my money-saving proposals in more
detail, ranging from the largescale (energy saving: the ambient
temperature in the main hall was now on average one and a half
degrees cooler than a month ago. Naturally, the children haven't
noticed the change, and I've provided the staff with warm
sweatshirts sporting the park's logo) to the smaller scale (I

repainted the Loopy Ladder in Caper Castle by myself, which is evident in the splashes of paint on the wall behind it, but the saving was not insignificant).

I crossed the road and walked into the car park. My mood improved with every step because all the pieces were finally falling into place, both in general and individually, in the long term and on a day-by-day basis. The equation was beginning to take shape. All was well.

This was my life now. And most importantly of all, my life was orderly again.

A series of brisk steps brought me to the main entrance, the sliding doors slid open and I stepped into the foyer, which was well lit and decorated in bright colours. This was always the point at which I felt like I was stepping into another world, and something akin to that happened now too. Alongside this, another feeling appeared too, one that I recognised right away. I realised that I felt at home. Was that what all this was about – that this adventure park had become a home from home?

Kristian was standing behind the ticket counter, handing a set of tickets to a tired-looking man trying to shepherd three shorter customers, all actively pulling in different directions. The man took his tickets, turned reluctantly, herded his flock, and together they all disappeared inside the main hall.

I bade Kristian good morning. I expected to see that broad, eager smile of his and to hear him give some variation on the theme of how fabulous or magnificent this particular morning was.

'Morning,' he said politely and continued staring at his computer screen.

Kristian was highly effective in his role as sales manager, and on the whole he was extraordinarily enthusiastic. He was in the habit of calling me and sending me messages, even outside of work hours. *Hi Boss, there's a SUPER-AMAZING surprise here waiting for you!!!* he might text, though upon arrival at the park I would learn that this super-amazing surprise was nothing more than the release of a new flavour of ice cream at the self-service counter at the Curly Cake Café. For Kristian, every day was a great day, and he never tired of telling me so. Now, however, he stood sullenly clicking his mouse. The clicks sounded like nervous little fillips. I glanced over my shoulder. There was no queue at the counter. By the volume of cars parked outside, I concluded that we had a moderate number of customers right now, just as one would expect on an unremarkable Wednesday morning in November.

'What a fantastic morning,' I heard myself saying and realised that the words came out of my mouth precisely because I hadn't heard them from anyone else.

'What?' asked Kristian. It was only now that he looked at me properly. He made eye contact with me, but his gaze was somehow unfocussed, as though while looking at me he had forbidden himself from actually seeing me. I was about to ask if there was anything troubling him, something pulling him closer and closer to the screen in front of him – he was stretching his neck in a most unnatural fashion – when I noticed the large clock in the park's foyer.

I was at the start of the Komodo Locomotive, and it was already eleven o'clock. The Komodo Locomotive was one of our oldest rides, a perennial favourite among our younger clientele. It was also one of the safest rides we had, suitable for those who weren't even old enough to ask to get in it. To increase security further, we had decided to install additional airbags in each of the seats. I thought this a bit over the top, but Esa was the park's head of security, and he believed we should prepare for any eventuality. I'd realised some time ago that when Esa says 'any eventuality', he really means it.

I found Esa behind one of the carriages. He was lying on his stomach, tapping it from underneath with a hammer. As always, the air around him was stale and thick. And even though he was lying flat on the floor, he looked as though he would be ready to leap into action at any moment. The sweatshirts of the US Marine Corps, which he had worn religiously until only a few weeks ago and which listed the bearer's years of service, might have had something to do with it. Though he had recently switched these sweatshirts with cosy-looking woollen jumpers, complete with colourful animal figures, I saw the same military demeanour and physical readiness that one might expect from a former US Marine.

'Aren't the airbags supposed to be on the inside?' I asked.

The hammer stopped in mid-air. Esa didn't turn or take his eyes from the underside of the carriage.

'All in good time,' he said.

'Meaning?'

'Once we've secured our position.'

I couldn't imagine what Esa was referring to, but this style of communication was typical.

'How long do you think it will take to ... secure our position?'

'Hard to say with our current intel. We're vastly outnumbered and constantly having to make do with inadequate coordinates. And seeing as there's no let-up in hostilities—'

'Quite,' I interrupt him. 'I have to take an important call at eleven-thirty...'

'It'll take longer than that,' said Esa, this time speaking more quickly than ever before, the words spilling from his lips in a single jumble of sounds.

I looked around. Getting the Komodo Locomotive up and running wasn't a matter of life and death. There were still only relatively few customers, and most of them were larger than the median passenger on the Komodo Locomotive, and in all respects it looked as though today would be a fairly quiet day. Just then, Esa audibly passed a cloud of noxious gases from deep within. I felt a warm puff of air on my face, stopped breathing through my nose so as not to trigger my gag reflex, opened my mouth and instantly felt a burning sensation at the top of my larynx.

'I'll come back later,' I suggested.

The hammer resumed its tapping. Esa said nothing.

I walked off towards the Big Dipper, and once I was sufficiently far away – in Esa's case, I considered a safe distance around fifteen metres – I filled my lungs with fresh air once again.

The Curly Cake Café smelt of salmon soup and pastries fresh from the oven. Our shorter clients were often at the louder end of the scale, and that was the case now too. Though the air conditioning had recently been enhanced and optimised, the café was still very warm. Taken together, the cumulative effect of these factors – the thick, greasy smells, the shrill squeals, the higher than usual temperature – made the place feel quite exhausting. I often felt conflicted when visiting the café, my mood a vexing combination of drowsiness and dread.

I walked up to the counter and saw Johanna in the kitchen. I took a butter-and-sugar bun from the glass cabinet and raised my plate so that Johanna could see it. She noticed me, lowered a batch of French fries into the vat of bubbling oil and walked to the other side of the counter. I was about to say I would pay for the bun and take it back to my office when Johanna cut me short.

'This one's on me,' she said. 'Do you want another one too?'

I looked at the plate in my hand, the bun sitting on the plate. Then I looked up at Johanna again. The very first time I had met her, several months ago, I'd been struck by the way her face made me think of a former convict training for an iron-man competition. I wasn't wrong. And the café meant everything to her. Here, nothing happened without her say-so, and nobody circumvented the rules, both the written and the unwritten varieties. But more to the point, she never, under any circumstances whatsoever, gave anything away for free. And now she was offering me a second bun.

'I only need one,' I said.

'Just a thought, in case a second one might come in handy.'

'By my initial calculation, one should be enough to sufficiently raise my blood-sugar levels,' I replied, and in a curious way I felt like a turtle that had been turned upside down: I couldn't move, and even if I could, it would have taken far too long.

'What about lunch?' she then asked.

'Lunch?'

'We have Sailor's Salmon Soup, Cock-a-Noodle-do, and today's vegan option is Tearaway's Tofu Tart. For dessert there's Spotted Quick and all the grown-ups' favourite, Caramel Cannons. My treat.'

'I think I'll be fine with this for now...'

'I meant later on,' she explained.

I was about to say something – I didn't quite know what – when I noticed a queue had formed behind us. Johanna seemed to notice this too. She looked at me and gave a curt nod. I assumed this meant I was excused, for now. I took the opportunity and, once my legs started obeying me again, left.

I walked towards my office, passing the Strawberry Maze and the usual cries and stampede of footsteps coming from inside it, then I turned right at the noisy, rattling Caper Castle, made my way around the Turtle Trucks, whose loud and over-excited drivers were currently changing seats, and headed towards the corridor, at the end of which was my office. I had only taken a few steps along the corridor and I was about to pass the office belonging to Minttu K, our head of sales and marketing, when she stopped me in my tracks.

'Hi,' she whispered. At least, I thought it was a whisper. The voice was gravelly and demanding, like a serrated saw against a plank of hard wood, only much, much lower. It was morning, but Minttu K's room already exuded the unmistakable scent of tobacco and gin. She raised her right hand and waved me over, beckoned me inside. 'Let's talk money.'

'The marketing meeting isn't until Thursday,' I said. 'It's probably best if we return to the—'

Minttu K shook her head and raised a well-tanned hand to silence me. Her silver rings sparkled.

'Honey, this Tesla waits for no man. Imagine – a real-life karate sensei. Thirty-five thousand followers on Instagram.'

Minttu K took a sip from her black mug. From her expression, it was hard to tell whether there was coffee in it or something else. The mug was as black as her blazer, which was at least one size too small for her.

'And why do we need a ... karate sensei?' I asked.

'Karate Kids,' she replied. 'There's plenty of them round here. All we need is a good slogan.'

Minttu K ruffled her short blonde hair. She seemed utterly convinced of whatever it was she was trying to tell me, which didn't particularly surprise me.

'First, this sounds like it could be a little dangerous, and the park isn't really a martial-arts college...' I began but started to feel a slight wooziness. I had to get to my office. 'We don't have the funds to cover any extra activities. As I've said several times.'

Minttu K twiddled a cigarette in her fingers. It had appeared there without my noticing.

'So you're just going to let this fish get away?' she asked huskily, and before I could say anything at all, she answered the question herself: 'Fine then. We'll forever be second best.'

I was genuinely taken aback. Usually Minttu K was ready to

fight to the bitter end, figuratively speaking. Now, barely seconds after the apparent end of our conversation, she was calmly sipping from her mug again, sucking intensely on the end of her cigarette and tapping her computer keyboard as before, as though she was reprimanding it for doing something naughty.

There was one final corner in the corridor.

The morning's encounters started replaying in my mind. And I realised that the brief wooziness of a moment ago had very concrete origins: it had grown exponentially with each encounter. Now everything was playing through my mind on fast-forward, getting stronger and sharper, taking on depth and life, and I started seeing and hearing things in these brief encounters that I hadn't registered at the time. Kristian wasn't bursting with enthusiasm, he hadn't suggested any changes or offered to make improvements first thing in the morning, the way he usually did; Esa was in no hurry to shore up the park's security, and instead he was carrying out repairs at a leisurely pace and without any sense of impending disaster; Minttu K caved in quickly and easily; Johanna offered me a second bun in case I needed it. As that last thought came into focus and began echoing more vividly through my mind, I felt the hand holding the plate with my bun begin to tremble.

I turned the final corner, stepped into my office and stopped in my tracks.

The butter-and-sugar bun leapt into the air.

The plate flew from my hand and smashed to smithereens.

The dead had come to life.

2

A pair of bright, sincere blue eyes, fair hair parted on the right, making his round head look even rounder, and a small, deep dimple in his chin. A blazer, a shirt (no tie), and that beaming, contagious smile.

The sounds from the hall carried into the office like waves, by turn fading then surging over me, as though their crests were crashing above my head. The children were running and screaming, banging and clanging on the rides, and above it all hung the thick, sweet, creamy smell of pastries and salmon soup.

The man held out his short arms, as if to introduce himself. There was no need. I knew perfectly well who he was. Thousands of images and memories hurtled through my mind – the most recent being the clearest. Standing in front of me was a man who had almost got me killed, a man who had left me with debts to the tune of several hundred thousand euros. And by the looks of it, he had risen from the dead.

My brother. Juhani.

Alive and well, and in my office.

He took two or three steps towards me. He said my name, wrapped his arms around me and bear-hugged me. I was a head taller than him, and the familiar smell of his aftershave rose into my nostrils like smoke from a bonfire. But the bear-hug had another significance too. It made everything real; his hug was the crushing evidence of it. My desire to snap out of the bear-hug was every bit as physical and as concrete as the arms around me.

Juhani brought our embrace to an end, took a step back and gave a characteristically sunny smile.

'This is brilliant,' he said. 'We did it.'

The speed of light is three hundred thousand kilometres per second. I was certain that something in me or in the room was moving at that speed, and I realised it must have been the decision I made there and then, in the blink of an eye. I moved, walked behind the desk and sat down in my chair.

'You're probably wondering where I've been,' Juhani said, still breezy.

'I haven't had time,' I said, honestly, and realised this was the first time I'd been able to speak. My voice sounded somehow more distant than usual. 'I assumed you were in Malmi. I buried you there myself, lowered you into the ground, shovelled sandy earth on top of you.'

'Yeah, thanks for that,' said Juhani and took a few short steps into the middle of the room. 'But no, I wasn't there. Anyway, moving on. While I was waiting for you, I did a little walkabout around the park. I chatted to people, tried to take in the vibe of the place. So, I've been thinking...'

I stared at him. Juhani looked and sounded as though this was a perfectly normal morning and we were perfectly normal brothers. In a certain sense, that was true, but in another – no, it was not, not at all. I had finally woken up. That's what it felt like.

'You deceived me,' I said.

Juhani stopped and seemed a little more serious now.

'That's putting it a bit strongly,' he said. 'But you're right, I owe you an explanation. I needed your help. As you know, the situation here had got a bit out of hand. We needed a mathematical intervention. Enter, my brilliant brother Henri, who can magically sort everything out. Meanwhile, I had to take a back seat for a little while. So, we both did what we had to do. You were here sorting out the park, I was lying low in a campsite. In eastern Finland. Rain, mosquitoes ... waiting for the life insurance to pay out. In vain, as it happens. I'll come back to that little problemo in a minute. But I'm sure you agree, the end result is a towering success.'

Juhani had been talking so quickly that by the time I'd fully understood what I'd just heard, he was already quiet.

'I could have died,' I said.

'That wasn't part of the plan though,' said Juhani, pulling a chair from beside the conference table and sitting down. He sounded almost offended. 'There's no way I could have predicted—'

'You were in debt to criminals,' I said. 'Very dangerous criminals. And I attended your funeral.'

'My lawyer thought a funeral would be a good idea.'

'Even though you weren't dead?'

'I wasn't far off.'

'But you were not dead. You were in eastern Finland.'

'If you saw the place, you'd know it's basically the same thing.'

'But it is not the same thing, that's what I'm trying to say. I had to clean up your mess.'

At first Juhani didn't say anything, then he gave another smile.

'But we survived,' he said, placing his hands together in front of him as though he were thanking some higher power. 'And here we are, victorious. And I'm absolutely bursting with new ideas.'

'Ideas about what?'

'This place. The park. I'm ready. Let's go.'

Everything seemed to be moving too quickly, as though someone had pressed fast-forward and there was no way of switching it off again.

'I don't know what you mean,' I said, and it was the truth.

'Henri, I've come back to liberate you,' Juhani smiled. 'To lift the burden from your shoulders, as they say. I'll take it from here. Full steam ahead. And a very grateful steam it is too.'

Had a cold November wind just blown through the room, or a

draught of chilled air, perhaps? The feeling was very real; it was powerful and bracing. My initial shock, my surprise and general confusion were gradually replaced with a cool serenity, the same composure I'd often thought it must take to work in a bomb-disposal unit, the same feeling I had experienced in my brother's company dozens, hundreds of times before. I looked Juhani in the eyes and remembered everything: our peculiar childhood, our parents and their constant financial chaos and general lack of life skills, the upheaval of our teenage years as we moved from one place to the next, then, later on, Juhani's string of failed business enterprises, my own trials and tribulations over the past few months and how everything very nearly imploded. And just as clearly, I understood what I had to do, what was required of me under the circumstances: I had to use mathematics and logic. Because they had brought the park balance, clarity, reliability and a positive outlook for the future.

'We are still going through a strict period of austerity,' I said. 'We've done away with everything unnecessary, and in the near future it's likely we may have to tighten our belts in other ways too. We have to consider any investments extremely carefully, and we need to raise our debt repayment capacity. On top of this, competition in the adventure-park sector is only going to increase in the near future. The good news is that there shouldn't be any nasty surprises coming our way – in the form of new criminal elements, for instance. If we hold our course and budget carefully, we have the chance not only to retain the staff we already have and maybe make the park profitable again, but, one day, we might even be able to pay everyone the Christmas bonuses you promised them.'

Juhani looked as though he had been listening to me intently and sincerely. His bright-blue eyes were wide open, his cheeks healthy and pink.

'This is exactly what I was expecting from you,' he said. 'All in all, excellent work.' He paused for a moment, then continued:

'Of course, I'll bear all this in mind once I'm back in the saddle again. I'll just add a little bit of my own magic too. Ideas, innovations, openness, happiness.'

We looked at each other.

'No,' I said.

'No?'

'No.'

'No ... what?'

'No ... everything. The park's long-term prosperity requires—'

'Henri, this is my park.' Again, he sounded offended.

'Which you left me on the verge of bankruptcy, not to mention that you'd taken out debts with a bunch of extremely dangerous gangsters. Then you ran away.'

Juhani tilted his head to the side. I knew this gesture. Nobody else tilted their head time after time in exactly the same fashion and in similar circumstances, after being caught out one way or another. And though this was only a microscopic shift compared to everything else that had happened in the last few minutes, the movement was like the hint of brightness that comes after a downpour. There it was, an admission, right in front of me. And if I needed any confirmation, it proved two things: my brother Juhani truly had returned and, what's more, he had returned with all his character traits intact.

'Okay, that's how you see things,' he said. 'I get it. We can negotiate. We're talking about a week or two, maybe a month at most?'

I thought for a moment, carried out some quick calculations.

'To be honest, I was thinking in terms of years. And even then, we're still only talking about share ownership and not...'

Juhani shook his head. 'I haven't got years,' he said. 'And neither does the park.'

'What do you mean?'

'Henri, can't you see what's happening out there?' Juhani asked, pointing a thumb over his shoulder. He was clearly shifting up a gear. 'Like I said, I walked around the place before coming here to wait for you. I heard all about the scrimping and saving, how you've put the park on ice so that everything will be groovy a hundred years from now. People don't like that kind of thing, Henri. They want things to be groovy today. I told them we'll be putting that right straight away.'

'Excuse me?'

'I want to bring back a bit of creative madness,' he said. 'You said yourself the park has to do a spot of penny-pinching. You solve that by increasing the volume of customers. And that means getting all our ducks in a row, as they say. Who wants to visit an adventure park where everybody is sad and crying all the time?'

'I haven't seen anybody crying, and besides—'

'Henri,' said Juhani, again gesticulating as he spoke. It looked to me as though he might be getting a little agitated. 'You have a tendency to get bogged down in the details. We've got to look at the bigger picture, assess the situation on the ground and … understand that one plus one isn't always two.'

'But it is,' I said. 'Every single time.'

'Henri,' he cried. 'I've come back from the dead!'

I was about to say that, for a whole host of reasons, this simply wasn't the case and that making fanciful claims that had no basis in material reality was typical of the same old Juhani who very nearly ran the adventure park into the ground in the first place. But I bit my tongue. Something about Juhani's expression stopped me saying it out loud. He spoke again before I had a chance to respond.

'Are you trying to get rid of me?'

The question took me by surprise, it hit me right in the

diaphragm. I realised I hadn't thought of it in those terms. The truth was that I hadn't thought of it in any terms. Everything had happened so fast. Juhani looked me right in the eyes. I found myself suddenly feeling a sliver of warmth and understanding towards him. Not so much towards his recent behaviour, but in general. He was my brother, I thought, and he was … Indeed, what was he, actually? He hadn't returned from the dead because he had never passed away in the first place. And he hadn't changed at all – rather, he seemed just the same as he always had been. He was Juhani. Of course I didn't want to get rid of him. I couldn't even if I'd tried.

'Our park manager, Laura Helanto, whom you know from before, has recently left us,' I said, trying to enunciate Laura's name in as neutral a way as I could. 'The position of park manager is both demanding and diverse, as you know, and it will certainly keep you busy. I know you weren't previously involved with the practical side of things – the day-to-day running of the park and our everyday routines, let alone repairs. But the position is free.'

Juhani looked at me for a good few seconds before answering. Then he smiled.

'I can start straight away,' he said.

3

I'd been sitting in the same position on a tall stool near the window in the room smelling of paint for more than an hour now. My task was to look like myself. Relaxed. At first it had sounded like an easy enough task, but the longer I sat there and the more I thought about how best to look relaxed, the more impossible the whole thing started to feel. I'd had time to think about different things over the course of the last hour, most notably the fact that, to be perfectly honest, I didn't think I'd ever *been* relaxed and wasn't sure what it meant or what it was supposed to look like. Which, in turn, made me wonder what I looked like right now; if only I knew that, then perhaps I might relax a little. And this, in turn, meant I was trying to do something that I fundamentally didn't understand and couldn't control. I was like a ski jumper placed in the cockpit of a jumbo jet, simply because he too knows a thing or two about soft landings. It could have been the other way round too: I was a pilot pushed at full speed from the top of the ski-jumping hill because his job saw him flying through the skies too.

What restless thoughts, I sighed to myself.

The same thing happened every time I met her, particularly when I found myself under her attentive eye, having to remain there, relaxed, hour upon hour.

I was sitting for Laura Helanto while she painted my portrait. She wanted to give me this portrait as a gift, and naturally I was very grateful.

Laura Helanto was on my mind even when I wasn't thinking about her.

The thought felt embarrassingly illogical, and of course it was.

But it was impossible to describe this phenomenon without resorting to – in the absence of a more appropriate term – somewhat poetic language. Which felt like a profoundly reckless way of approaching any subject. When I compared the relative reliability of mathematics and poetry when it came to the successful outcome of a given project – say, constructing a skyscraper or designing a cheese knife – I knew there was no alternative to mathematics. But when it came to Laura Helanto, I found myself behaving differently. It was as though in a fraction of a second I had forgotten everything upon which my life had been based. And strangest of all, this didn't seem to bother me nearly as much as I might have expected.

We had met each other only twice since she embezzled a sum total of one hundred and twenty-four thousand, eight hundred and sixty-one euros and thirteen cents from me. To be more precise, she didn't embezzle the money from me directly: the money already had criminal origins. Her actions had saved both me and the park; this became clear to me a few weeks after she had left her post. And me.

I wanted to imagine this was all in the past now. From now on … Yet again I had to step back and remind myself that we had only met twice since then.

We'd gone for a walk and a cup of hot chocolate with Laura's daughter, Tuuli. The walk had progressed in sporadic bursts, largely because Tuuli was setting the pace. She didn't seem interested in maintaining a steady rate of steps per minute or trying to find the optimal route between two points, principles that governed my own walks. Instead, we zigzagged here and there, and stopped for pauses of indeterminate length to marvel at this and that: children, adults, birds, rubbish bins, the tow bars on the back of cars. The purpose of these pauses never became clear to me. But I didn't need any explanations for our aimless wandering. I was in Laura Helanto's company, and I had the distinct sense that I would enjoy her company whether we were moving or stationary, in a sensible place or a less sensible one.

Laura's daughter asked questions that I would have gladly answered at length and more thoroughly than was possible. But I'd barely started my answer to one question, when she was already asking the next. Laura seemed to enjoy the conversation despite its occasional unruliness. She smiled at me, took my hand, gave it a few squeezes. And as I accompanied them to the metro station, she and I kissed. It wasn't a very long kiss, and not remotely like those that occurred during our night of passion, when our tongues had seemed to intertwine and lock tightly together. And though, for reasons of biology, physiology and evaporation, I knew it was impossible, I imagined I could still feel that kiss on my lips.

Her brush skated across the canvas, the smell of oil paints filled the room. Laura's trainers squeaked against the concrete floor.

It felt as though every second I spent with Laura Helanto existed on a different plane of relativity, that time was fuller and denser than usual. Of course, there was no quantum explanation for this, but...

'Henri. Hello? Henri!'

'What?'

'Are you uncomfortable?' Laura asked, and when I caught her gaze I was even more confused. Those blue-green eyes, framed and enhanced by her dark-rimmed glasses, conducted something akin to an electrical current through me.

'Not at all,' I said.

'Okay,' Laura nodded. 'You just look a bit ... pained.'

'Am I in the wrong position?' I asked.

'No,' she said, and I got the distinct impression she was holding back a smile. 'The position is fine. I just thought you might be getting a bit tired. Seeing as you're tensing every muscle.'

'I'm trying to look relaxed.'

'It's the trying bit that's the problem. You're tense. If you stop trying, you'll get it. He who doesn't seek, shall find. That's what they say, right?'

'I suppose someone might say that,' I admitted. 'But I've always found it a misleading and distinctly unscientific saying. The truth is the very opposite. It is specifically by seeking that we will eventually reach a solution. This is fundamental. Nothing would ever have been invented if people had simply shrugged their shoulders and waited for the right answer to fall from the sky, and if—'

'Henri.'

Now Laura was smiling. She placed her brush on the work surface next to her and started walking towards me. I tried to make my pose even more relaxed. Laura approaching me didn't help.

'I once said I'd never met anybody like you,' she said as she came to a halt in front of me. 'But that's an understatement.'

'I've never met anybody like you either,' I told her earnestly. 'Someone able to mislead me so profoundly in a matter of practical mathematics, and someone I was interested in for many different reasons. If I'm honest, it's the first time either thing has ever happened to me.'

Laura was standing in front of me. I could smell her wild, bushy hair, that familiar fragrance of forest flowers. She was so close that I could make out a tiny droplet of red paint on the rim of her glasses.

'That's just what I mean,' she said.

'Not to mention that these two things happened simultaneously,' I nodded. 'In any case, the probability of such a coincidence is so infinitesimally small that I haven't even tried to work it out, which is quite out of character for me.'

'That's not quite when I meant,' she said quietly, and smiled.

What happened next is what kept happening to me in Laura's company: I completely lost my thread. Very often, I had the sense that Laura's words, even those that at first seemed simple and appeared to have a purely practical function, in fact had many different layers, and they almost always referred to something other than what she had just said. The connections between them were either intentionally unclear or very hard to deduce. So I remained quiet, sitting on my tall stool, and simply enjoyed her presence.

I don't know whether one of us had leant our upper body forwards or whether we had both done so. Our faces were so close that I shut my eyes and prepared myself for two things: a kiss and telling her what was bothering me.

'Juhani is back,' I said, and continued leaning forwards.

And fell into thin air.

I didn't find Laura's lips, or Laura, or anything for that matter. I opened my eyes again. Laura had backed away and was standing a metre and a half from me. She didn't look like she was looking for my lips – which I noticed were still pursed in a kiss. I corrected the position of my lips and sat up straight.

'Juhani? Your brother ... Juhani?'

'That's right,' I nodded. 'He said, all that time he was supposed to be dead, he'd been living in a caravan.'

Laura looked at me. She opened her mouth, but no words came out. She tried again, and this time she spoke.

'Juhani is alive?'

'I'm quite sure of it.'

'When you arrived here, I asked how you were doing, and you didn't say anything about ... your brother.'

'Yes, I remember. I told you I was doing relatively well. I thought you were asking about me, all things considered. I didn't imagine you meant Juhani. I don't know how he's doing, other than that he's been staying in a caravan somewhere in eastern Finland.'

Laura looked the way I imagined she might look if I were to mix up her paints, then take a brush and daub it over her painting.

'You mean he just ... turned up?'

'Yes.'

'What did he say?'

'He wants the park back.'

'And what did you tell him?'

'That it wouldn't be at all sensible, either financially or practically, especially in light of the recent demonstration of his management skills and ability to take responsibility for his actions, but I told him he could have a good job at the park, which would give him a regular income and health insurance and accrue his future pension. He accepted my offer.'

'He accepted your offer?' Laura asked, as though she had just heard the most impossible statement in the world.

'The park manager's position has been free since you left.'

'Juhani will probably make an excellent park manager.'

'I'm still not sure quite how qualified he—'

'Henri, that was sarcasm. Irony.'

'Irony, sarcasm, right. I like them too.'

I didn't know why I added that last sentence. I realised I was a little off kilter and noticed that Laura seemed agitated.

'Doesn't it seem strange to you – that Juhani should turn up and take a job just like that, a job where you need to be really careful, always on site, always available, and where you have to take care of a thousand practical things all at once?'

I didn't have time to think of an answer, let alone say it out loud, before Laura was speaking again.

'Henri, can I ask you something? Did you talk about me?'

'Not at all. Why would we?'

And why did this conversation suddenly feel so uncomfortable? And not just the conversation we were having right now. It felt as though there were two conversations going on at once, the first with these very words and the second somewhere under the surface, invisible and wordless, but every bit as audible. I felt as though I didn't understand either of them. Then I found something to grab hold of.

'Why are you so upset about Juhani and his return?' I asked. 'You don't work at the park anymore, and there's nothing in our bookkeeping to implicate you in any way in what happened.'

Laura glanced at the portrait she was painting. Then, just as quickly, she turned away. To me, it looked as though she wanted to give herself a little time to think.

'You've just managed to get the park's finances back on their feet,' she said eventually, still staring up at the tall windows. 'And now Juhani ... is going to mess everything up again.'

Once again, the way Laura stressed the words in her last sentence was such that I found myself listening in between the lines, as they say. At least, that's what I tried to do, because I imagined that was where the essential information might lie. And what I found didn't feel particularly pleasing.

'I have drawn up plans for both the long term and the short,' I said. 'And I've calculated everything thoroughly several times over, based everything on the facts and told the employees the truth about the direction the park is heading. I am the park's owner, and everybody knows that. Juhani is an employee. What could he possibly do?'

Laura didn't answer right away. She had lowered her eyes, and looked as though she was staring at a spot on the floor behind me.

'It's just ... he's Juhani.'

'What does that mean?'

'He is...' Again Laura seemed lost for words, and I was puzzled at what had just happened; she'd always been to express herself so fluently. 'You and he are ... different.'

I didn't know where the feeling came from, but I was sure that a great fire had just burst into flame.

'I've known him my entire life,' I said, perhaps more quickly than I'd planned. I was suddenly angry, almost livid. It had come over me by stealth. 'Nobody knows better than me that he and I are different. Juhani has demonstrated this in practice too, most obviously with regard to the adventure park. He hadn't even drawn up a preliminary budget proposal, he got into debt in the most nonsensical way, high-interest loans, criminal loans. Wastage, carelessness, unfounded promises, dangerous impulsive behaviour.'

'That's not what I mean ... Well, maybe that's exactly what I mean. That too. It's hard to talk about this.'

The tall, bright studio seemed to dim a little, as though someone had drawn a black curtain in front of everything. At the same time, my thoughts seemed to be darkening too. I looked at Laura and saw something I didn't want to see.

'When you say Juhani is different,' I began, and formulated the end of my thought just as the words came tumbling out of my mouth. 'What you really mean is that I am different.'

Laura didn't answer right away. She looked as though she didn't know quite what to say. That felt worse than if she'd actually said something – anything, in fact. She didn't look at me.

'And because I'm different,' I continue, 'you think I'm no match for a man who doesn't know whether he's coming or going, who lies, makes promises he can't keep and a conveyor belt of catastrophic decisions. A man whose actions are based on everything but reason. In that respect, I am very *different* indeed and I'm no match for a man like that.'

'Henri, you are—'

'Different. For your information, when I completed my

mathematics degree in record time, I heard people say I was different. And when, as an actuary, I was able to calculate things two and a half times quicker and more accurately than anyone in the company's history, they told me I was different. Maybe I'm different in a different way from how you think. Maybe I *am* a match for my brother.'

I stood up, walked to the steel coat rail by the doorway. I pulled on my coat, tied my woollen scarf loosely but carefully, so as to provide optimal heat above my tie. Laura Helanto was still standing there, by my reckoning almost diametrically in the middle of the floor space. I looked at her, and knowing her height I could easily have calculated a whole array of measurements regarding the distance and volume of the room, and perhaps even produced an equation that would bring these measurements together, or at least an expression to that effect, but I realised I didn't want to. This I took to be the clearest of signals, and I turned away.

The door was made of thick metal, but I didn't even notice its weight.

Outside, I chose the shortest route to the bus station and set off at a steady, leisurely pace of seven kilometres an hour.

4

The meeting was in Konala.

I arrived six minutes ahead of the appointed time, so I sat waiting in the van used to transport the park's equipment; the second-hand Renault Kangoo had lots of space and excellent capacity, its fuel consumption was reasonable and its appearance suitably unattractive, which lowered the risk of its being stolen, which in turn ensured that the vehicle's insurance premium and excess remained untouched.

The sun was shining horizontally into my eyes, so I lowered the sun visor and allowed the beams to warm my chest. Most of the traffic passing by consisted of vans and lorries bearing a variety of familiar and unfamiliar brands and logos. Most of the brands and logos overtook me, driving slightly over the speed limit, at a cautious estimate. Having spent my entire adult life immersing myself in statistics and probability, I accepted this did not mean that most of the residents of Konala were habitual speeders. This was the first time I'd ever visited this area of the city, and therefore my data set was deceptively small. It was considerably more likely that most Konala residents were responsible motorists and that traffic through Konala was, on the whole, very balanced and drivers dutifully adhered to the general rules of the Highway Code, and it would be wrong to generalise based on the rather lax behaviour of one or two or three Konala motorists and to extrapolate that to apply to all Konala motorists...

I shook my head and faced facts.

I was trying not to think about Laura or our encounter, so I was prepared to come up with almost anything to take my mind off it. I adjusted my tie and tried to shake Laura Helanto temporarily from my mind.

The offices and warehouses of Toy of Finland Ltd were ahead of me to the left, at one corner of the triangular plot. The company was a long-term supplier of adventure-park equipment, and YouMeFun was tied to a long-term contract with them. The contract was valid for at least the next three years. The existence of this contract had come as a complete surprise to me, as had almost everything else to do with the park.

Nonetheless, the contract, which had been signed two years earlier and which appeared to have been drawn up by Hannes Tolkki, owner and CEO of Toy of Finland, was very reasonable and beneficial to both parties. My own calculations confirmed that cooperation with Toy of Finland was profitable to both of us, particularly in the long term. What made this contract even more unique were the so-called exclusivity clauses that bound both parties, including Toy of Finland. As per these clauses, Toy of Finland was not allowed to supply adventure-park equipment to anybody except us within the boundaries of Greater Helsinki.

And therein lay the reason for my visit to Konala. Because I didn't understand the company's most recent messages and offers.

And because everything seemed to come back to the Moose Chute.

The Moose Chute was a unique piece of equipment, and I wanted it. Or, more specifically, I needed it.

The Moose Chute stood taller than any of our other pieces of equipment, and in every respect it was gigantic. This single device offered up to ten different activities. The most hair-raising of these was the possibility to leap from the tip of the moose's antlers right into a forest of trampolines positioned at its front. The other activities included various ways of climbing up to the tips of the aforementioned antlers and a giant slide ending at the bottom of the animal's back-left hoof. On the moose's back there was a balancing circuit with two parallel tracks, allowing the most competitive of our customers the opportunity to test their agility against one another. But most magnificent of all was the fact that the entire moose could be turned into one enormous rollercoaster. The circuit running through the inside and along the back could support several carriages, and the moose itself moved them along with the help of a powerful and fully carbon-neutral electric motor. Only one Moose Chute was manufactured every year; it was the crown jewel of the entire French and, indeed, the whole European adventure-park industry.

For YouMeFun, the Moose Chute would provide a much-needed competitive edge. The truth of the matter was, we were the underdogs. Our nearest competitor was expanding and had secured a whole slew of big acquisitions. We needed something to differentiate us from them, but all within the constraints of our current financial predicament. The Moose Chute was one such acquisition – if, indeed, we were able to acquire it. But the messages I'd recently received hadn't brought that acquisition any closer. After many attempts, I'd finally managed to arrange a meeting to discuss the matter.

I looked at the clock on the dashboard, checked my tie in the rear-view mirror, picked up my briefcase and stepped out of the car.

The office building was made of white-painted, roughcast concrete, it was on one level and clearly much older than the tall, grey, steel-and-aluminium construction behind it. I walked up to the dark-brown wood-panelled door and pressed a round buzzer on the wall. There were large windows on both sides of the door, their

Venetian blinds open a fraction. They had been pulled so that you could only see into the room if you lay on the ground and looked up, meaning you would probably only see the ceiling.

The buzzer sounded, and I heard the door's lock give a click. I pulled the door open and stepped inside.

I found myself standing at the end of a lengthy corridor, which meant that the office building was significantly deeper than it looked from the outside. Otherwise the impression was a neutral one. The interior was white, very brightly lit and office-like. The corridor was dotted with doors, most of which stood open. Just as I was about to call out and ask which direction to go in, I heard the sound of conversation and saw half a man's face in a doorway on the left of the corridor.

'This way.'

This way seemed to mean a conference room, a large table and the chairs around it. It might also have meant the men sitting around that table. There were three of them: two older gentlemen and one considerably younger. None of them was the CEO, Hannes Tolkki.

'Take a seat,' said one of the older men, and showed me to a chair. This was the same man whose face I had half seen a moment earlier. 'The park's chugging along nicely, isn't it?'

'Will Hannes Tolkki be joining us?' I asked. I was standing on the same side of the table as the man who had offered me a chair. The other older man was standing across the table alongside the younger man.

'He's retired,' I heard from beside me. 'I'm Kari Liitokangas.'

'Otto Härkä,' the other man introduced himself.

'Jeppe,' said the younger man, held a two-second pause, then added, 'Sauvonen.'

Kari Liitokangas, who was still offering me a chair, was a man of around fifty and of average height, and beneath his flannel shirt his prominent chest and shoulders seemed to dominate the rest of his torso, as though he had only succeeded in growing a few strategic muscles at the gym, but all the more thoroughly. His facial features were similarly curious: his broad chin and high cheekbones were almost cinematic, but the sections under his chin and above his nose revealed a penchant for beer. To sum up, one might say that it was hard to look at him only once; there was something about him that forced you to look again and check what you thought you'd seen the first time. Otto Härkä must have been in his fifties too; he was slender though still with something of a beer belly, and he sported a particularly impressive moustache. I'd seen topiary of the garden-brush variety a lot in recent years, though mostly on younger men who, I had been told, considered it an ironical fashion statement. And then there was Jeppe—pause—Sauvonen. He was tapping the table-top with his right hand, his left hidden somewhere deep under it. He had a serious, statuesque appearance, a dark monobrow and beneath it brown, smouldering eyes. He was wearing a black sweatshirt with the words *FUN MACHINE* in large white letters.

'Let's sit down, shall we?' said Kari Liitokangas. His words had immediate effect: we all sat down.

'I didn't know Hannes Tolkki was about to retire,' I said.

'It all happened very quickly,' said Liitokangas. 'But he left us detailed instructions. We want to continue along the same lines and respect the terms of our contract.'

'Good,' I nodded. 'That's what I was hoping.'

'Excellent,' said Liitokangas with a smile. Otto Härkä and Jeppe Sauvonen smiled too. I looked at them each in turn and began to feel distinctly ill at ease.

'Indeed,' I said eventually. 'Speaking of our contract—'

'I have it here,' said Liitokangas, and opened a plastic folder in front of him. 'Along with our catalogue.'

He slid the stapled pile of papers he called their catalogue across the table. I leafed through the bundle to find the product I was looking for, the one I wanted to discuss. As I turned the pages, my attention was drawn to the price of the devices and equipment. The prices had all risen, most of them quite dramatically. I reached the final page and turned it too. Then I looked up at the three men. They were all still smiling.

'I don't see the Moose Chute,' I said.

'There are plenty of other good items,' said Otto Härkä.

'Might I suggest the Crocodile Canyon?' said Liitokangas.

'That one's really great,' said Otto Härkä. The way he spoke the words 'really great' did little to convince me this was what he actually thought.

I looked at both men. 'The children don't like it,' I said. 'I've examined the data from adventure parks across Central Europe and the Nordic countries. A brief analysis and some rudimentary calculations are enough to tell you what works and what doesn't. Nowhere does the Crocodile Canyon reach even the top forty most popular rides, and most of the parks in my study have already got rid of it. It's an old piece of equipment, of bad quality, and simply too rough for the children.'

'Then get stronger kids,' said Jeppe Sauvonen.

'Excuse me?'

'What Jeppe means,' Liitokangas interjected, and somehow moved a little closer to me, 'is that this is a question of perspective, and perspective is a bit like sight in general: people see better with better glasses on.'

'I don't follow,' was my honest response.

'Let's look at the catalogue once again, shall we?' said Liitokangas, shook the pile of papers before us and opened it at the page showing the Crocodile Canyon. 'Here it is, and if we round this down a bit like so, there's our final offer.'

As he spoke, Liitokangas took out a ball-point pen, scored out the highly inflated price of the Crocodile Canyon and wrote a new price underneath it. I looked at it and began to understand.

'You've written the same price again,' I said, and looked up at the trifecta of smiles in front of me.

'That's today's price,' said Otto Härkä. 'It's up to the minute.'

I shook my head. 'This is not … Our contract doesn't…'

'Precisely, dare I say, our *exclusive* contract,' I heard a voice right next to me say. Liitokangas was so close he was almost touching me. He slid another sheet of paper in front of me. 'There.'

I'd seen our contract before. I'd read it many times. I knew it in detail. I didn't need to start examining it again now.

'I know what our contract says. I want the Moose Chute. I have no intention of buying the Crocodile Canyon. And certainly not at that price.'

The men looked at one another. Then, like in a slow-motion film, they all turned to look at me.

'Well, this is a bit of a change of mood, and not quite the one we were expecting.'

'A change of mood?'

'Yes,' said Liitokangas, who, to all intents and purposes, was now right up against me. 'It's come to our attention that the changing of the guard between you and your brother didn't go quite according to the rule book. Now, I'm not insinuating anything here, but I'm sure there are one or two things you'd rather keep locked in that briefcase of yours.'

The room fell eerily silent. I realised that I hadn't heard any sounds from the other offices in the building. I hadn't seen anyone else when I arrived. I hadn't noticed the sounds of work, no office hubbub, no conversation or telephones, nothing. Where were all the other Toy of Finland employees?

'My brother is not responsible for park acquisitions,' I said. 'And whatever he might or might not have said or promised you is—'

'Interesting?' said Otto Härkä. 'Alarming?'

In one respect, Otto Härkä was right. Alarming was the word I would have used too. I began to see how everything that had happened before had led me here: the dogged attempts to sell me the Crocodile Canyon, the price that wouldn't budge though the product was ugly and had been rejected by most children. Of course, it must be Juhani.

'My brother...' I began and tried to find the most apt way to describe the matter '...doesn't always know what he's talking about.'

'We're more than aware of that,' said Liitokangas with a chortle. Otto Härkä chortled right after him. Jeppe Sauvonen again spent two seconds thinking things through, then he chortled too. I noticed I didn't like the situation one bit, and I knew why. Juhani could be reckless, irresponsible, had a tendency to open his mouth before engaging his brain, he might even leave people in mortal danger and bring companies to the brink of collapse, but he was my brother. The catalogue in front of me was still open at the page showing the Crocodile Canyon. It looked even more dejected than before.

'I want to buy the Moose Chute,' I said.

'It's not for sale.'

'I know you have it in your warehouse.'

'And we know what we know,' said Liitokangas. 'And we're offering you the Crocodile Canyon.'

'No,' I said.

'No?'

Liitokangas leant away from me, and as he did so his facial features seemed to come into focus. His face was more angular than I'd thought at first.

'Do you think everything in that briefcase would stand the light of day?'

I glanced at my briefcase. I realised he didn't mean the literal briefcase. He meant the adventure park, the way I'd put the criminals behind me, what I'd had to do to save the park and myself. And now I was convinced that Juhani had told them something he shouldn't have. I could tell: Kari Liitokangas's assertiveness, Otto Härkä's smile, and the burning coals beneath Jeppe Sauvonen's thatched eyebrows. His sweatshirt unrelentingly shouted the words *FUN MACHINE* at me, but to my mind nothing about him suggested fun, mechanical or otherwise.

'Let's look at the facts one more time, shall we?' said Liitokangas. 'At the end of the day, we have a contract that is pretty straightforward. Either we work together or one of us will have to pay the other for breach of contract. The settlement will be in the region of the adventure park's annual turnover. Give or take. We don't want to breach this contract.'

'Under any circumstances,' said Otto Härkä. 'In any way.'

Jeppe Sauvonen chimed in after a short pause: 'Think of the children.'

Before I could ask what he meant, Liitokangas once again took charge of proceedings.

'We suggest that you buy the Crocodile Canyon and that we, in turn, deliver it to you with exclusive rights.'

Though part of me sensed that something very unpleasant was about to happen – much like when a company holds an unannounced press briefing at three o'clock on a Friday afternoon – I continued all the same.

'Or what?' I asked.

'Osmala,' said Liitokangas, as though he were offering me condolences that he didn't really mean. 'Pentti Osmala. I gather you two are acquainted.'

I said nothing. Detective Inspector Pentti Osmala of the Helsinki organised-crime and fraud units. Acquainted was one way of putting it. In fact, we were so well acquainted that he probably still suspected me of something – in part justifiably. The case was complicated: I had been defending myself and my adventure park, and in doing so had resorted to some extra-mathematical tactics. Meanwhile, Osmala certainly knew a thing or two about my non-actuarial undertakings, but at the time he'd seemed content that I was merely helping him in his investigation. We'd never discussed the matter further. I imagine this putative conversation would have taken me far beyond what people called their comfort zone. But every bit as important was what the mere mention of Osmala's name meant. The three musketeers here knew more than they should, more than should have been possible.

'Who are you exactly?' I asked.

'We're Toy of Finland,' they replied in unison.

5

The noise from the great hall, carrying through the closed door, sounded like a distant construction site as I sat crunching the numbers again. The budget estimates I had drawn up before my visit to the premises of Toy of Finland Ltd now felt hopelessly out of date.

I'd spent hours trying to come up with a financially viable solution to the park's current predicament. I slid my chair slightly further from the desk, looked at the piles of papers, the calculator. The more I counted and the more I found raw facts to support my conclusions, the clearer it became that we needed the Moose Chute, and that there was no way we would survive with the potential short- and long-term costs and inevitable permanent losses that acquiring the Crocodile Canyon would entail. I'd also gone through the contract between the park and Toy of Finland one more time, scrutinising every detail and all the small print, but the contract was exceptionally clear: it wouldn't help us one bit. After much calculation and examination, it looked as though I would either have to pay for something I didn't want and that would ruin the park's finances, or give in to our cut-throat competition and wait for eventual destruction, which would occur sooner or later. And given how aggressively our competitor on the other side of town was expanding their portfolio of equipment, that destruction might come very quickly indeed.

The long and the short of it was that we *had* to acquire the Moose Chute, just as we *had* to avoid the Crocodile Canyon. Sadly, my calculations alone couldn't tell me how to do this.

I stood up and walked to the window.

Afternoon in November. Overcast, dry, a hint of dusk.

My eyes moved from the horizon to the car park and inched closer to the entrance, which was on my right. I saw a woman dragging a much shorter person, presumably one of our customers. They had left the park only seconds earlier, they walked towards me and came to a halt at a red Volvo parked right in front of my window. The smaller customer was exceptionally dirty. Her trousers and the T-shirt beneath her unzipped coat looked as though she'd been rolling in a vat of paint. Just then I saw another customer being frogmarched to a car. This one was covered in muck from head to toe and seemed to have clumps of something stuck in his hair. Halfway through the frogmarching, he stopped, doubled over and was promptly sick. At the same time, the red Volvo angrily pulled out of its parking spot, turned right in front of me and accelerated towards the exit and the intersection up ahead. I unrolled my shirt sleeves, buttoned the cuffs and straightened my tie.

I found Kristian behind the ticket desk in the foyer. Apart from him, the foyer was empty, so I got straight to the point.

'I've just seen two customers leaving the park covered in paint, and one of them looked distinctly queasy,' I said. 'What's going on?'

In recent days, Kristian had taken to staring at his computer screen and clicking his mouse ever more frantically whenever I approached him. This time, however, he didn't do so, and the change was remarkable: he stood to attention and smiled; his row of whitened teeth sparkled, and his great, broad muscles seemed to stretch the fabric of his YouMeFun sweater even more vigorously than usual.

'Conceptual fusion,' he said.

I looked at Kristian, then the exit, then back at Kristian. 'I don't understand.'

'A fusion is like a combination of things,' he said. 'You take two different things, two concepts, and kind of ... put them together—'

'Thank you, I get the general principle,' I interrupted him, and at that moment the truth began to dawn on me. 'And whose idea was this ... conceptual fusion?'

'Juhani's.'

'Do you know where I can find him?'

'Yes.'

Kristian's smile might have been just a fraction less self-assured, but his bodily vim and eagerness were undiluted.

'Could you tell me where he is, please?'

'Yes,' he nodded, seemed to think about something, and finally answered me: 'He's at the Big Dipper.'

I was about to turn, then looked at Kristian again. 'But there's no paint at the Big Dipper,' I said. 'How...?'

Kristian did something quite astonishing: he managed to nod and shake his head simultaneously. He smiled too, and there was a sense of jubilant liberation in his smile.

'I tell you, Juhani is a real business genius,' he said. 'He's got so many...'

I didn't hear how Kristian finished his sentence. Instead, I ran.

The Big Dipper was one of our most popular activities, one of the park's classics, shall we say. It was a gleaming steel construction that comprised nine different slides, and everybody wanted to get to the top of it. Looking from the entrance, it was situated behind the Strawberry Maze.

I walked around the Strawberry Maze, passed the Doughnut, where our little customers ran in circles inside a giant plastic tube and collided with the padded walls. The Doughnut was our all-time classic; it was the very first apparatus we had ever acquired. Even now, quickly walking past it, I marvelled at the cost-effective union of kinetic energy and centrifugal force. The machine cost next to nothing to maintain; all the fun, allure and attraction was secured by the fortunate position of our planet within the Solar System and our customers' own enthusiasm. But the fleeting sense of satisfaction was gone as soon as the Big Dipper came into view.

I could smell what I most feared.

Warm milk.

And something more pungent too.

And the Big Dipper...

...looked like a giant had used it as his own personal ice-cream tub, then left half the contents uneaten.

I stopped in my tracks.

The soft-ice-cream machine had been moved from the café and placed at the bottom of the Big Dipper. The machine appeared to be free for all our customers to use. They pulled the levers, the machine churned out three flavours of soft ice cream – chocolate, strawberry and Ye Olde Vanilla – from a total of six taps in a continuous, uninterrupted stream into punnets, cones and everywhere besides. The customers snatched their ice creams and dashed to the steps of the Big Dipper, then came careering down all nine of the slides, ice creams in hand. Every one of the slides was covered in ice cream, and so were all the little sliders. After sliding out at the bottom, the customers ran to the machine and pumped more ice cream for their cups. If the cup had disappeared somewhere inside the Big Dipper or if their cones had become soft and squashed against the walls, they simply pumped it into their hands, from which they proceeded to shovel it into their mouths and smear it all over the park. The air was filled with shrill, piercing squeals.

Several dozen of our customers looked as if they were experiencing the same sugar rush all at once. Others seemed to be beyond the point of no return. I watched two of our customers repeating what I'd already seen in the car park and expelling the vast amounts of ice cream they had eaten. One of them was coming down the longest of the Big Dipper's slides as it happened. The bumps along the slide gave each gastric spasm some added power, and the most vigorous of the expulsions were like something straight out of a physics textbook: an optimal combination of speed, mass, density and thrust.

I forced myself into motion and headed towards the ice-cream machine, unsure of what needed to be done first. The machine stood right in the middle of an enormous brown puddle dotted with patches of pink. The short, frenzied customers were besieging it, splashing through the puddle and jostling to reach the taps. I raised my hands and readied myself to shout something, though I still didn't know what, when I felt a hand on my shoulder.

'Now look at that, Henri. That's customer satisfaction for you. That's what running an adventure park is all about.'

I turned. Juhani was beaming. He looked particularly pleased with himself. I tried to say something, but words failed me.

'In the past, I think I was a bit too hands-off,' he said. 'But here on site, ideas start bubbling up like you wouldn't believe.'

Juhani gestured at the Big Dipper and gazed at it proudly. I did another 180-degree turn.

'You won't get an experience like this anywhere else,' he continued. 'This is exactly what we need. Quick, open-minded decision-making. Conceptual fusion. Slides and ice cream. And whose idea was it to combine these two things that so obviously go together? You can thank me later. But I'll tell you something for nothing, not a single one of those kids will ever forget this. Some memories live forever.'

I managed to take my eyes from the Big Dipper. It was hard, not least because the volume of destruction seemed to be growing exponentially.

'Do you have any idea how much this is going to cost?' I asked.

'I've already thought about that,' said Juhani, and he still sounded satisfied. 'The ice cream is basically free anyway. And the Big Dipper was just standing there waiting.'

I shook my head.

'I mean the cleaning.'

'Cleaning?'

'Yes,' I said. 'It's going to cost thousands to clean this up. Every join in the Big Dipper is filled with bucketfuls of milk, and it'll soon start to smell. This is beyond the scope of an average evening tidy-up. What on earth were you thinking?'

'I was thinking about the park, of course,' said Juhani, and he looked perfectly genuine. 'And our competitive edge, just like you are. The customers, the footfall, the atmosphere, giving people unforgettable experiences. You can see for yourself how happy they are.'

I looked at these human saplings, shrieking as they wound their milky way down the slides, coated in sugary sludge.

'They're not happy,' I said and turned to face Juhani. 'They have taken leave of their senses. And given the carnage, I can't help thinking the same applies to you.'

Now Juhani looked as though I had offended him in a most unspeakable way.

'Your world is so narrow,' he said. 'Always has been. When was the last time you laughed?'

'I laugh whenever I think there is reason to do so and when the moment lends itself to such a course of action. What has that got to do with this catastrophe?'

'What did you do when I came back, when I told you I wasn't dead after all? Instead of being happy and ecstatic that your flesh and blood was still alive, you started lecturing me and trying to teach me a lesson. You told me the future looks bleak and there'll be nothing but problems and more problems and doom and gloom until the end of time. You're as sour as an unripe lemon and as tight as a Scotsman's purse, and you insist that everybody else is as miserable too.'

'That is not—'

'And you're jealous,' Juhani continued. 'You always have been. You've just hidden it by pretending to know everything about everything. You're jealous now too because I saw an opportunity and I took it, and because I get along with everybody. You should have seen how the kids shouted and clapped when I told them there was free ice cream all round.'

'That is precisely the kind of—'

'I give people joy and happy memories,' said Juhani. 'And don't you forget, I'm the one that founded this park.'

'That's one of the main reasons I want the park to survive in the—'

'There you go, *survive*,' he said as though he'd tasted something exceptionally foul. 'When I was running the show, we set our sights a bit higher. Some businesses understand the importance of thinking outside the box and really making an impact.'

'In some businesses,' I said, 'this sort of behaviour would be sufficient grounds to terminate your contract.'

Juhani took a breath, stood up straight, pursed his lips together so that the area around his mouth formed one crinkled, pouting, sulking whole. It all happened at once, and I'm not sure I would have noticed it if I didn't know Juhani.

'I think you should let me do my job the way I see fit,' he said. 'You're the one that made me park manager. I assume organising the clear-up is the park manager's responsibility. And that's what seems to be your biggest issue here, right? The cleaning?'

I glanced at the Big Dipper, smelt the sea of milk.

'Most acutely, yes,' I said. 'But—'

'Done,' said Juhani. 'When you come to work tomorrow morning, the Big Dipper will be spotless. Park manager's honour.'

I said nothing. Once again, Juhani looked and sounded utterly sincere.

Had I been too harsh on him, I wondered, or somehow unreasonable? Had I always been like this? I didn't know where the thought had come from. It just appeared, in a flash, and suddenly it was great and bright in my mind, and it was followed by a feeling that spread right through my body. The feeling didn't seem to dissipate as I stared first at the Big Dipper then at Juhani. And just then I realised where the root of this new feeling might reside. Juhani seemed genuinely horrified at the thought of being fired. Surely this told me how much he valued his workplace? Which suggested he might be willing to change his behaviours after all.

'You promise to take care of it?'

Juhani nodded. 'When duty calls, the park manager will always rise to the occasion.'

I wasn't entirely sure what these words had to do with what we'd just been discussing, but I decided to let it go. I asked when he was planning to get around to clearing up, and he said he would do it immediately. I had a nagging feeling that there was something else I should have said, but I didn't know what. Eventually, I forced myself to walk away. It was reasonable to say I had mixed feelings about the situation.

Maybe Juhani was right. Maybe I just needed to relax.

6

I was a great connoisseur of closing credits.

I watched one film every week. I found this an optimal frequency, given how complex an event this could be. The film I ended up watching was the result of a thorough selection process. There was an almost infinite number of factors that had to be taken into consideration, although these could be whittled down to a handful of crucial ones, meaning that the groundwork could be done in about a week. I followed a number of what are loosely termed 'film reviews', but only to get an overview of what was on offer. Very rarely did I agree with anything the reviewers said; to my mind they didn't focus on what was important.

For instance, only very few film reviews provided a good understanding of how many people appear on screen, on average, at any given moment. And I rarely ever saw any list of budget expenses, let alone any that were itemised in a satisfactory manner. I was never warned in advance how many minutes and seconds a particularly praiseworthy scene would last. This had a disproportionately negative impact on my overall viewing experience: everything was up in the air and regrettably unclear, and thus enjoying the scene playing out in front of me was impossible from the outset. Another thing I never found in reviews was information about exactly how many people had taken part in the film's production. This was an essential piece of information as I took my seat in the cinema or made myself comfortable at home in front of a streaming service: how many staff hours was I about to watch, and how did the team's overall productivity compare to that of other, similar projects?

Furthermore, how was the length of the film divided between the subjects it portrayed?

In the case of one particular thriller set during the depths of winter, the calculation was very straightforward: snow – 34%, depressed police officer – 21%, the cunning criminal mastermind hurtling around on a motorbike – 15%, the police officer's resourceful spouse – 11%, hand-held weapons – 9%, overpriced winter trousers – 6%, coffee and other refreshments – 4%. Indeed, one of the most interested features of going to the cinema was comparing how these percentages varied from one film to the next.

Then there were the closing credits.

Everything about the film was crystallised in the credits. They were the film's heart. I was finally able to find out what had really happened. Good, informative credits were the turning point, the moment when the film really grabbed my attention – if this happened at all.

This time it did not happen.

I had only barely been able to follow the story of two singers and their love affair. I hadn't actively paid attention to the proportions in this film because they didn't seem all that interesting, and the credits didn't change this fact. What's more, I realised that a film in which a famous singer was portrayed by a far less famous singer was already doomed to asymmetry and internal incoherence, and not even the credits could repair the damage.

'Infatuation'. 'Falling in love'. 'Love story'. 'Happy ending'. I didn't normally pay much attention to advertising slogans like these. The events of the previous week had clearly affected my judgement.

Schopenhauer was asleep at the other end of the sofa. Outside it was still November, but without the rain. All should have been well, and in other circumstances it might well have been well. But things had become ... complicated. All of a sudden, in the blink of an eye. And I wasn't thinking only of Juhani (I still couldn't bring myself to think dispassionately about his return) or the fact that Toy of Finland had turned from a trustworthy supplier to a blackmailer and potentially destructive business associate, if I could use a term like that in these circumstances.

I thought of Laura Helanto.

I hadn't heard anything from her since I'd left her studio in a mood that was hard to interpret.

All evening, I'd been aware of the fact that my telephone was on the coffee table in front of me. I'd seen it out of the corner of my eye while ostensibly paying attention to the singer's extra-marital affairs. I knew I wasn't at my best on the phone. But something had to be done, and I didn't know what. In this respect, I could relate to the singer. She darted from one song and one mattress to the next without achieving any equilibrium in her life. I glanced at the picture on my wall – one of Gauss's equations, in his own handwriting. The equation was one of the most beautiful ever written; it was the fruit of many years' work. But I wasn't thinking about that right now. I was thinking about getting started; after all, there was a time when even Gauss had to put pen to paper for the first time. I picked up my phone.

'Hi.'

'Henri Koskinen here,' I said.

'I know.'

'It's in your contacts.'

'What?'

'My phone number.'

'Yes, that's right, it's saved on my phone.'

'That shows you've been thinking about me.'

Silence. It was moments like this that made talking on the

telephone so difficult. If I had seen Laura's face, I might have been able to draw some conclusions from it. Now it was as though I was at the bottom of a well: I could hear my own words like an echo, and all I could see around me were the same empty walls as always.

'Really?' she asked eventually.

I felt instant relief. 'A certain number is associated with a certain person,' I said, and confirmed this with a little nod. 'The thought process doesn't have to be long, and naturally it doesn't always leave a permanent trace, but nonetheless it is essential with a view to the final result. In conclusion, therefore, you've been thinking about me.'

'What about you?' she asked. It was as though her voice had changed ever so slightly.

'I've been thinking both about you and your number,' I admitted.

'Good to know it's both.'

'Perhaps less about your number.'

Was that a little laugh? The sound was short and soft, but it reminded me of laughter.

'So, everything is fine,' she said after a short pause. Both the pause and the laughter had made me doubt myself.

'No,' I said candidly.

More silence.

'Is it something to do with Juhani?'

'Why…?' I began but felt the first claws of agitation and realised this was something I would have to skirt around for now.

'It's to do with you,' I said.

'In what way?'

I thought about this for a moment and looked up at Gauss's equation. It began, it presented the solution, and it ended.

'I'm not sure I like what you said the other day, but I want to see you again because I enjoy your company.'

For a moment, Laura was silent.

'I've been thinking ... along the same lines.'

And there it was again: something happened. My heart emptied, right down to the last drop of blood; that's what it felt like, because I was suddenly dizzy.

'What do you want?' asked Laura.

The question took me by surprise, and just as surprising was the way an answer formed in my head without my even thinking about it. This time I didn't have to look up at the equation.

'I enjoy your company,' I said. 'I've noticed that I'd like to increase the proportion of that company in my life.'

'I'd like to increase the proportion of you in my life too.'

'By how much?' I heard myself asking. 'I don't expect you to give an exact number or percentage, just a rough estimate, the approximate value being...'

'A rough estimate? Let's say that double would be a good start.'

'In that case, the four hours we spent together last week would be—'

'And what about you? How much would you like to increase it by?'

Again, my heart. This time it was trying to leap out of my chest.

'Me?' I said. 'I'd like to increase it a thousandfold.'

Please, someone stop me, I wanted to shout. I do not talk like this, in such imprecise terms, and especially not in irrational factors.

'That was beautifully said.'

'It is, of course ... the roughest of rough estimates...' I began, and didn't know what I was saying. My cheeks felt warm, almost burning.

'I understand,' said Laura quietly. 'Still, or maybe because of that, it was beautifully said.'

I didn't say anything. All of a sudden I couldn't trust that what came out of my mouth would be sensible.

'Perhaps we can move in that general direction,' she said. 'Somewhere between double and a thousandfold.'

'By a quick calculation, that would be—'

'Saturday?'

It took a moment to realise that Laura's question was simultaneously a suggestion. She told me she had a short but important appointment on Saturday morning but that the rest of the day was free. I was about to hang up, the phone by my ear was like a redhot coal, and my arm was cramping.

'Everything fine at the park?'

Laura's question brought me hurtling back to reality. The difference from our previous conversation was like that between a beam of summer sunshine and a gust of icy wind. I realised quite unequivocally that I didn't want to mix Juhani or Toy of Finland, or anything to do with the adventure park, with *this*. They didn't belong in this part of the world anymore. I felt the decision forming in my mind, like a complicated equation suddenly coming into focus: I would not talk to Laura about park business ever again. But I didn't want to lie to her either. Therefore, I had to change perspective slightly and look at the bigger picture.

'Everything will be fine,' I said.

7

The Big Dipper was gleaming like a brand-new mirror, and the first customers of the morning were already hurtling down its slides. I took a deep breath, inhaled the cool air inside the hall, and concluded that it smelt fresh.

I looked around.

There was a good number of customers, though the doors had only just opened. What's more, the customers seemed to be behaving much more tidily than yesterday. I rubbed my eyes, which were dry with fatigue, and was about to head to my office when I stopped. At first, I didn't know what had made me stop. I allowed my eyes to pan across the hall. Customers, machines and rides working impeccably, a modest volume level. I waited for a moment, but nothing changed. Then I walked into the middle of the hall to see a bit better, or at least to see things from a slightly different perspective, and I saw everything I had seen a moment ago, nothing more, nothing less. Still, I had an inkling there was something I simply hadn't noticed yet. But what? Then, as though an overhead projector had switched from one slide to another, I saw the difference. I shouldn't have tried to note what I could see, but what I couldn't see.

The staff.

I realised I had walked past the ticket desk, seen the sign in which a photograph of Kristian – in a typically smiley pose – said he would be back in a jiffy. I'd noticed that the door to Esa's monitor room was closed; recently he had taken to keeping the door open, which I'd assumed must be because even he couldn't cope with the sulphuric sauna in there. Samppa wasn't in his usual spot behind the Turtle Trucks, situated in front of Laura Helanto's mural painted in the style of Helen Frankenthaler, holding the first psycho-developmental playgroup session of the day. And when I looked towards the administration wing, even Minttu K's office looked dark, though the marketing manager's lights usually shone round the clock and on most days the aroma of cigarettes and *lonkero* wafted all the way out into the park. Now there wasn't the faintest glimmer of light, the slightest pong of alcopop. There wasn't even the usual whiff of menthol cigarettes and the curious sensory dissonance they caused, a fine balance between Polos and a pulmonary aneurysm.

Something had happened.

I spun around just as a herd of short customers sprinted past me. I almost lost my balance, but regained it at the last moment.

I saw the light.

The Curly Cake Café was open. I could smell the first aromas of coffee, porridge and today's special offer, stuffed baked potatoes named Fire and Grimstone. That meant Johanna must be here.

Johanna was level-headed, I thought as I paced towards the café. She would never do anything irresponsible, she wouldn't leave the park unstaffed ... And immediately afterwards, I was reminded of the way Johanna had behaved on the morning I discovered Juhani alive in my office. She had offered me a second bun, which was completely unprecedented. Only now did I realise what I had in fact witnessed. By her own standards, she was beside herself.

I walked up the steps, arrived at the entrance to the café and stopped at the door.

They were all sitting around a table, listening to Juhani. I heard his voice but couldn't make out the words. He was gesturing wildly and seemed very enthusiastic about something or another. Every member of my staff was watching him and listening intently: Kristian nodding keenly, his mouth slightly open; Samppa constantly adjusting the position of his scarf and ponytail; Esa expressionless, his arms folded rigidly across his US Marine Corps sweatshirt; Minttu K spluttering and sipping something from her large coffee mug; and Johanna – Johanna! – perhaps betraying a hint of a smile.

Esa was the first to notice me. I don't know how he did it, but word got round the table in an instant. I wondered if he might know some secret communication technique that only special forces knew how to use. The others quickly turned, looked towards me, then just as quickly turned their attention back to Juhani. Only Juhani looked right at me. I reached their table and was about to ask why they were all sitting in the café during their shifts, but I didn't get the chance.

'Nice job, isn't it?'

It took a second or two to work out what Juhani was referring to.

'Yes...'

'Sparkling like a diamond.'

'Yes...'

'Sparkling like these good people here.' Juhani raised a hand as if to introduce the employees to me. Still, not one of them so much as glanced in my direction.

'That's what I mean,' I said. 'We need someone in the foyer, and the main hall too. All the other jobs are at a standstill. You should all get back to work.'

Nobody moved. Juhani's blue eyes looked up at me.

'You heard the boss,' he said after a beat, looking each of the employees round the table in the eye. 'Let's make this the best adventure park ever. Keep up the good spirits, guys. *Vamos.*'

The employees stood up. Nobody said anything. The group silently dispersed around the park, all with the exception of

Johanna. With a swing of the swinging doors, she slipped into the kitchen and appeared to be looking disheartened daggers at me. I couldn't be entirely sure because there was a vitrine full of sandwiches between us, and part of Johanna's face was obscured behind a row of feta-and-pesto baguettes. Juhani stood up.

'I really like these people,' he said. 'They've got a great energy going. I inspire them, and they inspire me back. The more we talk and share things, the more ideas we'll have. I love being park manager. Thank you, Henri. What do you say about the Big Dipper?'

'It's clean…'

'Just as we agreed,' Juhani added quickly, and walked around the table. I caught the smell of his aftershave from a distance. 'It feels like I'm starting a new life. And I suppose I am. I was dead, to all intents and purposes. It's unbelievable, the effect that can have on you.'

Juhani was about to walk past me, then he stopped.

'A little extra budget…' he began. 'It might come in handy. The crew that came in to tidy the place up last night, they usually clean operating theatres. They're good, and they're all about the hygiene, but they certainly know their own worth. As they should. Anyway, I'm needed in the hall.'

I'm not sure whether I was about to say something, but by the time I had regained my powers of speech, Juhani had already disappeared and I was left standing by myself in the middle of the café. Johanna was busying herself in the kitchen, and a dozen or so children and adults were enjoying snacks and refreshments. I strode off towards my office. Just then, my telephone rang. I didn't recognise the number.

'Afternoon. Otto Härkä from Toy of Finland here,' came the man's voice.

An image of the fifty-something man with the imposing

moustache like a damp, yellowed garden brush on his upper lip flashed through my mind. I said good afternoon and waited, then turned into the corridor leading to my office.

'Just calling to ask how I might get hold of you, that's all.'

'Get hold of me?' I turned and stepped into my office.

'Yes, I mean, where does the CEO of the adventure park spend his afternoons when he's not...'

I saw him sitting at my desk with his back to me, his phone at his ear.

'...in his own office?' I heard these last words in stereo, from the phone and right in front of me.

Otto Härkä was alone. He was dressed in the same way as at our last meeting: black blazer, blue shirt, loose corduroys and a pair of laced, black winter shoes. I couldn't decide whether he looked more like a regular at the betting shop or something else altogether, something more threatening.

'I thought we could have a look at our catalogue one more time, right here at your desk,' he said once I had reached my chair and sat down. He leant down to his briefcase and took out the same meagre catalogue that I'd already seen.

'Does this mean the Moose Chute is available after all?' I asked.

'It doesn't quite mean that,' said Otto Härkä, and opened the catalogue and slid it across the desk. I saw the one thing I didn't want to see.

'I am still not interested in the Crocodile Canyon,' I said.

'Well, interest isn't really how we measure these things now, is it?' he said. 'I think you and I should come at this from a slightly different perspective, don't you?'

I looked Otto Härkä in the eyes. They didn't reveal anything. His manner of speaking didn't bring me any clarity either. His sentences were both cryptic and deceptive: at face value, you might get the impression of a jovial salesman, but listening more closely and stripping away the bumbling and the obfuscation to reveal the heart of the matter, you realised the conversation was ultimately very straightforward.

Otto Härkä had come here to repeat his threats.

At the same time, the fact remained that the adventure park's budget couldn't withstand an acquisition like the Crocodile Canyon, let alone the financial repercussions – one of which would be that we wouldn't be able to acquire any new equipment for a long time. Not to mention that we would miss out on the Moose Chute. Then, almost simultaneously, the equation inverted itself. After a quick calculation, I realised that Toy of Finland might be in the same situation, only the other way around. I don't know why I hadn't thought of this earlier, and yet, I did know: I'd had other things on my mind.

'Is Toy of Finland in trouble?' I asked.

For the first time, I saw something happen in Otto Härkä's eyes. A fleeting flicker.

'We're here to talk about your park now, and how magnificently the Crocodile Canyon will fit in, and of course it'll fit because this is where it belongs, am I right?' he said. 'And because it belongs here, then you and I ought to agree on a delivery date right here and now, and that's exactly what we're going to do. No point mulling it over when there's nothing to mull, right?' Otto Härkä was speaking a little faster than before. And, if possible, he was bumbling more too. 'I tell you what, I'll put a note in here to get the Crocodile Canyon delivered extra quick because I know you want it so badly, and the customer's always right,' he continued. 'Let's have a look at the calendar, shall we?'

Otto Härkä stared at the white-painted office wall to my right. There was nothing on the wall, let alone a calendar.

'That's what we'll do. Now, if we take a look at Friday...' he continued, and looked up at me. 'Well, what do you know? Friday is a very good choice, if I may say so, so we'll take that. Friday it is, then. One Crocodile Canyon will be coming your way on Friday, and the price is the same one we discussed when we showed you the catalogue the other day. Well, that's that sorted. Nice doing business with you. It's been a real pleasure.'

I said nothing. Otto Härkä took the catalogue from the table and returned it to his briefcase. He stood up. With the briefcase in his hand, he looked like a civil servant on his way to the office, but at the same time it looked as though someone had played a prank on him and glued the handle to his hand and now he was wondering how to get his own back.

'What happens if I refuse?'

Otto Härkä stepped towards the door.

'What's there to refuse,' he answered without turning, 'when this is the final offer?'

8

Only a few days ago, I'd imagined that my life was finally in order again. The thought hadn't come out of nowhere: it was founded on a realistic assessment of the situation and the facts at hand. The truth was that, at the moment I thought it, my life was in order.

But I couldn't say the same about the current state of affairs.

I rolled over in bed, though I knew the relief it gave me was only illusory. Soon enough, this new position would be just as uncomfortable as the previous one, and sleep would be as distant as when I had started tossing and turning. I heard Schopenhauer take a deep breath at the foot of the bed. From the time he was a kitten, he had a tactic of falling asleep once and once only during the night, and he resorted to that tactic now too.

It felt as though the park was somehow slipping from my grasp, out of reach. Or worse still: as though I had already lost my grip and only just realised it. It was hard to explain the feeling in concrete terms. I was still the park's owner, and I still made all the decisions about new acquisitions; all changes, large and small, required my consent. But despite this, it still felt as though I'd drifted from the shoreline and found myself up a certain creek without the proverbial paddle.

Juhani's return still flummoxed me. I was understandably angry at him, but I was still happy and relieved that he was alive, as silly as it sounded in the light of all that had happened. At no point had he actually been dead – he had been fast asleep in his caravan in eastern Finland while I was fending off his criminal money-lenders with a giant, plastic rabbit's ear. And while he was doubtless roasting sausages on an open fire and exchanging pleasantries with the other happy campers, I was left with no option but to hide the considerably heavy body of one of these dangerous crooks in the adventure-park freezer.

And what was Juhani talking to the staff about? Was the change I'd noticed in their behaviour a result of his influence? Did Juhani talk to them the way he talked to everybody else – feeding them irresponsible, unfounded and, more to the point, untrue notions and ideas?

These questions brought me back to Laura Helanto and what she had said about me and Juhani.

Those words spun round and round in my mind, and so did my reaction to them. Of course, I was aware that Laura Helanto caused me varying degrees of agitation, but losing my temper like that, as well as developing a sudden reluctance even to count things properly, was something I really didn't know how to process and couldn't have anticipated in any way. I could see, and later had concluded, that this sense of agitation was akin to what people called happiness – the emotion I felt when I was around her – only this emotion was a negative one: it was just as powerful but positioned at the opposite end of the spectrum.

My emotions continued along their rollercoaster ride: I found myself at times strangely disappointed, only to feel hopeful again a moment later. I was perturbed by what Laura had said I was. On the other hand, it seemed perfectly possible that at least one of us was mistaken in our assessment of the situation.

The restless night and the hours lying awake failed to provide any clarity on the matter.

It was still dark when I set off for the train station. Wind whipped across the platform, whistling around me in the rickety shelter.

And perhaps the strength of the wind, the way it tugged at my coat and ruffled my hair, had a cumulative effect on me. The night seemed to merge with the wind, irrevocably, and I found myself wondering whether I'd overreacted – in every respect.

The train arrived on schedule, and the connecting bus slowly glided to my bus stop a full minute earlier than usual. This sealed one of my decisions: when it came to internal affairs at the park, I could talk to the staff too, just like Juhani. In these conversations, I would stick to the facts, lay out what was sensible and, where necessary, invoke the inviolable authority of my carefully compiled calculations. For, ultimately, what can possibly be more convincing than the truth? Whatever Juhani had told them, the truth would prevail. By the time I started walking from the bus stop to the adventure park, I didn't notice the wind at all.

I found Esa sitting at his monitors. The only light in the room was that emanating from the multiple screens in front of him. There was something laborious and instantly exhausting about staring at these faint, blurry images. Having said that, they seemed to have the opposite effect on Esa. Again he was wearing his Marine sweatshirt, which provided details of the owner's years of service and which, again, I found highly improbable.

'There's a minesweeper on camera two,' he said, and pointed at one of the screens. 'The kid in the dinosaur T-shirt. One metre fifteen, fair hair. Lightweight little trooper. There he goes, running, looking for cover, pants down, then plants the mine. My guess is he doesn't want to tell his commander he's got an upset stomach, so he isn't taken off active duty.'

I looked at the monitor. At that moment, our young customer

wasn't leaving behind a trail of destruction but was instead climbing at a ferocious pace up the so-called Velcro Palm.

'We need to eliminate the enemy,' Esa continued. 'Or before long we'll have half the battalion in the field hospital. Do you want me to call in the cavalry?'

Esa was already pulling the microphone attached to the monitor table towards him, aiming it at his angular, square goatee, and his right hand was nearing a row of buttons.

'There's no need,' I said quickly. 'I'll take care of it. Esa, I wonder if I could have a word.'

Esa stopped, leant back from the console. 'As I've always said,' he nodded, 'when the park calls...'

'You will answer the call of duty. Well, this very much affects the park ... Or, let's say for now that it *might* affect the park. As you know, my brother Juhani has returned.'

'That was a surprise,' said Esa. 'But I didn't let it distract me. There are still men coming back from Vietnam.'

'Indeed,' I said, though I wasn't sure I wholly agreed with him. 'I've noticed that he's been talking to the staff, as a group and maybe even one on one. Perhaps he has spoken to you too?'

Esa maintained his composure but somehow retreated into his chair a little too. Moreover, he didn't say anything, which was most out of character. Not that Esa was one for small talk – far from it; but I'd become used to him having an answer for everything. Not this time, though. He only responded after an extended silence.

'We discussed the park's security and defence protocols. I planned this myself long ago. In fact I started the minute I began working for the park four years ago. Back then, we didn't even have a security camera, so I patrolled the park by myself. Long stakeouts, terrible provisions, unclear lines of attack.'

'Right,' I said, before Esa could sink any deeper into his

memories. 'Did Juhani have anything to say about the park's current ... protocols?'

'He agrees with me that the defence budget needs increasing.'

'Does he?'

'In fact, he agrees with me about everything else too,' Esa continued, and it sounded unmistakably as though this thought pleased him greatly. 'Like me, he recognises the need to extend our operations beyond the park itself. There are a number of large blind spots all around us. A few unmanned aircraft should do the trick, I think. A fleet of drones. Of course, this is a big investment and will require a significant expansion of my job description. But when we spoke about it, Juhani was assured that this is exactly what we need.'

'Juhani doesn't make the decisions,' I said so quickly that I heard my own words before I'd even been able to think them through. 'What I mean is, he doesn't have that sort of position in the park.'

Esa's usually unflinching gaze inched its way towards the row of monitors.

'He has some good ideas,' said Esa.

It felt as though, just as the oxygen levels in the room were dropping, the temperature was rising. It shouldn't have been possible, either biologically, physiologically or thermodynamically. The phenomenon was clearly the upshot of Esa's steady methane production, which in a variety of ways had a cumulative, deleterious impact on his surroundings.

'Esa,' I asked after a short pause. 'Did Juhani tell you how all this would be paid for or where the extra money is going to come from?'

Esa looked down at his monitors. 'He mentioned it,' he replied, still not looking at me.

'And?'

'He gave the impression that things might be different if he came back to run the park.'

I had come to Esa first because I'd imagined he would think of Juhani's return with the same neutrality as he did when, say, one of our customers broke a shin. Perhaps I was wrong.

'Esa,' I said as calmly as the turmoil Juhani was causing within me and the stuffiness of the air allowed. 'Even if Juhani were to start running the park again, which is a highly theoretical proposition, this would not in any way increase the amount of money at our disposal.'

I believed I had expressed this fact as clearly as it could possibly be expressed. Now Esa looked me in the eyes, adjusted his position in his tall chair with the large neck support, and regained his characteristic dourness.

'There are several waterways nearby too,' he said. 'The Vantaa River is less than a kilometre away. Juhani pointed this out; I hadn't thought of it myself. He suggested investing in an amphibian defence team too, maybe even with some underwater reconnaissance capabilities. Why would he say something like that if we couldn't afford it?'

The sight and smell of today's lunch, Frolicking Fish Fingers, was so strong that I had the distinct sense of wading through breaded cod as I walked along the corridor towards the café. The noise was as potent as the smell. To my mind, eating and shouting at the same time was an impractical combination, but it didn't seem to cause the children any difficulty.

I walked through the swinging doors into the kitchen and found Johanna sliding a tray of Scoundrel's Scones – small strawberry toffee muffins – into the oven. She closed the oven door and turned to look at me. Her expression didn't flinch.

'Do you want something to eat?' she asked, tucking a few

strands of long red hair behind her ears. 'I'm frying ten eggs for myself. I can fry the same for you, if you want.'

'Ten...' I said, bewildered. 'No, thank you, I don't need ... ten eggs. There's something I wanted to ask you about.'

'I can cook and talk.'

Johanna always got straight to the point; she was a woman of few words.

'Very well,' I said, and looked on as she cracked the eggs into the frying pan quicker than I could blink. 'As you've probably noticed, my brother Juhani has come back.'

'He eats all his meals here, from breakfast right through to supper.'

'Indeed,' I said as the eggs sizzled in the pan. 'I wonder if he's spoken to you, one on one?'

'He eats here. Sometimes we eat together. Are you sure you don't want an egg?'

'I'm quite sure I don't want an egg,' I said, and noticed I was getting a little agitated. I feared Johanna might have noticed it too, though she didn't so much as glance at me. 'While you've been eating together, I wonder whether the subject of the park has ever come up.'

'Of course,' said Johanna, and peered at me. 'We both work here.'

I was keenly aware of what I'd just heard from Esa.

'Would I be right in thinking he has some plans for the café too?'

Almost imperceptibly, Johanna raised her shoulders. 'He sees a lot of potential in the Curly Cake, the kind of potential I see too. The kind of things I've already mentioned to you.'

'I'm afraid, right now, opening a French-style bistro at the other end of the park simply isn't possible,' I said.

'Juhani says he and I share many of the same dreams,' said Johanna as she moved the spatula under the eggs with the same precision and lightness of touch as a brain surgeon. 'And together we can make those dreams come true, he told me. He says he might know a suitable vineyard where we can order quality vintages directly. Château Platini, it's called. And he has a potential contact with Mitterrand, an importer specialising in artisan pâtés. Juhani said good ideas pay for themselves many times over, and you should always look bravely to the future, and a lot depends on the attitude you have to getting things done.'

This wasn't the Johanna I knew, I thought to myself. That Johanna would never talk like this. I looked on as she slid the flawless yolks and dazzling whites onto a plate, picked it up and carried it to the table.

'And he stressed to me,' Johanna continued as she ground black pepper over the eggs, 'that any French bistro worth its salt should always have fresh squid on the menu. How did he know that's my favourite food too?'

Samppa was just rounding off his action-story lesson. A dozen children were listening to Samppa's story and moving – or rather dashing, bashing and climbing – to the words. There were certain sections in the story where the children's actions lost focus a little. From time to time, the story's hippopotamuses and albatrosses spoke in rather abstruse psychological terms, and I wasn't sure whether the scene in which the albatross and the hippopotamus came face to face at a divorce hearing was suitable listening for six-year-olds. I could see that Samppa thought this was an important moment in the story, and he wiped the corner of his eye as he read out a section in which the albatross and the hippopotamus divided up their belongings in a way that, even after much agonised self-reflection, the hippo still found terribly unjust.

I waited for Samppa to finish his lesson and send the children back to their parents. Then I walked up to him and asked outright what he had been discussing with Juhani. Samppa shook his head so vigorously that I was certain I could hear his feathered earrings whooshing in the air.

'That's confidential,' he said. 'I wouldn't tell anybody else what *you* say at my surgery.'

'Surgery?'

Samppa quickly scratched his temple and didn't answer right away, so I managed to ask my next question.

'You mean your current job?'

Samppa looked pained. 'Think of it this way, I'm providing a service,' he said eventually.

'Samppa. If you can't talk about Juhani's affairs, surely you can talk about your own? What service are you providing, exactly?'

'My surgery,' he said quietly.

'But you work here. You're paid a monthly salary. You should be doing the job you're paid to do. You give the children various themed sessions. That sort of thing.'

'That could change,' he said, and I sensed a new weight and determination in his voice.

'Did Juhani promise that you can open your own surgery once he starts running the park again?'

Samppa was silent.

'Juhani appreciates my holistic approach to play,' he said after a pause. 'The kind where adults can experience the healing powers of play too. Grown-ups' playtime. It's a form of therapy I've been developing. I suggested I should have the chance to refine this new therapy in practice, full-time, and Juhani said that sounded fantastic.'

'And who will do your regular work, then?'

'Juhani said everything will work out once—'

'He starts running the park again,' I finished the sentence for him.

Samppa said nothing.

I stopped on the threshold of Minttu K's door. I could hear her snoring and caught a warm, acrid note of alcohol and grapefruit in the air. She was fast asleep on the short, dark-red sofa in her office, in a particularly uncomfortable-looking position and still wearing her jet-black, tight-fitting blazer. I didn't walk into the room, and Minttu K's passed-out whiff wasn't the only reason I changed my mind. I could imagine what Juhani had promised her: the doubling of the marketing budget and a pipeline from the Hartwall brewery giving her an unlimited supply of *lonkero* on tap.

I wondered whether I should try talking to Kristian, too, and decided against it. I already knew enough. And everything I knew led to one and the same place.

9

The story about the caravan might well be true. It would be the first true thing since the resurrection.

I checked the address that Kristian had given me one more time, then looked out towards the sun and the sea.

November. The most misunderstood of months.

The sun never rose very high, but when it shone from a clear blue sky, as it did right now, its light was like an endless cascade of white gold and silk. On windless days, the temperature was very pleasant, perfect for any kind of activity, be it jogging or building a house. The harshness of winter hadn't yet pierced the air, and the dampness of autumn had finally evaporated. The leafless trees didn't yet feel final, but simply served to clarify the view. There was a history of entrenched – and, it should be noted, mostly emotional – stereotypes about November, which severely dented its image, but in the cold light of facts and statistics, this was one of the best times of year, especially when it came to business and productivity. November was the Lasse Virén of the calendar: like the great long-distance runner, it stumbles, falls, then jumps to its feet and takes the gold.

I knew why I was thinking things like this. I was trying not to think about what had brought me to the entrance of a campsite by the seashore in eastern Helsinki.

Juhani.

Who had told me he would be working from home today. I didn't know quite what this meant in practice, especially when it came to the park manager's roles and responsibilities. The park manager's job was to resolve any acute problems that arose and

sort out anything that needed doing in the actual park, and he
was responsible for making sure everything ran smoothly.

I noted that I both did and did not look forward to hearing
Juhani's explanation.

I walked through the gates of the campsite, leaving the reception
hut behind me and turned left. The site looked like a cross
between an English terraced street and a camping exhibition.
While the narrow, street-like pathways were soothingly identical,
you could still tell them apart both from the numbers and the
different caravans and mobile homes parked along their lengths.

Row eleven. I turned right.

I smelt the proximity of the sea and a smoking sausage on a
solitary, unmanned barbecue. There weren't very many campers
at this time of year, but there were a few. I clearly wasn't the only
one who had looked beyond the calendar and the sales pitches. I
arrived at the end of the row; a seagull squawked above me. To
my left there was woodland, and beyond that the sea. To my right
was plot number 161.

The caravan wasn't new.

It was small and beige except for a hem of faded yellow running
around the edge, and in front of it on the narrow patch of garden was
a charcoal grill – old, battered and spattered like the one I'd seen
before – and a flimsy-looking round table with plastic folding chairs
on both sides. In a curious way, everything was as small as possible, as
though the owner had gone out of his way to find miniature versions
of everything. The caravan had a window facing the pathway, and the
curtains were open. Still, all I could see in the window was a reflection
of the blue sky, and I didn't know whether I was being watched or
whether I was watching someone I couldn't actually see.

I walked up to the door of the caravan, noted the electric cables dangling adventurously from the door and knocked, perhaps a little louder than necessary. The caravan was a lightweight fibreglass box, it wobbled and rattled when I rapped my knuckles against the door. I heard the thud of footsteps, the creak of plastic, and the door opened.

Judging by his attire, Juhani was either about to leave or had just got home. He was wearing a smart white shirt and grey tracksuit bottoms. The upper part suggested a blazer and life outside the caravan, while the tracksuit bottoms told a different story, one about what went on inside the caravan, perhaps. He'd hunched over to open the door. Juhani was just over twenty centimetres shorter than me, but even he couldn't stand upright in his new home.

'I've come to talk to you,' I said. 'And hopefully to make a proposal.'

'By all means,' he said, then beamed at me. 'Come on in.'

He stepped back from the doorway, and I followed him inside. This required an amount of concentration, because I had to crouch down and propel myself forwards at the same time – this simply to get through the door – then, my shoulders hunched, I crept towards a microscopic bench and a table bolted to the floor, and finally folded myself in between them.

Juhani lodged himself at the other side of the table. Our feet and shins kept bashing into each other. Eventually, we found a position whereby neither of us was kicking the other. We were sitting as diagonally and as far apart as possible, and yet we were probably closer to each other than at any time since our childhood.

I felt like a giant. The table and the benches and everything in the caravan seemed to come from the same extra-small catalogue as the garden furniture, and everything looked just as worn out. The caravan smelt of coffee and the chemical toilet.

'How can I help?' asked Juhani.

'I'm hoping we can have a serious conversation.'

'Sure.'

I looked at Juhani. I knew he could say 'sure' to almost anything, but it didn't necessarily mean much.

'I've been talking to the staff,' I began, 'and it appears you have been giving them a misleading impression of how—'

Juhani raised his right hand to interrupt me. 'Hang on a minute. Who says it's misleading?'

I looked at him. 'The facts,' I said. 'The budget, which I have calculated many times. The funds at our disposal. The number of customers at the park. The concrete, immutable facts.'

Juhani was quiet for a moment.

'But none of the staff?'

'No,' I admitted.

'You see?'

'See what?'

'What you can do when you inspire people,' he said. 'They start thinking positively. All I had to do was open their minds, show them some new perspectives, encourage their good ideas and suggest a few of my own. They're great people. Incredible amounts of positive energy. All the gloom is gone, the moping is history. They can see opportunities again, Henri. They can see the future.'

I knew this was one of the challenges one often experienced talking to Juhani: long before the other party realised what was happening, Juhani had already moved the conversation as far as possible from the original point.

'It has to stop,' I said in an attempt to steer the conversation back on track. 'The lying. It's got to stop.'

Juhani's face froze as though I'd just let a dreadful slur out of my mouth. As he had done many times before, he tilted his head ever so slightly and looked at me as if from a wholly new angle.

'I haven't lied to anybody about anything, ever.'

'You're lying now telling me you never lie.'

'Here we go, typical Henri, splitting hairs again,' said Juhani as though addressing an invisible audience beside him. 'And all so he can win the argument. I guess he'll take out a pen and paper next and draw an equation to show how I've always been wrong and always will be.'

'There is truth and there is untruth,' I said. 'And both can be proved in mathematical terms.'

'My own brother,' he said quietly.

I paused for a moment.

'I want to help you,' I said eventually.

Juhani looked as though he had just woken up or knocked into something. He looked genuinely confused. The position of his head had corrected itself too.

'Henri,' he said. 'It's the other way around. I want to help *you*. That's exactly what I'm doing. I'm trying to make the park a happy, open, successful place again. I want to show you the way.'

'The way ... where?'

'I suppose you're wondering why I've been working from home today.'

'It had crossed my mind,' I reply honestly.

'Pensioner Play,' he said. That familiar sparkle had returned to his eyes.

I said nothing and waited.

'Kids alone aren't going to be enough to get our customer numbers up where they need to be,' he began. 'And besides, there aren't all that many kids in Finland. I don't know a single one. What I mean is, there aren't very many of them compared to our most abundant natural resource: the elderly. And where do we keep the elderly these days? Behind lock and key. What happens there? Happiness shrivels on the vine. We're going to bring happiness back with a bang. We'll invite pensioners into the park. Imagine the joy, the happiness. Not to mention the exercise, the companionship, the fun. We bus them in from the old folks' homes, ice creams all round, and off to the slides they go. Everything I've read about dementia works in our favour here: people regress to the level of a child. And I've thought of the financial side too. Imagine this: Caper Castle full of geriatrics who will take hours to find their way out again. We get the full entrance fee, but only one apparatus has any wear and tear and needs repairing. If they're quicker on their feet but still don't know what day it is, that's not a problem either. The park doors can be locked from the outside too, you know. It'll be cost-effective, and everyone's a winner. Just imagine it.'

I did as Juhani asked: I imagined the scenario. I saw senior citizens stumbling, panicked, bashing into one another, falling from the ladders and climbing frames. I saw broken bones, fractures, the endless stretchering of patients. I saw lawsuits.

'I don't think this is a particularly good idea,' I said.

Juhani either snorted or exhaled forcefully through his nose. 'Because it's my idea,' he said. 'You treat me just like our parents. You were always trying to talk them out of things too.'

There was a new tone to his voice, perhaps a hint of bitterness. I didn't want to discuss our parents under any circumstances, but the subject now seemed both unavoidable and inevitable. What's more, Juhani's monologue concerned me so much that I realised I was becoming agitated.

'Yes, because their projects were nonsensical,' I said. 'They founded a puppet theatre with the aim of performing action films to huge audiences. Do you remember the premiere of *Rambo*? The audience consisted of one drunk, and the final scene culminated in him attacking the Rambo puppet. And before that, the fire-crackers used as hand grenades set the props on fire.'

'That's innovation for you,' said Juhani. 'Open-mindedness.'

I shook my head. 'They opened a herring farm,' I said, 'though at the time we lived in the driest, most land-locked forest in southwest Finland. All through the summer, the place stank so much it made your eyes water. Nothing ever made any sense.'

'Passion, a love of life,' said Juhani, gradually raising his voice. 'There were no shackles, no pigeon-holes. They followed their dreams. My dreams...'

I knew I shouldn't open my mouth; I knew I was all-too close to losing my temper.

'Your dreams are bankrupt dreams,' I said. 'They always have been. You are a walking bankruptcy, one that's always spawning new bankruptcies, that go on to create little bankruptcies of their own. The Wikipedia entry for bankruptcy has a photograph of you and no text. Whenever a company files for bankruptcy, all they have to do is mention your name and everybody knows what's happened. If there's ever a bankruptcy Olympics, it'll have to be scrapped right away because you would take gold in every category. You're the mayor of Bankruptville, King Bankrupt the First.'

We stared at each other.

'Was this the serious conversation you came all the way out here to have?' Juhani asked.

'No,' I said honestly. 'I wanted us to consider alternative ways of going forward, of how we can take stock and—'

'I just gave you plenty. Alternatives. Stock-taking.'

'Juhani...'

'Let's continue on our respective paths. You can be the sensible one. It looks like it does you good. You seem happy and content. Relaxed.'

'Thank you,' I said. 'Happiness and contentment come from being responsible.'

'It was a joke, Henri. You're about as relaxed as an iron bar stuck in the tundra.'

I didn't understand what was so amusing about Juhani's previous comment, and I didn't see much resemblance in this metaphor either. I began to sense that the atmosphere in this small fibreglass box might not be the best, but I wanted to outline my proposals.

'As I said when I arrived, I want to discuss—'

'That's what we've been doing,' said Juhani.

'I believe I have a balanced and rewarding proposal that will benefit all parties,' I continued, 'especially in the long term.'

Juhani shook his head again.

I looked him in the eyes and spoke. 'I've been thinking that, if in a year's time, or in two or three years' time, once we are certain of the growth in sales and footfall, and the park's finances are in good enough condition that we can think about considerably updating our equipment and making a number of large infra-structure investments, at that point you could take the lead and oversee the next phase, because as park manager you will have experience of the park's day-to-day operations on a grassroots level, you will know the park from the smallest bolt right up to the financial side of things, where I can guide and help you. At that point, we can talk about some form of joint leadership. That is my proposal.'

Juhani said nothing. A full minute passed.

The fact was that I had said what I had come here to say, and there was nothing to add. The only appropriate move now was to leave, and to this end I began shuffling my shoes under the table. After an amount of fumbling, I managed to extricate myself from between the table and the bench and stood up. Still hunched over, I made my way to the door, opened it and glanced over my shoulder. This required careful coordination. Juhani was sitting on the bench facing the window, his eyes fixed somewhere distant but clearly defined.

'Juhani,' I said. 'I want the park's employees to fulfil their dreams too – to the extent that those dreams are realistic. But now is not the time. There simply isn't any extra money. I don't want you to give them any more unrealistic ideas. If the situation escalates any further, I don't know what will happen or what people will be prepared to do.'

Now Juhani seemed to be listening to me. His head turned, and he looked me in the eye. His gaze was so sincere that it took me back to our childhood.

'Those dreams are alive now,' he said. 'You can't extinguish them all.'

10

Schopenhauer was following me around, asking questions. Very quickly I realised I didn't have any satisfactory answers. I gave him a plate of gamey food rich in minerals, prepared breakfast for myself, too, and sat down at the kitchen table. First I had two pieces of ryebread with sliced turkey, then a glass of live yoghurt sweetened with honey, and drank a cup of tea. I clicked away the business pages on my iPad and readied myself for the next phase of my morning routine. But I didn't stand up. Instead, I stared out of the window and into the dark Kannelmäki morning. Before long I had the distinct impression that the darkness was looking back at me. Of course, I knew this wasn't factually correct, but there was another dimension to the sensation: it told me how I really viewed my current situation.

Only a moment had passed since Juhani had reappeared. Only the blink of an eye ago, everything was fine, everything was in order, and everything looked promising. Now chaos and disorder threatened to ruin it all.

Sometimes putting everything in a timeline helped to clarify my thought processes. I placed the problems to be solved along the line in order of importance and urgency, and after this I categorised them depending on the resources they required. This way, I was able to come up with a strategy, and all I had to do was follow the strategy and trust the multiplier effects as I went: the planned and desired goal awaited right at the end of the timeline. I tried to do the same now too, but time and again it became clogged up right at the outset, started to curl, then wound itself into a knot that I couldn't undo.

I stopped staring into the darkness and resorted to manual arithmetic, as far as was possible without pen and paper.

First things first, I had to respond to Toy of Finland. I believed I had almost solved this problem altogether. I had calculated a number of possible scenarios, and had then decided to combine two of them into one. Now I had a concrete proposal whereby both parties would, yet again, come out as winners. And despite the fact that Toy of Finland had threatened me and even insinuated that they might send Detective Inspector Osmala in my general direction, the thought didn't worry me or cause me nearly as much anxiety as the immediate threat coming from closer quarters.

If Juhani's vague promises had managed to cast a spell over all the staff in such a short space of time, what would his next move be? How far were they all prepared to go? Why did nobody seem to care that the pipe dreams Juhani encouraged would be quite simply impossible to implement? Why did nobody care to listen to plans that were based on long-term realism, careful calculations, market analysis and concrete facts? Why didn't my staff, who only a moment ago had seemed perfectly content, just tell Juhani that what he was promising them was impossible?

My staff.

The assignation was deliberate because I still thought of them as such and – and this is how I interpreted the sentiment – I still cared about them. I'd thought of them as the closest friends I'd ever had. And now...

Schopenhauer rubbed himself against the back of my leg. He'd said something that I hadn't heard, and now I noticed there was power in the way he pushed against me. I understood. I got up, opened the balcony door and let him out to observe the events of that cool November morning. He could see in the dark too, which meant that the darkness could never see him. The thought snapped me awake. I went into the bedroom and began getting dressed.

As I stood at the mirror knotting my tie, I recognised the fact that had been staring me in the face all this time: everything came back to Juhani, sooner or later everything would wind itself around him and – as I had noticed many times in practice – things would get so complex that even mathematics was of little use. The central question seemed to be: how far was Juhani ultimately willing to go? This was a hard question to answer, for many reasons.

Juhani had always been vague and remorselessly avoided using logic in anything he did, but he'd never been quite this irresponsible before. On the other hand, he'd never been this proactive either: in a very short time, he had engaged in group and one-on-one discussions with all the staff and, judging by the results, with great determination too.

All this together made him even more erratic and his next moves all the more unpredictable. But following this particular timeline in the opposite direction, from the end back to the beginning, we might make a discovery that could tell us something relevant to the current situation. What did this greater unpredictability and urgency tell us? One answer was: despair. Juhani had to act the way he was acting. This would explain the new-found harshness that I had sensed in him and that I couldn't account for in the moment I saw it. He found himself without any alternatives, again. The last time this happened, he had died. What would he have to do this time?

My tie was straight, the knot symmetrical in both width and depth. I pulled on my suit jacket and glanced at the framed image on the wall. I didn't know how many times I had quickly looked at Gauss's equation only to stand there staring at it for longer. Something about the equation reminded me of Juhani. I knew it inside out, but somehow it always managed to surprise me.

I could almost hear Juhani promising all these things. It happened virtually by itself. It was as though Juhani had lit a bonfire, and the more enthusiastic people became, the more logs he added. The crazier people's ideas, the more Juhani encouraged them, egged them on to go faster and faster. Eventually, a now-familiar turn of events would occur. Juhani would come crashing into a reality that was still far removed from ... reality. Realising the plans required one essential factor: Juhani himself, who had to be able to steer the course of events. It was actually astonishing how many times he had succeeded in this. And it seemed he had succeeded now too. He had sold the park's employees their own impossible dreams and presented himself as the key to them all coming true. The same must have happened with Toy of Finland. Juhani had said too much, promised too much, and got himself into a situation where he didn't have any options left. And now I had to clean up the mess.

I let Schopenhauer back inside, and he gave me his report. After this, he glanced at me once more and headed to the sofa without looking behind him. His consistency and steely nerves were an example to us all. I pulled on my shoes and coat, wrapped my scarf round my neck, and thought that I too had everything I needed: meticulous calculations, a realistic plan and a carefully prepared schedule.

I wrote the email as soon as I got to the park. My offer was fair, reasonable and mutually beneficial in the long term. I offered to buy both the Crocodile Canyon and the Moose Chute, in one purchase and for one price. There was only one stipulation in the offer: I would only buy the two products together. I had drawn up a detailed payment plan based on the fact that the added revenue created by the Moose Chute would improve the park's solvency in the years to come, and therefore the monthly repayments to Toy of Finland would increase over a two-year period. At the same time, I would be able to offset the dent in our finances brought about by the acquisition of the Crocodile Canyon at the start of the repayment period. But best of all, this offer would tie YouMeFun and Toy of Finland into exclusive collaboration for many years to come and would guarantee our mutual success. I read the offer through one last time, attached the spreadsheet with my detailed calculations, and pressed send.

I took off my jacket and went through into the main hall. I was on the move early. In the list of repairs that needed to be done, there was a note that the pedals in the last carriage of the Komodo Locomotive were twisted. Our customers might have been short and slight, but many of them seemed to have the destructive energy of a small neutron bomb. I decided to address the matter myself. The hall was quiet, save for the banging and clanking of my tools.

The spot where I was working gave me an unobscured view of one of Laura's murals, the one painted in the style of Dorothea Tanning but with Laura's own twist and subject matter. Because the mural was situated so close to the Komodo Locomotive and because Laura had wanted each of her six murals to communicate with their immediate surroundings, this piece was entitled *Tanning Takes the Train*. I'd spent a long time standing in front of each of her works, but this was possibly my favourite. Seeing it this morning made me think that Saturday, tomorrow, the day we were supposed to meet, was somehow desperately far away; it might as well have been on a different continent, another whole season in the future. I couldn't say where this idea had come from, but it was powerful and there was something particularly unpleasant about it. I concentrated on the Komodo Locomotive.

I managed to straighten the right-hand pedal and began working on the left. Working at the adventure park had taught me to use my hands, and I suspected this might have been one of the reasons I felt a growing sense of attachment to the place. These days I was more than familiar with hammers, screwdrivers, wrenches, pliers, Allen keys, chisels and saws, and I'd come to realise that, in the best possible way, manual tools represented a direct extension of mathematics. Everything had to be calculated before starting to screw, tighten or saw; once everything was in place, to use a tool was simply to draw an equals sign.

The left-hand pedal turned out to be more of a problem. I fiddled with it for some time but soon had to face facts. The pedal would have to be replaced and the spare parts ordered from Toy of Finland Ltd. I detached the twisted pedal, put in a temporary bolt and a tarpaulin over the pedal, and suddenly noticed something I should have noticed earlier.

There was no smell of food in the air. Neither morning buns nor preparation for lunch. I peered towards the south end of the park.

The Curly Cake's sign was lit up and the lights were on inside. So Johanna *was* there. Which made the matter all the curiouser: by this time of the morning the hall was usually full of smells, and I knew Johanna took great pride in having everything ready on time. I inhaled again and expected all the familiar smells to rush into my nostrils: cinnamon buns, today's lunch special, Marching Meatballs, gravy, coffee. But no. All I could smell was the grease from the Komodo Locomotive's chains and disinfectant from the nearby polystyrene foam pool. I gathered up my tools and returned the kit to the storeroom. I washed my hands and walked back to the café.

It was a strange sight.

The doors were open, but the glass vitrines were empty. I couldn't see any sign of food, and still couldn't smell anything. The adventure park was supposed to open its doors in forty minutes, so by now the shelves should be filling up, there should have been clanking, hissing and boiling sounds coming from the kitchen. I walked across the café and stepped through the swinging doors into the kitchen.

Johanna was in the kitchen, but she wasn't in her work clothes. She was holding her phone to her ear, and when she saw me she held up her forefinger, which I took to mean wait a minute. I looked around. At this point, one minute was neither here nor there. The kitchen was still sparkling from last night's clean, and the counters were empty. The ovens and hobs were cold, the cookers and blenders stood idle, waiting.

Johanna said yes, twice, and ended with, 'You're not wrong, bye.' She looked at me, and before I could ask why nothing was being prepared, she said simply:

'Industrial action.'

'Excuse me?'

'We're striking in protest.'

One of Johanna's most endearing traits was her ability to call a spade a spade. I assumed she must be doing so now too, and I was doing my best to understand quite what she was saying. Without much success.

'Striking? In protest?'

'Yes. Until midday.'

Even on a normal day, Johanna's face was slender and sinewy, and her resting expression was such that anyone who didn't know her might describe it as rude. Now I felt as though I didn't know her either.

'Striking for what?'

'A better future.'

'Against what?'

'Stagnation.'

'And who is involved in this ... industrial action?'

'Us. The staff.'

Us. That tiny two-letter word helped open up the conundrum. Or so I thought.

'Does this have something to do with Juhani's promises?' I asked.

Just then, I heard the swinging doors swing open behind me. I turned and saw Kristian, who almost froze on the spot when he saw me. He said a subdued hello, avoided eye contact and sheepishly crossed to Johanna's side of the kitchen.

'Our eyes have been opened,' she said, 'to new horizons.'

'Sounds like Juhani,' I said. 'And I suppose I represent stagnation, then?'

Neither of them replied. Johanna looked me right in the eyes, Kristian continued staring down, either at the floor or his trainers.

'Is everybody involved?' I asked.

'Yes,' said Johanna.

'I don't understand,' I said, and it was true. 'We are going through a very difficult period right now, and we have to continue following the same—'

'The same old models,' she said. 'That's precisely the problem. We want change.'

Kristian's giant muscles were tensed, his face was glowing bright red. His eyes seemed to have fixed on the food processor on the countertop.

'Kristian,' I asked. 'What has Juhani promised you?'

Johanna turned, but she was too late to stop him.

'The board,' he said quickly.

'Sitting on the adventure park's board doesn't actually mean anything, it's not even a paid position,' I said, and now Kristian looked up at me for the first time. I didn't know whether I had ever seen a more confused human being.

'Can't you see?' I asked, speaking primarily to Johanna, but to Kristian too. 'He promises you things you can never have; he's just full of words that don't mean anything.'

'His promises feel cool,' said Kristian, again quite quickly.

'Cool?'

'It makes us feel good. The atmosphere is better and—'

Johanna raised a hand to stop him, and this time Kristian obeyed.

'We don't want to be unreasonable,' said Johanna. 'We just want to send a clear message.'

I knew I shouldn't show how incensed I was, but by now I couldn't stop myself.

'What if Juhani doesn't start running the park?' I asked. 'Not now, not ever? What if, after your industrial action and everything else that's been going on here, I'm still in charge?'

My questions seemed to land with both of them. They landed in different places, but both of them reacted. Kristian looked on in horrified disbelief, as if he had just heard that an oasis in the desert was in fact a hundred kilometres further ahead. A layer of tiny muscles tensed Johanna's cheeks even further. Neither of them said anything. I turned and walked away.

I opened the park's doors myself, sold tickets myself, and ran back and forth across the main hall: I checked the machines, handed out equipment, oversaw safety and security. Outside, the sun was shining and it was an unseasonably warm day, so there was only a modest volume of customers. Still, keeping the entire park running by oneself was too much. I had barely located a sobbing child's shoe from inside the Strawberry Maze when I had to explain to a tired-looking father why his child wouldn't be able to take part in the advertised music-therapy class today and why, at the same time, he would be unable to sit down at the Curly Cake Café for a cup of coffee and Clown Bun. A queue quickly formed at the ticket office. At the Trombone Cannons, someone started shooting the other players in the back, and I didn't have time to consult the security cameras and serve as a referee because I still had to wash and disinfect the Doughnut of trace evidence left when one of our customers ran headfirst into the plastic wall and broke her nose. There's surely more blood smeared across the wall of the Doughnut than there is left in our metre-tall customer, I thought.

Finally – just as I was about to run out of energy and found myself standing exhausted in the middle of the hall, not knowing where to run first – the clock struck twelve, the staff returned to their respective jobs, and my phone beeped as an email arrived in my inbox.

I opened the message.

Toy of Finland had declined my offer.

I walked off towards my office and peered over my shoulder. Both Esa and Samppa glanced at me surreptitiously. It looked to me as though they wanted to make sure I was finally walking in the right direction. Away from them.

As though I were the obstacle, to everything.

NOW

1

The rain has become heavier and more intense. This is my first observation after I manage to stand up straight again. I try to steady my breath, and maintaining my balance is still an effort. My forehead is throbbing and it feels hot, as though it has just been battered against a metal grille – which, of course, is the fact of the matter. I look at the man with the balaclava pulled over his face standing at the loading bay fifteen metres away. He, meanwhile, seems to be watching the man lying on the tarmac below with a plastic strawberry on his head, the man currently being washed by the rain driven in heavy waves by the wind.

Only a moment earlier, the strawberry flew through the air, and the night, leaving an arc of blood behind him. Now the flaming-red plastic berry is lying dejected on the ground, shining through the rain like a light outside a nightclub.

I look at the balaclava again. For what seems like a long time, he stands motionless. Then, as he turns to face me, I am more startled than at any point in the last three and a half bizarre minutes. I recognise the way he turns, the way he walks as he steps closer to me. It appears that what has just happened is affecting his legs too. And I don't doubt it: he arrived at a terrific pace, practically appeared out of nowhere, and with a part of the Strawberry Maze he struck the man who was threatening my life very precisely and strategically in the upper body, then set off running after what looked like a panicked strawberry. The familiar steps come to a halt in front of me, and he pulls the balaclava from his head.

'There are plenty of positives here,' says Juhani.

I am a great supporter of public transport. Recently, however, I've come to realise that there are sometimes good and convincing arguments for the occasional use of a private car. This applies particularly well to the adventure-park business and its various transportation needs. This thought occurs to me as I find myself turning the park's Renault van in the car park.

My head is aching. I realise that the night is at most only halfway through and that all assessments I would normally present at a moment like this will naturally only be provisional data points: interesting in and of themselves, but at best only vague and without any certainty as to the final result.

Juhani and the man who died twice – he seems to have died both from blood loss and a broken neck – are waiting for me behind the adventure park. Juhani is standing under the small roof above the loading bay, sheltering from the rain, while the dead man is currently hidden beneath the bay itself, still with half a strawberry lodged over his head. I pass them, stop the car, turn the steering wheel a little and reverse almost right up to the loading bay. Then, just when I am about to jump out of the car, I stop.

I glance in the mirror. I can see Juhani and the pile of equipment he has gathered. It looks like more than enough. But this isn't the reason I stop. Juhani is.

He saved my life.

That is an incontestable fact.

And there's something else I realise too, something that feels much more onerous. What was Juhani doing behind the adventure park at eleven o'clock on a Friday night? It's a simple question, and it's a justified one. The rain is pounding on the roof and the bonnet, shining and sparkling in the glare of the headlights. I keep my eyes on the side mirror. Juhani doesn't move.

I understand only too well that I didn't think this a moment ago. Juhani had just saved my life, and all I could think about were the next essential steps for our survival. I gave Juhani quick, simple instructions, I went inside, washed my face and pulled a baseball cap deep over my face to cover the marks the steel grille had left on my forehead. I was guided solely by my instincts. My behaviour was doubtless partly down to some level of shock, partly informed by my previous experiences at the adventure park. This isn't the first time I've faced the challenges of running a small-to-medium-sized business.

I open the door and step out into the rain.

We wrap the man in a length of fabric taken from the Teddy-Bear Trampoline, an item that is no longer in use, and lift him into the spacious boot of the van. This sounds much easier than it actually is. The man is heavy, tightly packed and shaped like the world's largest cannonball. The rain seeps through the fabric. I am soaked right down to my underwear. Eventually we manage to get the man into the back of the van. We haven't spoken more than is absolutely necessary.

The rain lashes the tarmac and the part of the loading bay not protected by the shelter. We gather up the remaining shards of plastic strawberry and place them in the same bin liner as the leftover packaging materials. Then we lug the heavy steel legs of the Banana Mirror, also removed from use, and lift them into the vehicle too. The back of the van is now full.

I glance around one last time. There is nothing to suggest what took place on the loading bay only an hour ago. I tell Juhani I know a place where we can offload our cargo and tell him that I know the place because I almost ended up there myself while I was attending to *his* debts. We look at each other in silence, then climb into the car and set off.

The air conditioning is breathing warm air into our faces. The seat heaters are roasting us. We've been driving for six or seven minutes in complete silence, and my fingers have finally come back to life. My forehead is still throbbing as though part of my heart has been transplanted and is now beating painfully in the cramped space between my skin and my skull. I can still hear – or rather, feel – a low-pitched humming in my ears that has nothing to do with the car or the fans or any other external factor. Without the streetlamps lining the road and the car's headlights, the world would be as dark as the far side of the moon.

'I think what's most important now is to keep positive,' says Juhani.

I glance to the side and catch Juhani's blue, sincere eyes.

'To look to the future,' he continues. 'I don't see any use in standing, staring at the pit we've fallen into, pointing at it and arguing about who dug what, who stepped where, whose knee hurts the most. By far the best alternative is to stand up and carry on side by side.'

I realise Juhani is speaking in metaphors. But everything is wrong with these metaphors. Knowing who dug the pit is absolutely essential, as is knowing why we both stumbled into it. Besides, neither of us has fully climbed out of it yet. I say nothing.

'Another way of looking at it,' he continues, 'is from the park's perspective. This kind of thing happens all the time in adventure parks. Accidents happen, people get hurt. When you're busy and active, there's always a bit of rough and tumble. It's inevitable. Of course, someone might say this precise kind of accident happens only rarely, but right now I don't think that's a very meaningful argument. There's no point blaming the park every time somebody comes a cropper.'

'That would be unnecessary,' I admit, because, as far as I can see, in this last respect Juhani is quite right. I steer the car to the intersection and put my foot down. I glance in the side mirror and realise that there's no need to speed up or slow down. The road is empty. I continue at the same pace.

'And I'd like to add,' says Juhani, now more slowly and quietly, 'that I didn't mean ... I mean, what happened was an accident.'

Again, I glance to my side. Juhani is staring right ahead.

'I understand,' I say after a beat.

We arrive at a crossroads. I click the indicators on and steer the car sharply to the right. I'm certain I can feel Juhani's eyes on the side of my face.

'You do?'

'It's very clear cut,' I say. 'He would have killed me. You saved my life. Thank you.'

A short silence.

'Exactly,' says Juhani. 'You're welcome.'

Twenty-six minutes later I guide the car onto a narrow, bumpy pathway, and for a few minutes I drive slowly and with extra caution. The Renault jolts from side to side. A faint knocking sound can be heard coming from the boot.

The last time I was here was with Lizard Man and AK. Both men tried to kill me but ended up killing themselves instead. I arrive at the final fork in the road, which is more like a fork in the path, and take the way that I remember. The car rolls down towards the shore at a steep angle, and the surface of the water dances its black dance in time with the rain, and all around us it's as dark as the shadows of outer space. I switch off the engine and all the lights. Darkness engulfs the car. I reach into the back and find a torch in the footwell, but I don't switch it on just yet because I realise something crucially important.

I haven't accounted for everything. Perhaps this shouldn't be so surprising, given the circumstances. After all, this is the first time I've been by the shores of this remote pond with my brother, my forehead covered in scratches, and a body in the boot of the car.

'What now?' Juhani asks as if sensing something is wrong.

I flick the torch into life. Juhani is right, something is wrong. The pond is right in front of us, but we have no way of getting out there.

'Right now, it's important to think positively,' I say, and open the door.

We walk along the pathway, the light from the torch bobbing in front of us. The path follows the contours of the pond, at times running along the shoreline, at others illuminating the undergrowth between the trees. The ground is wet, in places our feet get stuck in the sodden earth. The rain shows no signs of letting up. On the other hand, it means we stop paying it so much attention. I'm already soaked through. Eventually I see something that gives me hope.

A small cottage has been locked up for the winter. We pass the cottage and walk down to the shore. No boat, no ... But there is something. This isn't a difficult calculation: we have to consider the man's weight, the weight of the steel legs from the Banana Mirror, my and Juhani's combined weight, the estimated bearing capacity of the object we have found – and the fact that we don't have any other options.

A jetty.

A pontoon bridge that's been dragged ashore for the winter.

It takes us about thirty-five minutes to get the jetty into the water. We find an old oar propped against the west-facing outer wall of the cottage. Until now, Juhani has done as I've told him, but now he seems a little reluctant and asks what we need the jetty for. I tell him the truth: that the man has to be rowed out into the middle of the pond because that's where it's deepest. I omit what Lizard Man told me once before: there are others there too.

We test the jetty for balance and conclude that it will be best if we lie flat on top of it. This we do one at a time. Once we are both on our stomachs on the jetty, we carefully shuffle away from each other and towards the edges. Eventually, the jetty is floating, as balanced as can be.

Juhani is first on rowing duty.

The weather is our friend. The rain stops once we've rowed roughly halfway back to where we left the car. An old jetty is a slow mode of transportation, but we get there in the end. When we reach the shore and I stand up from the wet planks, my body temperature feels colder than ever before. Moving is hard at first but the idea of offloading our cargo warms me – as grim and unpleasant as it is.

Once I have propped the torch in the embankment at a suitable angle, we unroll the fabric from the Teddy-Bear Trampoline right by the water's edge, then grab the man under the armpits and haul him up onto the jetty. Next we carry the legs from the Banana Mirror onto the jetty and tie them to the man's legs. The result is that his new shoes weigh around sixty kilos each. We work in the shallow waters by the shore. After this, I switch off the torch. The rain clouds have passed or dispersed, and now the moon lights the pond like a dim, cosy lamp.

The November water is freezing, the mud at the bottom exudes an almost prehistoric chill. By the time we position ourselves on the jetty for a second time, my feet are already numb.

The jetty is hanging deep in the water, so progress is slow. We row and use our hands both as an extra oar and a rudder. My back and shoulders are cramping from the exertion and the cold. Finally, we are floating diametrically in the middle of the lake.

I quickly calculate the distribution of weight on our little raft and plan the various stages of what must happen next at the end of the jetty. This might well be the first time in history that Juhani has followed my instructions to the letter. He moves his hands and feet as necessary, turns when he has to and moves only fractionally, so as to maintain our fine, precarious balance. Eventually, we are both lying on one side of the jetty, while the man and his shoes press the other side down just enough that, in adherence with the laws of physics, he eventually slides over the edge and into the water. As the man leaves the jetty, Juhani immediately slides over to take his place.

We lie there for a moment in silence, the moon casts its bright sheen across the surface of the pond.

Then, without a word, we row back to the cottage, pull the jetty back onto the shore, replace the oar against the cottage wall, walk back to the car and open the boot once more. We strip off and stuff our wringing, muddy clothes in a bin liner. I open the bag of dry clothes that Juhani brought with him. The adventure park's lost-and-found cupboard contains piles of woollen jumpers, sweatshirts and tracksuits – even adult ones. I pull on a pair of thick, black, comfortable but all-too short jogging bottoms and a loose, light-coloured woolly jumper with a giant dark-red rose across the front. Juhani is left with a soft, dark-grey sweatshirt and a pair of flannel trousers that look almost exactly the right size for him.

We look as though we've been enjoying a relaxing evening at home.

But we have not.

It's almost five in the morning, it is November, and even a quick calculation tells me that the relationship between me and my brother has just entered a new phase.

2

I awake to the sound of my phone, and yet my first thought is that I haven't slept at all. I have no recollection of dreams or anything else after finally getting to bed at six in the morning. I sit up and notice that every muscle in my body aches, and there is still a residual sense of hypothermia in my hands and feet. I fumble for my phone and answer.

Laura Helanto tells me that she has completed her morning work and now she's free. I tell her I haven't forgotten the matter – which is true – and that I always uphold my end of a deal. Laura says she knows this and suggests I pack a small bag with me. We agree to meet downtown in one hour.

Before I can get to the shower, I have to face Schopenhauer. He doesn't hide his disappointment and lets me know he is annoyed. I understand only too well. I have upset his sleeping patterns too.

It's half past twelve.

In the afternoon.

I don't even try to explain why all this happened – problems at the adventure park, a nocturnal attacker, my brother, a wintry pond, a pair of steel boots – but I accept his rebukes and answer every meow with, yes, you're right, I'm very sorry, this won't happen again. And I mean it. Schopenhauer has saved me from many sticky situations with his unflinching example and his cool, rational mind; he doesn't deserve such a jumbled, disorganised life. I give him some food and leave the balcony door ajar.

In the bathroom, I encounter something that will be even trickier to hide. My forehead looks like I've held it against a hot waffle iron, several times over. It is swollen, raw and distinctly chequered.

I look at it for a moment and weigh up my options – a new and peculiar hairstyle, bandaging my head then hiding it with a hat or baseball cap – but these solutions all share one common feature: they are only temporary. All I can do is accept the mathematical inevitability of this matter too. A given equation will provide a given result, and there is no way my forehead will stop being my forehead any time soon. I'll have to take it to our meeting just the way it is.

I shave, tidy my hair and get dressed. I give Schopenhauer a little treat, then leave.

It's only once I'm on the train that I properly wake up.

Why didn't I just ask Juhani what he was doing behind the adventure park late on a Friday night? Why didn't I bring up the matter, even in passing, as we were driving back to Helsinki and to the gates of the Rastila campsite as hot air from the heater whirred through the otherwise silent car?

The list of possibilities is short, and it was the same as last night, but I still think it is logical:

1) I realised I was too tired. The frigid, November water and the night spent performing a number of unwanted chores had sapped my strength. My alertness levels weren't where I needed them to be to have a thorough conversation.

2) I wanted evidence. I still do. I need something concrete before deciding how to proceed.

3) I wasn't sure how Juhani would react. Early that same evening he had grabbed hold of a giant plastic strawberry with fateful consequences.

And so, I'd just leant forwards, gripped the steering wheel and kept my eyes fixed on the road ahead. Thinking back on it now, I realise I acted just as the situation demanded.

But who was the attacker, and why did he attack me?

It's quite unlikely that this was simply a customer disappointed with the adventure park's services. I didn't recognise the man, neither did he say a word throughout the encounter by which I might have been able to identify him. It could, of course, be a random, lone-wolf attack, an individual acting on motives that would now forever remain a mystery. However, I must also consider the possibility that someone was supporting him, encouraging him, or even paying him to attack me.

And if it is the latter, several theories come to mind right away.

Toy of Finland is top of my list of suspects. They declined my offer, which was above all an attempt at reconciliation. They still refuse to sell the Moose Chute and are still trying to force me to buy the Crocodile Canyon at an inflated price. What's more, they know something about what happened before. It is perfectly possible that they might seek to speed up the process by sending someone to shape my opinions – not to mention my forehead – to fit their demands.

The park's employees are suspects now too. This is far from a pleasant thought. But if we consider how radically and rapidly their attitude towards me and their designs for the park have changed, the idea isn't entirely implausible. Particularly if we imagine that, in order to secure their future interests, they made a shared investment and hired a man who had the potential to help them achieve their goals. Naturally, I don't know the going rate for actual bodily harm, but I imagine a respectable sum of money wouldn't be beyond the means of five or six combined salaries. And if the park's employees have indeed decided to hire someone to carry out their dirty work, there remain only two options: either the man was supposed to scare me – in which case he succeeded quite well – or he was tasked with taking me out of the picture altogether. The latter option feels especially unjust. I think I've been a fair boss, I've always stood up for my staff's interests and the park's long-term outlook. In every conceivable way, yesterday's feedback is over the top.

The third option, of course, is Juhani. But thinking of him is like trying to grab hold of a bar of soap in a barrel of oil. Juhani has plenty of personality traits that make him susceptible to risky and short-sighted solutions. With this in mind, he could easily have hired someone to advocate for him in the middle of the night. But if we assume that he knew about the attack in advance, why would he turn up himself? Then there's the even bigger question: why would he have tried to alter the course of events? If, on the other hand, we assume that Juhani *didn't* know about the attack, it's still unclear what he was doing behind the adventure park with a balaclava over his head. Every thought of Juhani raises a reaction, a follow-up question; the bar of soap slips endlessly back and forth inside the barrel.

In addition to all of the above, I have to take into consideration the possibility that there is a completely different explanation for the attack.

In each of these scenarios, the end result is the same: I need more information. I can't dash here and there without a clear plan. Besides, anything that might arouse the suspicions of Detective Inspector Osmala obviously falls outside my repertoire of available options. At the very least, I don't know how I could possibly explain the strawberry. *We hired a seasonal worker who slipped over in the Maze, and because he was a freshwater diving enthusiast, we gave him the kind of send-off he would have wanted.* No. Just, no.

One thing is crystal clear, beyond doubt. As far as the park goes, I'm on my own now.

Sunlight seeps through the clouds, as though filtered through a thin, brittle concrete gauze.

The train judders to a halt at Helsinki central railway station.

3

Laura Helanto is sitting on a sofa at the back of the café, reading a book. I've walked briskly through the main section of the café, passed the ship-like counter in the middle of the space, taken the few steps up to the backroom, when I suddenly stop at the top of the short flight of stairs, about six and a half metres in front of her. She hasn't noticed me yet, the book must have swept her away. I recognise this phenomenon from mathematics: I'm often so caught up in my calculations that I only snap out of it when I'm about to faint with hunger or when I notice the sun has set or, as has also happened, when it rises again.

The winter evening's light is coming from behind her, it merges with the electric lights of the café and the small candle flickering inside a glass dome on the table in front of her. The room feels somehow softer than many rooms often do, and it is much quieter here than in the front section of the café. Laura Helanto's hair is like a vigorous bush, her glasses have slid slightly down her nose and the skin of her neck is a little red. I find myself thinking that she is both the most beautiful and the most important person I have ever met.

Of course, this realisation takes place primarily in my imagination, but it has a concrete dimension too: it is simple but strong, like a steel bar. At the same time, I am all the more resolved not to discuss park business with Laura anymore. I want to keep her as far away from YouMeFun as possible, in all respects. This decision feels suddenly essential, but I don't have time to think about it any further because Laura notices me. I move again, she smiles, closes her book and places it on the table. I take off my coat but leave my woolly hat on. I've seen younger people doing this – wearing thick, warm woolly headpieces in heated indoors spaces – so it shouldn't attract too much attention.

We – in fact it would be more correct to say simply Laura; right now I'm unable to formulate coherent conclusions about anything – exchange our respective assessments of the weather, talk about which modes of transport we used to get here today and note how quiet the café is and how pleasantly surprising this is, given it's a Saturday afternoon and how, for a variety of reasons, this might lead us to assume it should be almost full. Then she pauses, the brief hiatus seems to shift the mood in the room, and she says:

'I'm glad we managed to get over that little bump in the road.'

By bump, I imagine she means the circumstances under which I left her studio the other day.

'Me too,' I say, and because it looks as though she is expecting something else too, I tell her what I think. 'Because you are the most beautiful, most important person I have ever met.'

Laura Helanto appears to have some kind of seizure: she looks as though she is bursting into laughter and starting to cry all at once. Her cheeks quickly turn red and her eyes gleam.

'Oh, Henri,' she says eventually. 'Nobody has ever said anything like that to me before.'

'I can say it again if you'd like.'

'There's no need. I mean, you can say it if you want, and I'm happy to hear it, but I believe you. That was a lovely thing to say. And actually, it might be a good idea to talk about our ... status.'

A shiver runs from the bottom of my stomach right up to my neck. I vividly remember how, the last time we talked about this subject, Laura Helanto told me that what we had was over. Since then, we've kissed a few times and arranged to meet up, we've talked through the large-scale embezzlement between us and come to an agreement about the hiding of a body and other events in the day-to-day running of an adventure park. I say nothing.

'How do you see this?'

It takes a moment for me to realise that this is a question and to work out what the question might pertain to.

'Our status?' I ask, my mouth suddenly and oddly dry.

'Yes. You said on the phone that you'd like to increase your proportion ... our proportion, or my proportion in your...'

At this, I feel as though there is ground beneath my feet again. Laura Helanto surely wouldn't talk like this if, instead of increasing the time we spend together, she wanted to decrease it.

'We can think of it as interest,' I begin. 'Then as compound interest. So, if your initial investment is one, then in a year's time you have one plus the interest, but the year after that you have one plus the interest plus the interest on the interest, and the year after that—'

'Next year?'

'Yes, interest per annum,' I nod. 'For instance.'

'I mean, you're looking quite a long way into the future...'

Green and blue flicker and shimmer in Laura Helanto's eyes, like tiny pebbles at the bottom of the sea on a sunny day. She truly is the most beautiful, most important person in my life.

'The investment horizon is often the most important factor,' I say. 'When it comes to a significant investment like this, I think it is reasonable to think of how things will pan out over the longest possible period. For my part, we can think of this as a thirty-year mortgage, not in the sense of negative equity, but still proportionally, in that we can expect the value of the original capital to grow alongside the compound-interest factor. When I say I want to increase the proportion of your company in my life, I mean in a cumulative sense.'

I've been speaking quickly. Then something stops me in my

tracks. I feel an unpleasant pain somewhere deep inside, and as if out of nowhere my mind is suddenly flooded with dark slurry. I remember the doubts I had at Laura's studio. That she and Juhani...

'Of course, you've probably heard all this before,' I hear myself saying.

Laura Helanto shakes her head. 'I can assure you I've never heard anything remotely like this before.'

We look at each other. The dark, nauseating wave starts to recede as quickly as it had appeared. I don't know exactly what the sensation is or where it comes from; it arises whenever it wants.

'Thirty years,' Laura says after a pause.

'Given that the initial capital already exists and there are sound reasons for the investment...'

'Are you ready for something like this?'

'I wouldn't suggest an investment on this scale unless it was based on the most precise calculations one can make,' I nod.

'Is that ... a yes?'

I think I've already been more than clear. But because this is Laura Helanto, I am prepared to condense my answer even further.

'The profit outlook could not be more attractive,' I say. 'Yes.'

Laura holds out a hand across the table. When her fingers reach mine, as well as all the aches and pains, my body seems to let go of the permanent chill that I realise has been following me ever since the incident at the freezing pond.

'Yes,' says Laura, and squeezes my hand in a way that sends warmth radiating through my entire body. I respond to her squeeze, and I am about to say that one of the benefits of a carefully considered, long-term investment like this is that the small ups and downs of the market won't disrupt the overall yield prospects, but Laura is quicker.

'Did you pack what I told you to?'

'Yes,' I say again.

This second yes seems to make her every bit as happy as the first one.

'There's something I want to show you,' she says.

We have been walking against the stubborn wind through early-winter Helsinki, and I have tightened my scarf so many times that its warming effect only barely surpasses the looming sense of asphyxiation. We have arrived at a small peninsula in the middle of the bay, with the Hietaniemi cemetery and the beach behind us.

I find myself thinking that this place is more understandable in winter. All around us everything is empty and quiet, and death is equally distributed: the trees are black, the reeds are brown, the residents are calm, their behaviour predictable. In the summer, this ambiance is a little conflicted, to put it mildly: part of the peninsula is populated by loud, gleaming, sun-lotioned, half-naked sun worshippers running here and there, while the full-time residents are slowly decomposing in the bosom of the earth, beyond the reach of the thumping bass and the factor fifty. The former group can't imagine ever ending up with the latter, while the latter group knows what lies in wait once the sun sets for good. The tension between these two demographics makes the whole peninsula illogical from June until August: it's hard to decide whether to take your shirt off or to pick out an appropriate urn.

I don't say any of this out loud, and I don't have time because Laura Helanto opens a gate in a wire fence and turns to me.

'This place is important to me,' she says. 'I've been coming here for years, all year round. I'm a paid-up member, and you're my guest. Members can bring one guest with them. Usually, whenever someone comes as a guest, they end up becoming members of the ice-swimming club themselves.'

Laura Helanto glances at me, and it starts to dawn on me what is about to happen. There's no way Laura would know that I'm already freezing cold because only the previous night I was hiding a body in plunge-pool conditions. We pass the sauna building and walk onwards, the peninsula becoming narrower all the while. Right at the end of the peninsula there is a little cabin painted white, to the right of which is what looks like a jetty, and at the end of that a railing and a ladder. I get the distinct impression that the *something* Laura Helanto wanted to show me is the churning, green-cold Baltic Sea.

She stops at the cabin door. 'This is so much more fun together.'

I'm not a swimming-trunk sort of person, not even in summer. But now it's winter and very blustery. My swimming trunks are old; I bought them at the sales a long time ago, just in case. I notice that their style stands in stark contrast to the surroundings. Their primary colour is bright red, and on the left leg there is a tall, curved and very leafy palm tree with eyes, a laughing mouth and a pair of hands giving me the thumbs-up. Underneath the palm tree is the text *SWING IT*. I'm unsure what these swimming trunks are trying to communicate, but I hope in future I can spend time with Laura Helanto in something other than bargain-bin swimming trunks in conditions about as cold as an industrial refrigerator.

I pull the drawstring tighter around my waist, take the creaking wooden steps from the changing room down to the lower floor, trying to banish all feelings of disorder and discomfort from my mind.

Laura Helanto is waiting for me in front of the cabin. She glances at my swimming costume and the palm tree, and at first it seems as though her smile is growing wider, but then she looks up, her expression now quizzical. I realise why almost immediately. My forehead is still partially chequered, partially swollen. Before she has a chance to ask about it, I tell her the truth.

'The loading bay behind the adventure park,' I say, then add: 'And some considerable velocity.'

Laura examines my forehead and perhaps is about to say something, but decides against it. She lowers her gaze and looks me in the eyes.

'It could have been so much worse,' she says.

I can't disagree with that. She doesn't ask any more questions, and perhaps the winter winds play their part in blowing the subject away. She is wearing a simple and sensible black-and-white swimming costume and a pair of rubber swimming shoes. In this too, I admire her clear, logical mind.

We walk towards the sauna hut, and the wind cuts right through me. Laura tells me how wonderful it is to go swimming outdoors in the middle of a blizzard. Then, just before we reach the sauna, I realise I am listening to her so intently that for a moment I haven't given a second thought to ponds, criminals, bodies or anything else associated with the adventure park. And this reminds me of what's most important: this part of my life is right here with Laura Helanto, while the other part of my life is at the adventure park. And from now on, the twain shall never meet again.

'These works would be on display in the park alongside the murals,' she says as she throws water on the stove. 'They would be sculptures, in a way, or more like installations that will turn the existing murals into three-dimensional works of art. Sort of. But I'm going to try and make them new, independent works in their own right, so that they can be exhibited later on without the murals.'

I wipe the sweat from my brow. The situation has escalated quite quickly. We arrived at the sauna approximately seven minutes ago. We have been alone since a man who had sauna-ed himself fifty shades of crimson left four minutes ago, and it was then that Laura Helanto began presenting her new idea.

'This time I would use different materials,' she continues. 'Mostly wood, a little light metal, fabric, lots of fabric, even some plastic, unfortunately, just a little bit. And I'd like to use materials that the adventure park would otherwise have thrown away. We get through a lot of stuff – things are constantly breaking and being replaced. I'd like to recycle those materials in these artworks. In fact, that's one of the themes in the work. *Tanning Takes the Recycling Train*. Figuratively, if not literally.'

Laura throws more water on the stove.

'I've already done the preliminary sketches,' she says, and neither the ninety-degree sauna, the humming stove nor the constant water and steam seem to slow her down at all. 'And I'm ready to get started right away. In fact, the only thing the project needs now is...'

Laura Helanto glances up at me and her expression changes.

'Oh no, Henri,' she says. 'I think I got a bit carried away. Let's go for a dip.'

We make the journey between the sauna and the sea a total of three times. In the sauna I warm up, in the sea I cool down. It turns out this surprisingly simple procedure has an untold positive impact on my physical and mental wellbeing.

More people appear in the sauna, and Laura Helanto seems to know them all. She has stopped talking about her art project and doesn't even mention it as we walk back towards the city centre. It's a relief. I don't know what I would say to her, how I would break the news that, at least for the time being, there's no way she can start work on an art project at the adventure park. Not while the park is threatened, both from within and without, or while I might still be in mortal danger. And I cannot, under any circumstances, tell her that one of the people I suspect might have something to do with it is Juhani. I've even made a point of telling her that Juhani won't cause me the least bit of trouble.

We have just enough time to give each other half a hug before Laura hurries to her bus. I catch my train and ride home to Kannelmäki.

4

It's the kind of memory I've never spoken to anyone about, not even Juhani. Despite the fact that he shares it with me. The memory combines conversations that I remember clearly, word for word, and fragments of less clearly defined moments, but all the same it is like an old photograph that I can take out whenever I want and check what kind of jacket someone was wearing or how much their cheeks tightened or their lips narrowed when they smiled. And what makes this all the more jarring is that Juhani was the only person smiling that day, and by the time the day was out, even he had stopped.

We were in Lahti, burying our parents. Our mother had died only three and half days after our father. They had both died of old age, exhausted from all the years of wild dreaming, though they had only reached what might be called late middle age. I didn't know why or how they had ended up in Lahti. I didn't think they knew anybody in that area.

I was neither surprised nor unsurprised by the number of people who attended the funeral. Our parents had always attracted people wherever they went, even if only briefly. In their own way they were attractive, positive and open people; my former boss would doubtless have said they had a strong, positive, dynamic forward vision and the guts to dive headlong into the unknown. The flip side of this, however, was that their entire life was one long series of diving from one burning boat to another. Judging by the fact that I only counted twenty-four people at the wake, I assumed that our parents had only been in Lahti for a very short time.

The funeral itself was suitably short, and the priest who gave the eulogy had clearly received his instructions from Juhani. Nothing the priest said about our parents' lives was factual, and the handful of things that were partly true were presented in a distinctly one-sided manner. I wasn't planning on bringing it up and didn't want to comment on the arrangements at all. Juhani had organised the event, and he was allowed to do it the way he saw fit. For me, organising a funeral would have been impossible: I was a student of mathematics and my monthly budget was very carefully calculated. Juhani, on the other hand, was a successful businessman. Or so he'd said many times.

We moved from the chapel through to the church hall, where there was tea and coffee, sandwiches and cream cakes. A few people came up and squeezed my hand, and I learnt what had brought our parents to Lahti in the first place. People were sad that my parents never had the chance to open their private tram line connecting the world-famous ski-jump tower at Salpausselkä with their very own pizza village, a growing community of pizza restaurants situated on the outskirts of the city, where visitors were able to stay at pizza hotels and spend time at the pizza spa whenever they weren't patronising one of numerous other pizza restaurants. The potential, an elderly gentleman explained to me, his eyes darting from side to side, was in mass tourism during the ski-jumping week and in the direct tram line. When I asked the man whether the pizza village or the tram line existed yet or whether they were even under construction, he told me that my parents had already bought a giant pizza oven and there was a model tramcar lying in the middle of the living room of their one-bedroom apartment.

At some point, Juhani had disappeared. I noticed it as the funeral guests were starting to leave. The room became empty and quiet, and his full coffee cup on the table next to me seemed to have cooled and a clear growth ring had appeared on the inside of the cup, slightly above the level of the liquid.

Eventually I found Juhani in the foyer.

'One small problem,' he said. 'Nothing dramatic, but it's going to need a bit of … juggling.'

First he took me to one side, then into the chapel. He carefully closed the door behind us, and we found ourselves standing in a quiet room, warmed by the soft afternoon light, along with our parents – only one of whom was in a coffin. It didn't require a degree in applied mathematics to work out that it was our father.

For a moment, I felt as though I couldn't breathe.

Our mother was lying on her back on a plinth, as though she'd just lain down for a nap. She was wearing a long grey dress, a dark-brown cardigan and a pair of black, polished shoes. Of course, she was quite pale, but in all other respects she looked perfectly normal. I had to look away.

'They went to find another coffin,' Juhani said quietly. 'There was a misunderstanding about the price of these services, the payment schedule and what was actually included in this package. I had to decide between the fish terrine and the coffin, but by then most of the terrine had already been eaten.'

'You swapped our mother for a cake?' I spluttered, and I could almost taste the salmon in my mouth. That and the shock. I knew that Juhani was always full of surprises, but this was a different level of magnitude. Perhaps it was the combination of surprise and shock that allowed me to remain calm so I was able to listen to him.

'The good news,' said Juhani, 'is that I haggled them down, and the digger is included in the new price, but that means we're in a bit of a hurry.'

'A hurry?'

'We'll have to carry the coffin to the graveside by ourselves,' he said. 'The digger will be here in twenty-five minutes. There's a funeral going on at the other side of the park too, and he'll do this one right afterwards.'

'I don't follow...'

'Henri,' he said. 'This, if anything, is pure mathematics.'

Mother was stiff.

We couldn't decide whether she should lie on top of our father on her stomach or her back. Both solutions felt wrong, for different reasons. Finally, we managed to roll our father onto his side, then there was just enough room for Mother to slip in beside him. Closing the coffin was a little more complicated, mostly because our parents were like blocks of wood: hard and, given their volume, surprisingly heavy.

I didn't think I was doing right, and I didn't feel good. But I couldn't see any other option: I was still penniless and, judging by everything I'd seen, so was my brother, the supposedly successful businessman.

My general wellbeing didn't improve as we hauled the coffin onto the same trolley that only a moment ago was carrying the exorbitant terrine. The trolley had been designed for use in an industrial kitchen, and I doubt it was ever meant to bear the weight of two adult humans in rigor mortis, let alone transport them along the sandy pathways of the cemetery. But, as we had established, this was the best we could afford.

The process of pushing and pulling the trolley turned out to be painfully slow and arduous. Its wheels kept getting stuck in the sand and the smallest dips in the path. The trolley itself kept sliding across the path from right to left and from left to right, as though it were drunk. It also seemed to want to spin around, switching its bow and stern back and forth.

We were both soaked through with sweat. It was late spring,

and a hint of summer warmth already hung in the air. We left our jackets on a bench by the path.

The trolley kept spinning, getting stuck, moving again, sliding a metre or two, then became stuck in a narrow ditch furrowed out by the rain, and lifting it out again took all the strength the two of us could muster. I was aware that time was passing, and I imagined Juhani must have been too. We didn't speak. Each time the paths reached a fork, we checked our direction from a print-out of the cemetery's plots. The grave was marked on the map with a red rectangle. It was situated as far away from the chapel as it was possible to get. We puffed our way onwards, the trolley creaked, the coffin was silent and heavy. The old spruce trees stood motionless and watched our progress.

Waiting for us was a hole in the ground: a wide, dark opening about one and half metres deep. The width was understandable: there was room for two. We saw the digger arriving from the other direction. Now we worked quicker than before: we improvised a set of straps – for budgetary reasons we hadn't been able to use the proper ones – and had to lower the coffin quickly and with lactic acid still coursing through our muscles from wheeling the coffin there in the first place. The tablecloths held out, and we managed to pull them from underneath the coffin and out of the grave just before the digger arrived.

This digger was like a miniature model of the real thing, and it seemed to create an optical illusion against the landscape: the man inside the digger looked like a giant, though he was of average size. This became clear after the motor was turned off and he stepped out of the cabin. The driver adjusted the position of his baseball cap, greeted us, walked right up to the edge of the grave and peered down, then looked up at us.

'Says here there's supposed to be two,' he said. 'Where's the other one?'

We stood there in silence, still sweating, and tried to hide the tablecloths behind us. I thought our travails might be about to get the end they deserved: exposure, shame, punishment. I was going to say something when I heard Juhani's astonishingly clear and sincere voice.

'She's actually feeling much better now,' he said. 'She'll be coming along later. So, it's just one today.'

The man looked at each of us in turn. Then he looked down into the grave, stepped back into his digger and started moving the dark-brown earth back from whence it had come.

On the way home, neither of us said a word.

5

The more banal, the more suspicious, I think to myself on Thursday morning as I unload equipment behind the park. The sky is like a sea of lead, grey and oppressive, and there's something between rain and fog in the air – a light, cold damp that you only really feel on your skin once it's too late: by the time you hold out your hand to feel if it's raining, your clothes are already soaked through. I lift the items I've bought from the hardware store out of the van and onto the loading bay and think about my brother.

I have seen Juhani countless times since our nocturnal activities with the jetty. I have received exceptionally accurate reports from him about the park's current situation and listened to his sensible suggestions about what measures we might take to address it. Neither of us has mentioned our trip to the cottage in any way, shape or form. I have my own reasons for that, and I don't doubt that he has his.

What's also noticeable is the employees' behaviour: it seems as though the sternest resistance might have subsided slightly. None of them looks entirely content yet, but at least there haven't been any new protests or anything leading them to down tools. Of course, I've been criticised for my new belt-tightening measures: I have cut money from the wrong places at the wrong time, and everybody thinks I have cut more from their department than from all the others. Each time, I have returned to the facts, my calculations and the data we have to hand, and stressed that equality should be the guiding principle in everything we do. I have even offered them the opportunity to go through the numbers with me, but this hasn't inspired much enthusiasm: thus far, nobody has signed up for my course entitled Fundamental Principles of Adventure-Park Mathematics.

I lift the last box out of the back of the van and place it on the loading bay. The boxes are heavy. They contain parts and tools that I plan to use to repair the park's machines. These aren't official parts, and there is a reason for this. The official parts would have to be ordered from Toy of Finland Ltd. I haven't heard anything from them in a week, and I don't want to be the one to make contact with them again. I consider it very likely that they are the ones who sent the attacker my way. And I don't think the kind of gadgetry supplier who sends subcontractors to batter a client's head against a steel grille should be first in line when it comes to scouting out potential new business partners. The downside of sourcing these parts elsewhere is that we will have to build the spare parts ourselves from components bought here and there, and this will be slow and quite expensive, once we factor in the working hours that could have been put to better use doing other work around the park. It looks worryingly likely that, if internal sabotage and various forms of external attack don't scupper the park, their cumulative effect threatens to do so in the long term.

I close the van's back doors, and I'm taking the stairs up to the loading bay when a car swerves around the corner. The car is moving almost silently. It's an electric car. First it swerves in a wide arch a little further off, then its front wheels turn sharply, and the car starts coming right towards me. There is only one person in the car: the driver. I stand on the loading bay, looking down on the car from such a height that I can't see the driver's face. But the grey jacket and blue-and-white checked shirt tell me all I need to know. They are the same as the last time we met.

Detective Inspector Pentti Osmala of the Helsinki organised-crime and fraud unit takes up one half of his electric car, and it seems to me as though the car is slightly tilting towards the driver's side. I don't think it's necessarily a good thing that I recognise him so easily. I'm pretty sure he knows at least some of what happened in the park after Juhani left it to me and how I survived at the hands of the criminals he too was looking for. However, I don't have any proof of this, and the way Osmala talks to me certainly doesn't provide any.

The engine stops humming, and Osmala steps out from behind the steering wheel.

As if his stocky, broad-shouldered frame wasn't recognisable enough, with the exception of his shoes he is dressed exactly as before. And his shoes, when I finally see them, don't match the rest of his outfit at all. They are new, brown and polished. They look small and delicate on his feet, like a moose wearing a pair of ballet shoes. For some reason, I assume he must have bought the shoes at the same time as his new electric car, that these purchases must have something to do with each other and that it would be impossible to say which came first – the hybrid or the brogues.

Osmala appears to notice neither the rain-fog nor the November greyness. He stands by his car in his blazer and looks calmly at me and my pile of boxes. There's something deeply un-comfortable about this scenario, and the fact that he is looking at me from below certainly doesn't help matters. On the contrary, I feel as though I were standing on a plinth, exposed and under investigation.

'You're a busy man,' he says. It doesn't sound like a question, but answering him seems a better option than standing here letting him take stock of me.

'Wear and tear,' I say. 'Spare parts come in handy.'

'Business is booming, I see,' he says, and this doesn't sound like a question either. 'You won't mind if I come up and take a look.'

Osmala takes the steps up to the loading bay, and I can feel the whole steel structure trembling beneath me. He stops next to me, his eyes light-blue and ponderous, his eyebrows as though they have been worn away.

'Would I be right in thinking you've had plenty of visitors?'

'Our figures are quite satisfactory,' I answer truthfully. 'Naturally, we hope to increase footfall further, but it's not easy.'

'Easy,' he says. 'No, I'm sure it isn't. When you say your figures are satisfactory, what kind of figures are we talking about, on a day-to-day basis?'

It's relatively clear that, if Osmala had come in a purely personal capacity, he would have left his electric car at the front of the park, walked to the main entrance in his new shoes and bought a ticket like everybody else. I present him with the most accurate estimate of our daily figures based on averages taken over a long period. I mention usual daily variation and remind him of the median figures, which often tell us more than the simple average. Osmala nods, and it takes a moment before he speaks again.

'That's a lot of customers,' he says eventually. 'But I suppose most of them are children.'

'The adventure park is designed to cater to their needs, primarily,' I admit.

'So, you'd say there are fewer adults.'

'Indeed. Quite.'

'How many fewer?'

I give a detailed assessment of the distribution of tickets sold in the different categories (children's tickets for the children, adult tickets for the adults) but stress that these figures fluctuate wildly, especially at weekends and during school holidays. Something about my answer clearly doesn't satisfy him. I wonder whether I ought to clarify further, when Osmala interrupts my train of thought.

'That's still quite a considerable number of people,' he says. 'I imagine it might be hard to remember one particular adult among the crowds. Especially as this adult's ticket was sold last Friday, almost a week ago.'

Last Friday. In a fraction of a second, Osmala's words vividly bring back the chill of that black pond. The tremors run the length of my body in great surges, like a train stuck between the tracks. I don't think it shows outwardly – I'm not trembling and my teeth aren't chattering – but the freezing water is suddenly inside me again.

'You've probably sold thousands of tickets since then,' says Osmala, 'going by your figures.'

'It's the most accurate assessment I can—'

'Twenty-eight minutes past four in the afternoon,' Osmala interrupts. 'Did anything out of the ordinary happen then?'

'Last Friday at twenty-eight minutes past four in the afternoon,' I repeat to be as accurate as possible but also to buy myself some time. I don't like lying, it is the deliberate dissemination of incorrect information and goes against the best principles of mathematics. And so, even with Detective Inspector Osmala, I try to avoid ending up in a situation that would require me to tell an outright lie. 'Not to my knowledge.'

Osmala appears to be thinking about something.

'No accidents or anything like that?'

I realise at some point I'll have to ask where all of Osmala's questions are heading. In my estimation, now is my last chance.

'What exactly happened,' I ask, 'at twenty-eight minutes past four last Friday afternoon?'

Osmala still doesn't seem to notice the November chill. I wonder if he dresses the same way all year round. The idea feels perfectly plausible.

'At that time, one of the police's old acquaintances bought a ticket for your park,' he explains. 'Yesterday, that same individual floated to the surface of a remote pond – with the ticket in his back pocket. And we can confirm that drowning was not the cause of death. He'd already died several times before hitting the water.'

The icy water inside me starts to freeze. At first, I can't understand what could have happened to the legs from the Banana Mirror, then I remember who tied the knots that were supposed to attach the mirror's legs to the man's legs: Juhani.

'That sounds terrible,' I say, sincerely, and realise that we are standing almost exactly at the spot on the loading bay where the strawberry-headed man leapt into the late-autumn night.

'That's professionals for you,' Osmala nods. 'They don't leave anything to chance.'

'Quite.'

'Perhaps there's a connection between the ticket and his ... demise,' he adds. 'Then again, there might not be. And if this individual simply visited the park and nothing untoward happened during that time, then...'

Osmala shrugs his considerable shoulders.

'Last Friday was a very ordinary day,' I say, and that too is true. It only became extraordinary at around eleven o'clock that night. I don't know how to ask my next question so that I don't sound too interested. Finally, I realise there is only one way to approach the subject, and that is head-on: 'You said the man was an old ac-quaintance?'

Osmala's eyes might be lethargic as they move from one spot to another, but that only makes the movements all the stronger. Now he looks me right in the eye.

'Torpedo, they call him,' he says. 'He's part of the gig economy of the criminal underworld, you could say. A real jack of all trades. For the time being, he remains a person of interest.'

'For the time being?'

'For a while now, I've had my eye on a three-man outfit in the hostile-takeover business: one way or another, they take over companies, weigh them down with debt and sell off the company's assets to their partners at inflated prices, and it goes without saying they don't pay any tax on this income because all the money has disappeared and the company eventually goes into liquidation. What I'm most interested in is how this happens. I suspect they employ a good deal of intimidation and even violence. They might even hire subcontractors like the man in question.'

Osmala has just described the new owners of Toy of Finland so precisely that they might as well be standing here beside us.

'The reason I'm telling you all this,' Osmala continues, 'is that there's a chance you might come into contact with them.'

Osmala finishes his sentence, I realise that, but I can't help thinking that something has been left unsaid. He is clearly waiting for me to ask something.

'And if I do?'

'If you do, you'll know what I'm talking about,' he says.

We stand there in silence for a moment, then Osmala looks elsewhere.

'Any new masterpieces in the offing?' he asks. 'The wife and I really liked those murals.'

I think of Laura Helanto and her plans, how far she has got with them and how she will soon be at the park putting them together – in the middle of all this mess. And knowing her...

'Quite soon, I'd say.'

'Excellent news,' says Osmala. 'That means we'll be seeing each other again soon.'

He turns in his small, brown shoes, making the loading bay shudder again – the moose still getting used to its ballet shoes – then squeezes himself back into his electric car and drives off.

6

I empty the boxes onto the counter and gather the pieces I'm going to need to build a new pedal for the Komodo Locomotive. The storeroom feels like the best place to be right now: I can be by myself – I've stopped what I'm doing twice to look around and make sure of it – and it means I can do something with my hands. But the pedal I'm working on is only my secondary project. The primary one is assessing what Osmala's little visit entails going forwards. And as so often over the last few weeks, my thoughts seem to return to the same place.

Juhani.

Juhani knows everything. And he could reveal the whole truth to Osmala with a single sentence. Besides, knowing Juhani, one sentence would just be the opening gambit. The question is twofold: would Juhani do something like this and, if so, what would cause him to do it? In my experience, the answer to the first question is unfortunate: maybe he would – assuming he thought he had no alternatives and therefore had nothing to lose. And what would make him think that? The answer to this brings me back to the starting block when he returned from the dead only to find he still couldn't get what he wanted.

I know I'll have to keep Juhani happy, while at the same time protecting the park from him and – as now seems the case – from a variety of other threats too. And when Osmala makes good on his promise to visit the park again, he mustn't see anything that might confirm his obvious suspicions.

This isn't going to be easy.

Even the pedal turns out to be a more complicated affair than

I had anticipated. I continue fiddling with it and realise I've lost my train of thought, when I hear footsteps behind me. I place the half-finished pedal on the counter and turn around.

'Hard at it, I see,' says Juhani. 'You're an example to us all; a good boss should always know how to get his hands dirty, as it were.'

Juhani's voice and expression are light and breezy. Instinctively, I realise this has never been a particularly good sign. Besides, he seems to have undergone a larger kind of metamorphosis too: he is wearing a red-and-orange floral shirt beneath a light-brown blazer, white jeans and a generous splash of aftershave. Generous enough to fill the entire storeroom like a damp cloud. He is like a walking botanical garden.

'Can I suggest you take a little break?' he says. 'I've booked us a table at the Curly Cake.'

'I didn't realise they took reservations,' I say, though right now that certainly isn't the thing that feels most out of the ordinary.

'I want us to have somewhere quiet to talk,' he says.

I glance at the countertop.

'This will only take about half an hour...'

'He's a busy man, and he's here right now,' Juhani adds quickly.

'What do you mean?'

'He's waiting at the Strawberry Maze.'

'Who?' I ask. 'Who's waiting?'

'Kuisma Lohi.'

My thoughts wend their way back to the business pages of last week's newspaper, then a little further back in time, then return to the storeroom and Juhani.

'The investor Kuisma Lohi?' I ask.

Juhani smiles like a game-show host who has just heard the right answer.

'I've already ordered Captain's Cordial and Chocolate Monster Muffins for three,' he says.

There are some people whose age it is simply impossible to estimate in any reasonable fashion. Of course, we can say a person is between twenty and ninety, but this doesn't really narrow things down with any accuracy. And so, instead of trying to work out Kuisma Lohi's age, I resign myself to thinking, or imagining, that Kuisma Lohi must have been born looking exactly as he does now, and one day, a long time from now, he will die still looking exactly the same. Kuisma Lohi is dressed in a dark-blue pin-striped suit, a white shirt and a yellow tie with small black dots on it. He has very short light-brown hair combed in a meticulous right parting. He sports a pair of round glasses and a small, thin, trimmed moustache. He is slender and his face is gaunt in every respect: he has a small mouth, a small nose, no cheekbones to speak of, not a particularly wide chin. His eyes are light blue and seem devoid of any kind of discernible emotion.

'Henri Koskinen, I presume,' he says, or asks. I'm not sure which.

'That's me,' I say. 'Koskinen, Henri Koskinen.'

He tells me he is Kuisma Lohi, which both of us know already. Then he looks past the Strawberry Maze and towards the Big Dipper.

'They finance that, you know,' he says.

I look at the Big Dipper, where our customers are squealing as they slide down a variety of steel tubes at different angles.

'Generally it's their parents that pay,' I say.

'Yes, but they make it happen,' says Kuisma Lohi. 'They're great extortionists.'

We sit down at the table, and I see that Juhani has gone to a lot of trouble to set up our impromptu coffee meeting. The table has been moved slightly further away from the others to ensure we can talk in relative peace and quiet, and the delicacies Juhani mentioned have been laid out in front of us. Johanna has excelled herself – doubtless at Juhani's behest. The muffins are large, chocolatey and fresh from the oven. The straws in our glasses of cordial are the long, bendy kind and the coolness of the ice cubes and the juicy slices of lime crown the beverage beautifully. There are coffee cups on the table too in case anyone would like some coffee, which has been provided in a steel Thermos. Kuisma Lohi is sitting opposite me and doesn't seem to have blinked once since we met.

'If I introduce you two to each other,' Juhani begins, 'then perhaps we can—'

'How about I introduce myself?' says Kuisma Lohi.

'That's an excellent idea,' says Juhani.

Kuisma Lohi appears to spend about a second and a half thinking through everything he wants to say one more time, analyses it for any potential flaws (but naturally doesn't find any), double-checks the order of events, then begins.

'I'm an investor,' he says, 'and I'm actively looking for investment opportunities in areas where I see the potential for growth – opportunities that are currently under-resourced and underperforming. The Finnish adventure-park market is a good example. I've been looking for a way to break into this market for some time now, and I believe YouMeFun could be at the forefront of new developments in the field, in reshaping the market, as it were.'

Kuisma Lohi pauses briefly. My mouth feels dry. The Captain's Cordial tastes so concentrated that I can almost feel the taste of pear right through my body.

'Another factor making YouMeFun such an attractive proposal

is its management structure,' says Lohi. 'An actuary serving both as owner and CEO. Interesting. I've looked at the numbers and done my own research. Everything seems to be in order. What's more, you're considered a meticulous man whose word is his bond. From an investor's perspective, this is all very fascinating and compelling.'

I understand from Kuisma Lohi's words that he is trying to flatter me, though his expression doesn't tell quite the same story. His expression still doesn't tell me anything at all.

'When we take all the aforementioned elements together,' he continues, 'that is to say, the current underperforming of the adventure-park sector in general, the vast amounts of untapped potential both with regard to growing footfall and more effective leadership, and how YouMeFun might serve as a pilot scheme, a laboratory for how to create consistent success in the future, it's only natural that I'd want to make an offer.'

The Captain's Cordial feels cold in my hand. I quickly glance at Juhani. Not quickly enough, however, that Kuisma Lohi doesn't notice.

'When he contacted me, your brother stressed that you're the one who makes the decisions round here,' says Lohi. 'But he also said you have lots of shared interests when it comes to the park, and that you take each other's opinions into consideration in all the big decisions.'

I quickly realise the following facts: Juhani is essentially trying to blackmail me; Kuisma Lohi might know far more than he should; and our shared cordial-and-muffin meeting is far from cordial – in fact, it's a cold-blooded ambush. I decide to keep the conversation going until I can find a suitable way of making my excuses.

'What kind of untapped potential do you see,' I ask, 'at YouMeFun and in the sector in general?'

Kuisma Lohi looks at me for a moment before responding.

'This material, right here,' he says. 'This ... resource.'

'Resource?'

'I suppose "children" is the more accepted term,' says Lohi as though he is speaking to someone with less-than-average cognitive faculties.

'Do you dislike them so much that...?'

For the first time, I see a tiny movement in Kuisma Lohi's eyes. It's not quite a flicker, but something close.

'Noisy, dirty, revolting, repulsive creatures,' he says. 'Little monsters, every last one of them. It's hard to imagine anything more wholly unpleasant. But I admire their efficiency, their hidden potential.'

'In what sense?'

'In the sense of buying,' he says. 'And selling.'

There is a short, hollow lull in the conversation.

'Anyone for a top-up?' Juhani chimes in, breaking the silence. 'Or another muffin? We can share them if you'd prefer...'

'Children are like a sacred cow,' Kuisma Lohi continues as though he hasn't heard Juhani. 'Even for entrepreneurs. The same applies here. All forms of upselling stop as soon as they come into the park. All the children do is ... play. They should be steered towards effecting more and more purchases, groomed into future customers for our business partners. They should become indebted to us at as early an age as possible. In short, we need to squeeze more out of them.'

'They rarely bring their own wallets,' I explain. 'In the majority of cases, it's the parents who—'

'Of course,' Kuisma Lohi interrupts, and there's an iciness in his voice now, easily colder than the green drink in front of me. 'But have you ever heard one of those little brats whingeing for something from their parents?'

'Yes,' I say. For some reason the image makes me think of Juhani.

'Now multiply that energy by ten,' says Lohi. 'Or by twenty. Our job is to increase the pressure until it's unbearable for everybody: children, parents, grandparents, everybody. At which point, the only option is to do precisely what the whingeing, and ideally wailing, obsessive little dictator wants. As I've already explained to your brother, this excellent development can start right here.'

A group of little customers passes our table. It's loud. Kuisma Lohi visibly leans away from them, though there's at least a metre and a half between us. It doesn't look as though Lohi planned the reaction; it seems spontaneous, instinctive.

'In fact, there are two offers on the table,' he says. 'One in the short term and one in the long term.'

I say nothing and wait.

'The short-term offer is a simple cash injection,' Lohi continues. 'I will buy the park outright, immediately. My offer is seven hundred and fifty thousand euros.'

As Kuisma Lohi finishes his sentence, I can see Juhani stiffen. Everything about him turns rigid, even his permanent smile turns into something approaching a grimace.

'The long-term offer is, naturally, much bigger,' says Lohi. 'Additionally, it will tie you to the park for three years and will require the park to meet certain growth expectations. I will first make an initial investment by purchasing ten percent of the park's shares at a total price of one hundred thousand euros. This investment will commit both of us to a further contract. For every year producing over twenty-percent growth, I will pay another hundred and fifty thousand euros for a further ten-percent share in the park, and after three years, on the condition that we have reached our growth targets, I will buy out the rest of the park with a lump sum of one million euros.'

Kuisma Lohi leaves the sum hanging in the air. On purpose, I assume. And I expect he assumes I am currently calculating the true value of both his offers – both for me and my business. This I do right away, and very quickly I come to the conclusion that both offers might sound attractive on the surface, if I were thinking only about my personal interests and only in the short term. But if I think about the park as a whole and the interests of the staff, especially if I were to think further than three years into the future, I see that both offers contain the seeds of destruction. Not to mention the ways in which Lohi expects his growth targets to be met. I'm not at all sure I want to milk added efficiency from our underage clientele.

'You are an actuary,' says Kuisma Lohi, 'and I'm sure you want to do your own calculations first. If I have understood correctly, your brother is more inclined towards the first offer.'

Juhani's eyes meet mine. He looks at me only briefly, but I see three things at once: exposure, despair and an impatient desire for quick action. Naturally, I haven't forgotten the fact that I need to keep Juhani sweet, as they say. Which right now feels like a very ambitious task indeed.

'I certainly am an actuary,' I say, 'and that means I wish to familiarise myself with the matter in peace.'

Having said this, I look at Juhani once more. By now, his grimace looks as though it is set in concrete.

'By all means,' says Kuisma Lohi, and seems to notice for the first time that he has a Chocolate Monster Muffin in front of him. He looks sceptically – first at the muffin, then at me. 'Do you think they might have touched it?'

'Who?'

'Those filthy little urchins.'

I assume he is referring to our clientele.

'I don't think that's at all likely,' I say, and realise I'm a little offended on Johanna's behalf. She keeps the café in excellent, spotless order – right down to the freezers. 'We make absolutely sure nobody touches anything they shouldn't.'

As I finish my sentence, I turn to look at Juhani. He, in turn, quickly looks at Kuisma Lohi. Who, in turn, shifts his eyes from the muffin to the customers eating and shouting a little further off.

'I'll take it with me, if it's all the same,' he says.

Juhani and I accompany Kuisma Lohi to the front door. Juhani shows him the various parts of the park as we go. I walk behind them as though I were watching what they get up to and listening in on their conversation. In many ways, this is pointless. That conversation has already been and gone. Juhani has already promised whatever it is he has promised.

We look on as Kuisma Lohi and his Chocolate Monster Muffin get into a brand-new black Jaguar and drive out of sight at a speed that feels exaggeratedly slow. I wait a moment and make sure nobody else is within earshot. The entrance hall is empty, with the exception of Kristian, but he is approximately twelve metres away, behind the ticket desk. I'm about to say exactly what I think, but Juhani gets there first.

'That went well,' he says. 'Better than I thought. I'll admit, I was a bit nervous. Excellent negotiation. Very promising.'

There's a marked difference in Juhani's body language now, and his voice sounds different too, it's somehow lighter. I'm not as sure of my stance as I was a few seconds ago. It's as though I can't quite fathom everything that has just happened. Juhani turns to face me, and there's joy and excitement in his eyes, which reminds me of our first encounter after his surprise return.

'I'm sure you went through the will with my lawyer,' he says, 'so you'll remember the sub-clauses about selling the business.'

Suddenly I'm certain I do remember the sub-clauses. I hope I'm misremembering, but it's unlikely.

'Thank you, Henri,' my brother says.

'For what?'

'For being so constructive just now.'

'Constructive?'

'None of your correlations and cumulative conjectures and what have you...'

'I think you'll find that, technically speaking, there's no such—'

'My point exactly,' Juhani says, cutting me short. He smiles and taps me on the shoulder, then walks off towards the main hall. I don't understand what he means, in so many ways.

There's one matter I check as soon as I get back to my office. I take out the inheritance document that Juhani's lawyer handed me a few months ago and leaf through the pages until I reach the section about the possible sale of the business. I read it carefully and realise that, alas, I had remembered it correctly. The sub-clauses lay out quite explicitly who will be the beneficiaries, should the park ever be transferred into new ownership. According to the sub-clause in question, one of the beneficiaries will be me, the owner of the park. The other beneficiary is Juhani's representative, and that can also be ... Juhani himself.

The profits will be divided equally.

Half to me.

Half to Juhani.

7

Text messaging is a fine art. At times, it almost requires knowledge of a secret language. That's what it feels like. Laura Helanto is only too happy to communicate via text message, and I receive a great many of them throughout the day. I try to answer all of them, though sometimes I don't quite know what I'm responding to or how to answer a message that doesn't include any particular message, let alone questions, but instead consists largely of colourful images and figures. I give Schopenhauer his supper, sit down at the kitchen table again and try to select the appropriate figures to send back to her. At the same time, I know I'm trying to put off the main issue. Laura Helanto has suggested she start working on her new installations at the park tomorrow. She used the word 'suggest' herself, though we both know this is more of a statement of intent than a suggestion.

My tea has cooled while I've been weighing up my options.

Beyond my window, Kannelmäki has quietened as evening has drawn in. All the square windows in the rectangular wall of the building opposite are illuminated, and the effect is one of uniformity and careful planning. The symmetry causes me a little frisson of satisfaction. Once Schopenhauer has eaten, I let him out onto the balcony to keep watch. I tell him about the symmetry and boil some fresh water for my tea.

It is reasonable to conclude that, far from becoming clearer, matters are in fact becoming more complex. What is true of the park is true of Laura Helanto too. When it comes to Laura, the old saying (which I have always treated with healthy scepticism, because of the imprecise nature of its definitions) 'one step forwards, two steps back' suddenly seems like a perfectly serviceable assessment of the situation. One moment we are kissing, and everything feels balanced and settled, as though we are moving forwards together to the power of two. But the next moment, everything seems to have changed: we are two individuals, each of us alone, and it feels as though something or someone is digging a cold, black trench between us. *Two steps forwards, one step back.* To compound my confusion, there are times when I'm unsure which of these two theoretical steps I am taking.

My tea has cooled again. The phone rings.

Laura Helanto tells me that Tuuli is asleep and that she has a lot to do before the morning. I've realised this is her way of keeping conversations short. On occasion, I've also thought that we could achieve the same thing more easily and without lengthy explanations by agreeing the exact length of our phone calls in advance – say, eight and a half minutes. A bell would ring, and we would bid each other good night. I believe this would give us space and allow us to relax; I would certainly find it relaxing, as I wouldn't constantly have to wonder whether I've crossed some kind of unspecified line after which Laura Helanto will no longer be able to get all her work done by morning.

'I hope to be at the park around eleven,' she says. 'I'll do some preliminary work throughout the day – measurements, sketches – and think about the materials to be used. Tanning will be first on my list. Then after we close for the evening, I'll get started on the outline. There's still what's left of the old Peapod Swing in the storeroom; I could use that.'

Laura has stopped talking. I only realise this once the silence has lasted a few seconds.

'Henri?'

'Yes,' I say. 'The Peapod Swing ... is in the storeroom.'

'Is everything all right?'

I don't know how to say, in the most neutral way possible and without arousing any further questions, that I suspect my brother of plotting against me and my supplier of trying to murder me, and that a certain policeman, whom Laura knows too, has returned with fresh suspicions, and that I can now add to my list of woes one Kuisma Lohi, the investor who has clearly enthralled my aforementioned plotting brother, who in turn has a peculiar but very carefully drawn-up document on his side, and that in light of that document it is perfectly possible that my brother is trying to bring external facts to bear in order to speed up the sale of the adventure park. I am about to say something – or rather, trying to think of a way to avoid the question – when Laura speaks again.

'How is Juhani settling into the park?'

I'm confused by this question, but it is easier to answer than the previous one.

'Very well,' is my honest answer. 'He's very enthusiastic, very interested in how the park works. Why do you ask?'

'Well, because he's just taken on a new, challenging role.'

'He accepted the challenge,' I say, again sincerely.

Then the same unpleasant feeling, the one I always feel whenever we talk about Juhani, raises its head again. I'd much rather talk about—

'Toy of Finland,' Laura interrupts my train of thought. 'We could ask them to provide some of the materials. They might have some old stuff lying around that would fit the theme, something cheap maybe.'

'I'm in the middle of some rather fraught negotiations with them about our supplies,' I explain, and this is partly true. I leave out the bit about the hired assassin and some of the other details, such as the difficulty in acquiring the Moose Chute. 'So, perhaps we might leave those enquiries for a more opportune moment.'

'That's fine,' says Laura, and she sounds as though the matter really is done and dusted as far as she is concerned. 'Henri?'

'Yes?'

'It feels really nice to be working at the park again, but guess what feels just as nice?'

'I don't like to guess things. I don't find it a fruitful way of approaching matters.'

'Sorry,' says Laura Helanto, and I can hear from her tone of voice that she is smiling. 'I forgot. What I mean is, you and I will get to see each other every day. We could even nip into the storeroom for a quick kiss.'

Laura Helanto does this sometimes. She says something quickly and off the cuff, and clearly hasn't analysed her suggestion or thought it through in all its possible dimensions.

'I'm not sure the storeroom is an appropriate location for such activity,' I say. 'The space is mostly reserved for industrial use and storage purposes, and besides—'

'I'm just being silly,' she says. 'I'm just so happy at being able to start this project. Oh, wait. I think Tuuli was pulling my leg and she's not asleep after all. See you tomorrow.'

Laura hangs up. I walk out to the balcony. Schopenhauer is watching someone carrying a shopping bag from one side of the yard to the other and stepping into one of the stairwells. He knows what goes on around here.

8

The sound of my phone's alarm clock comes as a relief. Not because I'd been resting or sleeping particularly deeply; the relief is a response to my dreams being brought to an abrupt end. In recent days, my dreams have been restless, to say the least. One of them is still whirring through my mind, as I shave and see that my forehead looks to have healed a little.

I dreamt that I was trying to explain the current situation to a variety of different people: Laura Helanto, Detective Inspector Osmala, my brother Juhani and – for some reason that even by the machinations of the subconscious doesn't immediately feel logical – to Otto Härkä from Toy of Finland. In light of recent events, perhaps this is hardly surprising. But in this dream, all the characters seemed to have switched places, and I wasn't talking as myself but had instead taken on the characteristics of all the people above, characteristics that had become mixed with my own. The result was that in this dream I confessed my love for Otto Härkä and praised his artwork, I confounded Juhani with longwinded nonsense I'd learnt from Härkä, I pressed Osmala with an endless stream of police-like questions and ended up accusing Laura Helanto of short-sighted skulduggery.

I wash the remnants of shaving foam from my face, let the cool water wake me and freshen me up, and only then realise that there is something about the audio-visual cavalcade that played out in my subconscious during the night that can't be washed away. I quickly get dressed, leave Schopenhauer a snack and walk through the light drizzle to the train station.

The train journey is pleasingly predictable: the train arrives on time, stops at each station according to the timetable and leaves me at Aviapolis at the appointed time so that I can walk the 640 metres to the bus stop at a brisk but relaxed speed of seven kilometres per hour. It's only a few stops, so I stand in my wet coat; I don't want to get the seat wet.

I am about to cross the road towards the car park at the adventure park when I see something that takes me by surprise. Well, it's only surprising because it's happening right now. In other conditions, at another time, a delivery van belonging to Toy of Finland wouldn't seem out of the ordinary. The van is heading away from the park: at the intersection, it turns left, away from me, so all I can see is the passenger seat. I'm not entirely sure of the matter, but the man sitting there looks distinctly like Jeppe Sauvonen, the third, and clearly youngest, of Toy of Finland's new owners, the one who, when we first met, wore a sweatshirt declaring himself to be a *FUN MACHINE*. I look right, I look left, then right again, and though I usually resist and deplore such behaviour, I cross the road on a red light.

The entrance hall is empty, which is only to be expected. The park won't open its doors for another forty minutes. Perhaps I imagined I would bump into Kristian, who usually prepares the ticket desk long before the doors open. Now, however, the lights at the desk still aren't switched on and Kristian is nowhere to be seen. I hurry from the entrance into the main hall and stop in my tracks on the flying carpet in the doorway. It takes a moment before I locate the sounds I can hear. They are coming from far off, behind the Strawberry Maze. I walk closer. The Strawberry Maze effectively blocks my view. Behind it there is an area I have reserved for the Moose Chute. I've asked Kristian to dismantle the mini tennis court in preparation, and it sounds as though this is what he is doing. I pass the Strawberry Maze and expect to see Kristian taking the equipment down and clearing the area but...

Instead I see...

The Crocodile Canyon.

Bright-green crocodile-shaped canoes made of rubber and plastic allowing the children to row along a short, bendy stretch of river. The river is in fact a carpet of bright-blue rubber brush-heads that look like hedgehog spikes along which the sturdy canoes are supposed to glide smoothly. In theory, that is. In practice, almost everything about the Crocodile Canyon is wrong. The canoes are too heavy for the children and don't glide properly. The oars aren't proper oars, but sharp lances that the nimblest customers will quickly start using for improvised hand-to-hand combat. On top of all this, it is actually possible to drown in the river. After a fashion. The blue brush-heads are positioned so tightly and at such an angle that if you step into the river, getting your leg out again is a lengthy, painful operation, and usually requires the help of one or more adults. I know all this because I've read up on the matter and checked the security details with Esa, who claims to have worked in the adventure-park sector since the nineties. Which, of course, makes me doubt the veracity of his story about the US Marine Corps all the more. But that's another matter. The most acute matter is right in front of me.

The Crocodile Canyon.

And Kristian.

Who appears to be working with great gusto. As I step closer, he notices me and beams.

'The Crocodile Canyon,' he says and stretches out his hands as though he were presenting the unit to me personally.

'Yes,' I say. 'When did it arrive?'

Kristian's smile narrows a little but doesn't completely disappear.

'We started putting it together before six. They asked specifically. They came by here last night when I was closing up and asked when I could start work. You know I like to get to work early. The early business bird catches the business worm. That's my new motto.'

I have nothing to say about Kristian's motto. It's nonsensical, that goes without saying, but it isn't the only nonsensical thing in front of me right now and isn't a device the customers dislike, taking up room in the park. That would be the Crocodile Canyon.

'I don't understand,' I say. 'How did they just ... come into the park and start building—?'

'I helped,' says Kristian. He sounds both happy and sincere.

'How ... Why did you start building it?'

'They said they'd agreed the details with you, they showed me an order slip and a delivery notice and everything. Oh, and they left the invoice too.'

'The invoice?'

Kristian points to one of the canoes. I walk up to it and look inside. There is a pile of papers on the seat. I pick them up and read through them. The order looks legitimate, though I know I haven't filled out any papers like this; the quality of the forgery is impressive. Delivery has been carried out as per the timetable stipulated in the documents, a timetable I have never agreed to. And as for the invoice...

It could have been for a space shuttle. And it doesn't end at the bottom of the page, as I imagine at first. The list of costed items continues on the other side of the paper. In addition to the Crocodile Canyon, a number of extra charges have been added, itemised below: storage, delivery out of business hours, installation, guidance and instruction, spare parts, and finally the most expensive item of all: membership of an exclusive online forum for Crocodile Canyon owners. When everything is added up, the total price is over three hundred percent more than I originally feared. The payment is scheduled for today.

And this isn't our biggest problem, by any means.

That would be Toy of Finland.

My assumption – that they must have sent the man who attacked me – has been partially confirmed. This kind of action – the forced selling and installation of an old piece of equipment at a ridiculously inflated price – is something you do only if you think your opponent can't do anything about it, that he will have to swallow the rubber canoes with the lance oars and keep quiet.

I fold the papers and place them in my pocket, then look at Kristian, who is continuing to install the Crocodile Canyon. It's only now that I realise his behaviour is different from in recent weeks. He didn't seem nervous when I approached him, and he no longer seems to watch every word he says. In fact, it's now the opposite. I walk up to him. He is half inside one of the canoes, whistling as he works, though he is crouched into what looks like an especially uncomfortable position. It's baffling, as is the final result of his whistle. There is no discernible pitch or melody, and the cacophony of sound echoes around inside the confined space.

'Kristian,' I whisper. 'How do you enjoy your work?'

The whistling stops. Kristian backs out of the canoe and stands up straight. His face is bright red.

'Best feeling ever,' he says.

'You took part in a strike not long ago,' I remind him. 'And if memory serves me, you were quite unhappy.'

Now he looks as though something is finally bothering him.

'It just felt like ... you weren't really listening to us.'

I wonder whether there's any point explaining once again that we are in a particularly difficult financial situation and that we will have to do everything we can just to survive. I decide against it.

'But apparently now I'm listening?' I ask.

Kristian nods with his usual enthusiasm.

'You and Juhani are looking in the same direction now,' he replies. 'Juhani told me you and he make the decisions together. I've been going to business college these last few months, taking courses, just like you said, and let me tell you, that's a recipe for success. I call you guys the two-headed adventure-park eagle.'

'When did—?'

'This morning,' he says. 'I came up with it at about seven this morning while I was attaching that river to the floor.'

'I don't mean that,' I say. 'When did Juhani tell you that we … make the decisions together?'

Kristian looks suddenly unsure of himself.

'I'm not sure exactly. And I know how exactly you like everything to—'

'Give or take a day, that'll be fine,' I encourage him.

'It was Monday or Tuesday,' he says, and I can see he is really thinking about it. 'Yes, it was Tuesday. Because it was on Tuesday that I had my new introductory course on self-leadership and method-networking and—'

'Thank you, Kristian,' I say and return my attention to the hall.

Amid the lack of clarity, the lack of knowledge and lack of certainty, there are now a few things I know with utter confidence. Juhani has been preparing for Kuisma Lohi's appearance for some time, and he's been planning it on a number of fronts. Meanwhile, Toy of Finland has obviously escalated from the theoretical to the concrete, from threats, intimidation and blackmail to criminal direct action. And I suspect them of being behind my nocturnal tenpin-bowling experience, though right now I can't prove it. Kristian is obviously expecting something from me. His expression and his body language tell me he is waiting for me to tell him something positive, something along the lines of now that the two of us have got this much done already, the morning will continue in a similar upwardly mobile vein. But I've been thinking of my options, and I sense that what I have to tell him might be a little upsetting.

'I want you to start dismantling the Crocodile Canyon,' I say. 'We're sending it back.'

Kristian looks as though he hasn't understood – which is very likely the case. But I have to get him on side.

'There's been a misunderstanding,' I say. 'Correcting that misunderstanding will require some delicacy and a lot of responsibility, in short it's going to need what I believe is called soft leadership. We have to dismantle the device cleanly and smoothly, and without drawing too much attention. This operation will need a leader who can take the reins, and I hereby appoint you as that leader. But, you understand, this is completely confidential.'

'I don't understand,' he says.

'You mustn't tell anybody else about this new appointment,' I say. 'And you'll be working alone. This is your responsibility now.'

Kristian seems to be thinking it through.

'What's my new title?'

'Between you and me,' I begin, 'it could be leading—'

'Operational manager,' Kristian nods. 'That's good. Leading operational manager.'

I decide not to get bogged down in the element of tautology and tell him instead that I think the new title suits him excellently. Kristian tells me he will provide me with interim reports on how things are progressing, and I thank him again. Then I walk to my office.

'I decided to start with Frankenthaler instead,' says Laura Helanto and indicates a point on the concrete floor where I am to attach the end of a length of tape.

Laura's appearance at the park takes me a little by surprise, in that she hasn't sent me a text message telling me in advance when to expect her. At first I found this manner of agreeing a meeting, whereby we first agree a meeting, then send text messages a few moments before the meeting to confirm where and when we will meet, quite cumbersome, but now I realise this practice can have its benefits, especially in my current predicament. I pull the roll of tape across the floor and stop at the tip of Laura's shoe.

'I'm more familiar with this one,' she continues. 'And this morning, it just seemed to come to life. I want to give this one a physical dimension, a sense of what I experienced at my first Frankenthaler exhibition – that the work seems to leap out of the wall, sweeps me up and takes me somewhere, shows me something I've never seen before.'

I tear off the tape, stand up and look at the mural.

I think I like it more than ever before. This isn't an entirely unexpected phenomenon. Laura Helanto's works do this to me: I see something new in them every time, something that has been at once hidden and right in front of my eyes all the time; I experience a mixture of discovery and ecstasy, a heightened sensory perception. On a few occasions, I've tried to unpack the uncontrolled movements in my mind, in order to understand the phenomenon and myself better, but without success. Even my visit to the Ateneum Art Gallery didn't provide the great mathematical breakthrough I had hoped for. The beginning was promising: I could easily split the realistic works from the early twentieth century into their constituent parts (peasants + bales of hay + evening sunshine) and come up with what I thought was the essence of these paintings (southern German local agriculture before the Industrial Revolution). But cubism and abstract art made any attempts to understand them futile. Though they fascinated me, I didn't know how to process the different streaks, smears and splodges, and I found myself standing, staring at them for some time.

And right now, as I stand next to Laura Helanto and inhale her familiar scent – a combination of forest-flower shampoo and a pleasant perfume with perhaps a hint of the sea, citrus fruit and a few darker undertones – and look at her murals, I think I understand what she means when she says a painting can sweep her up and take her somewhere else. I notice I'm thinking that Laura's artwork may have the same origin as she does herself, that it springs from the same energy as the big bang that first set the universe in motion, the explosion before the explosion. And at the same time I realise that my thoughts have again lost their focus and usefulness; they have run away and are now floating far off, somewhere they shouldn't—

'Henri?'

Laura Helanto might have said something that I haven't heard. I glance at her and quickly realise this must indeed be the case. She is looking towards the Strawberry Maze, and naturally she can see the same as I can: in the foreground the Strawberry Maze, and inside it a cluster of customers colliding and bumping into one another. One of the customers is lying in front of the entrance to the Maze, either as a protest at the others or simply from exhaustion. And immediately behind the Strawberry Maze, the bright-green heads of giant plastic crocodiles. This is a pile of canoes from the Crocodile Canyon. The canoes that Kristian didn't have a chance to set afloat.

'I asked if that's the ... Crocodile Canyon?'

'Yes,' I tell her.

Laura Helanto turns to look at me.

'I've heard the kids don't much like it,' she says. 'And it doesn't even work very well.'

'Both statements are true,' I say with a faint sense of discomfort as I look at Laura's blue-green, always curious eyes. My discomfort is heightened by the fact that her experience of the adventure-park business is considerably longer than mine. 'We're sending it back.'

'Didn't Toy of Finland mention any of this when you placed the order? I remember it was always great doing business with them. They were really open about what worked and what didn't.'

This is not a conversation I want to be having. Of course, Laura is referring to Toy of Finland's previous owner and his previous way of doing business. I'm more acquainted with their current business model.

'A misunderstanding,' I say. 'It's only a temporary problem.'

At first, it's hard to read Laura Helanto's expression. Then she smiles.

'It's your park,' she says. 'For a moment, I thought I was still working here.'

All of a sudden, she leans forwards, kisses me quickly on the lips and pulls away again. An underground train rattles through my mind.

'Why go to the storeroom?' she says.

'I don't know,' I say, perfectly honestly. 'One generally goes there to fetch something – tools, materials...'

Laura laughs, I don't know why, then points at the roll of tape in my hand.

'Can you give me a hand measuring the de Lempicka too?'

The day doesn't turn out too badly after all – if we disregard the fact that almost everything to do with the park is either in danger, dangerous or simply wrong. Of course, I don't and can't dismiss these matters, but Laura Helanto's company pushes everything else into the background, so that none of it bothers me nearly as much as I might have expected, considering the number of problems yet to be solved.

One of my problems is, of course, Juhani, whom we don't see all day, for some reason. This is curious, but today of all days it feels right and appropriate. I don't mention the matter to Laura, and she doesn't bring it up either. When later that afternoon we are taping measurements on the floor in front of the O'Keeffe wall and I find myself measuring lengths of aluminium beams with characteristic precision, Laura smiles again and says we make a good couple.

I assume she means in the mathematical-artistical sense.

Five hours and twenty-two minutes later we are making love.

9

'Breakfast. My mum says you'll be late otherwise.'

This isn't like me, I think. In fact, nothing I see around me, in front of me or to the side is like me, and for a moment I don't know where I am or what has happened. Then I remember – everything. Naturally. There is nothing out of the ordinary about this at all. The only thing out of the ordinary is that I fell asleep ... blissfully.

First, we worked at the park, making plans and taking measurements. Then we took the park's delivery van and drove to my apartment, where I gave Schopenhauer some fresh food, water, dried food and a small treat and told him I would be away for the night, which didn't seem to shock him as much as I thought it might. Then we drove to Laura's place in Herttoniemi, where the babysitter and a sleeping child were waiting for us.

And eventually I too fell asleep, in Laura Helanto's arms, after engaging in a great many pleasant activities that both lifted our spirits (because I believe our time together was mutually beneficial) and relaxed me in a way I doubt I've ever experienced before. And I don't think this assessment is an exaggeration.

Tuuli is standing at the bedroom door. I'm in Laura Helanto's apartment, in her bed. I'm under her duvet, wearing a T-shirt she has lent me. Across the yellow T-shirt is a text in black lettering reading *THE PRETENDERS*.

'Good,' I say. 'Thank you for passing that on. I will be at breakfast in approximately eleven minutes' time.'

Tuuli stands in the doorway a moment longer and seems to be watching me. I wait for a moment, and she disappears. I locate my clothes, carry them into the bathroom, take a three-and-a-half-minute shower, comb my hair, get dressed and walk round the corner into the living room, where there is also a dining area and an open kitchen. Laura and Tuuli are already sitting at the dining table. Laura gives me a smile.

'There's porridge, bread, eggs,' she says and shows me the spread on the table. 'And coffee. There's hot water in the pot.'

'Thank you,' I say and sit down opposite her.

'Did you sleep well?' she asks, and there's a look in her eyes that reminds me of last night.

'Very blissfully indeed,' I reply.

Tuuli sniggers at my answer. I don't know why. I take some porridge and glance around me. The fifth-floor windows are level with the boughs of the trees outside, the old-town bay ripples past in front of us, with the houses of Arabianranta standing beyond it. The morning is at once light and dim. The living-room walls are a summery yellow, the furniture a mixture of old and new. I imagine this is deliberate. I'm not entirely sure what the word cosy means, but I'm minded to believe this room must be it. I take a spoonful of porridge and only then realise quite how hungry I am. It seems that art and intimate relations make us temporarily forget the importance of maintaining regular mealtimes. I'm about to say how much I have enjoyed the porridge and that I hold the porridge maker herself in high regard, but Laura beats me to it.

'Juhani called.'

I swallow. The porridge feels suddenly rough.

'Juhani? He called you?'

'Said he couldn't get hold of you.'

It's true; my phone has been switched off. I noticed the battery was low just as I was taking off my trousers last night. At that moment, the phone's battery was the least of my concerns.

'Apparently the two of you have an engagement later,' she

continues. 'That's what he said. They'll pick you up outside the house at ten past.'

I look at the black-and-white wall clock in the kitchen and keep my eyes fixed on it. Right now, that feels like the best option. I try to filter what I've just heard, and I remind myself that the park's problems have no place in this part of my life and that Laura Helanto doesn't need to know anything about them. Once I'm sure I can maintain my composure and continue eating breakfast, I look at her again.

'This porridge is delicious,' I say, because I want to tell the truth, but I'm also keen to change the subject. I'm aware that Tuuli is watching me just as she was a moment ago at the bedroom door. Her eyes are curious, perhaps a little inquisitive. Laura seems to notice this too.

'Tuuli remembers the way you calculated our bill when we were in the café. She's been doing arithmetic at school now, too, and she's very enthusiastic...'

'What's thirteen times sixteen?' Tuuli asks suddenly.

'Two hundred and eight,' I reply.

'What's three hundred and thirteen times fifty-eight?'

'Eighteen thousand, one hundred and fifty-four.'

'What's four thousand eight hundred—'

'Tuuli, you have to go to school in a minute,' says Laura. 'You can ask later on.'

'Just one more,' she pleads.

Laura Helanto looks at me. If my mouth weren't full of porridge, I would explain that multiplication is one of humanity's greatest achievements and that Tuuli has clearly understood this most excellently.

'What's eight thousand, three hundred and fifty-eight times four thousand, five hundred and sixty-one?'

I swallow my porridge.

'Thirty-eight million, one hundred and twenty thousand, eight hundred and thirty-eight.'

As I finish my answer, Tuuli squeals as though she has won something special and starts laughing. Laura Helanto looks as though, on the one hand, she would like to calm her down but, on the other, she is happy and proud of something. I eat my porridge. It doesn't feel the least bit rough anymore. Laura and Tuuli leave the table and walk through to the hallway and the door to Tuuli's room.

I eat an egg and a slice of ryebread, and drink a cup of tea, all the while watching the clock. Though everything is always in motion, I think, and though right now, on a personal level, time seems to be running out at an unfathomable pace, the passage of time feels different when I'm with Laura and Tuuli. My sense of hurry dwindles, and time restraints temporarily loosen their grip. I can't immediately think of an explanation for this, and I don't have time to think of one either. I try to prepare myself for what is, as I understand it, about to happen next: Juhani is going to pick me up and, presumably, we're going to drive somewhere. I'm not happy about this, but right now I can't change things one way or the other. Once Tuuli is ready for school, we stand in the hallway and pull on our outdoor clothes together.

My phone's battery is charged now. I switch it on to see whether anyone has sent me any messages or tried to call me. Juhani has not once tried to contact me, either by calling or by text message. Laura Helanto looks me in the eyes, she says she loves me, then kisses me on the lips.

In the lift on our way to the ground floor, I try to rationalise and make sense of everything I have heard. Unfortunately, my attempts produce nothing but undesirable outcomes.

10

The car doesn't belong to Juhani. A number of factors speak to this conclusion. It is exotic and expensive; we are sitting on the soft yet firm light-brown, leather upholstery in the backseat; and, what's more, we have our own driver. Everything is smooth and efficient, and we reach the eastern ring road before either of us says a word.

'Kuisma Lohi has invited us to lunch,' says Juhani.

I'm sitting behind the driver, and all I can see is the back of his head. His hair is short and dark and combed tightly back over his scalp. The air inside the car is a mixture of two strong, distinct aftershaves. I assume the one Juhani is wearing is the more pungent of the two – and the cheaper. I have a lot to say to Juhani, but most of it is very much between us. I dismiss several subjects before reaching the most suitable one.

'I don't recall being invited,' I say.

'You're a hard man to get hold of.'

I look at Juhani. He smiles somehow ... knowingly. I don't like the tone of his smile or what I think it must refer to. And I do not like the fact that he knows I've been out of reach, as it were, though he hasn't tried to reach me. As I see it, there is only one simple explanation for this: Laura must have passed Juhani the information. But that is one topic I certainly don't want to bring up in this fast-moving perfumery. I stick to what is happening right now.

'I assume the subject of this meeting will be the same as the previous one,' I say.

'You assume almost right,' Juhani replies. 'The subject is the same, but if I've understood correctly, now there are a few added extras.'

The house in Marjaniemi is new and massive. The car pulls up outside the front door, and the driver opens my door before I've even managed to take off my seatbelt. It's a cool morning, and I can sense the proximity of the sea, smell it on the wind. The white walls of the house stretch out in all directions. The front door is black and, just like the car door, it opens before we reach it. What's most confusing is that it's the same person who opens both doors: the driver. The man is around forty, impeccably dressed in a well-fitted suit, and utterly expressionless. In both his movements and his overall demeanour, he is like a successful cross between a flying superhero and a Merchant-Ivory manservant.

I am about to step inside when Juhani barges his way in front of me, meaning our entrance into the house isn't quite as stylish as it might otherwise have been. I'm sure we look as though we're vying for the affections of Kuisma Lohi, who is waiting to greet us. I surmise that this is certainly true of Juhani, because he praises everything in sight.

Notably the view, which is undeniably impressive: with its tall ceilings and a football pitch's worth of space, the living room features a wall made entirely of glass, giving a view out over the green and black waters of the bay. Juhani admires the paintings and sculptures, items that are certainly praiseworthy and that I would very much like to examine with Laura Helanto. And Juhani praises the timing of our lunch and lauds himself as he explains how, just like Kuisma Lohi, he too has been in business for many years and has a certain ... insight into these matters. And in his own topsy-turvy way, Juhani is absolutely right.

Without further ado, we sit down at the table. The driver appears out of nowhere, then disappears again just as quickly. Wine trickles beautifully and steadily into our glasses, even as the man is already moving away from the table.

Kuisma Lohi still hasn't said a word – Juhani has been waxing lyrical from the moment the car pulled up in front of the house – but now he looks at Juhani in a manner that makes my brother add that if Kuisma Lohi still doesn't have his own statue in downtown Helsinki, the council should erect one without delay. After this, Juhani finally falls silent, the same pained, grimace-like smile on his face as at our first meeting. The suggestion of a putative statue doesn't seem to impress Kuisma Lohi.

'I got some kind of food poisoning from that muffin of yours,' he says, and adjusts the position of his glasses, though they were perfectly straight to begin with. 'Besides, I thought it best we meet in more sophisticated surroundings this time.'

Yet again, I think, Johanna and her impeccably run café have been impugned most unjustly. So far, this morning has been full of surprises and deception, and Kuisma Lohi's words are, as they say, the final straw.

'Our muffins do not give anyone food poisoning,' I say, and even I can hear how harsh my voice sounds.

'I didn't say I ate it,' says Kuisma Lohi. 'Once I got home, I just looked at it and started feeling queasy.'

I lean forwards, I'm about to say something, when the driver-cum-butler's arm places a wide plate in front of me, its small inverted dome filled with steaming soup. Just then I hear Juhani's voice.

'We have lots of great things to talk about today,' he begins. 'As for Kuisma Lohi's proposal—'

'Perhaps I can present it myself,' says Lohi.

'That's a much better idea,' says Juhani.

I lean back in my chair and take a deep breath.

'Your brother contacted me after our meeting and told me your feelings on the matter,' says Kuisma Lohi. 'And your concerns about these large, though still theoretical changes.'

'Did he?' I ask, and look at Juhani. Of course, none of the above is true. Juhani knows nothing about my feelings, and I haven't shared any of my concerns with him. Once again, I think that if it weren't for our endeavours at the pond that night, I would get up and walk away. But the fact of the matter is that Juhani is trying to blackmail me. Juhani, who is again either grimacing or smiling. Or doing both at once.

'I appreciate you're worried about your staff,' Lohi continues, and from his voice I can tell that he doesn't appreciate anything in the least. 'You're worried about the park and its future prosperity. Perhaps I didn't make myself clear enough: I sincerely hope you will both continue running the park. And if it is what you both want, the current staff can remain in place too. Though everything will change, nothing will change. Not to the extent that there's any need for concern, and assuming we reach certain targets.'

Kuisma Lohi tastes his soup, slurps it almost inaudibly. I try to make sense of what I've just heard, while still retaining my composure.

'So, we would *both* continue running the park?' I ask.

'That's right,' Lohi nods. 'Your brother told me you want to use our arrangement to establish a new management structure and that this should be written into the contract. That's fine by me.'

I glance over at Juhani. He has ambushed me once again. He is looking out across the bay and sipping his soup. Then I look at Kuisma Lohi. Things have gone too far now, and it's time I said so and put an end to this nonsense.

'Then there's the fact,' Lohi continues, 'that I've adjusted my offer upwards slightly. And your brother has already accepted it.'

I barely taste the venison, our main course. Juhani appears almost liberated. He talks a lot, gesticulates a lot, the way he does when he is very excited. He lauds Lohi's business acumen and presents wholly unrealistic plans for the future of the adventure park. And the mere fact that Kuisma Lohi listens to these plans without commenting on them in the least, tells me more than enough. Kuisma Lohi has no intention of watching Juhani ruin his investment portfolio. My own assessment is that the minute the ink has dried on our contract, Juhani and every other member of staff will be made redundant and replaced, as is commonplace in such circumstances, with a brutal and hard-headed manager and new staff who are as poorly paid as possible, the Curly Cake Café will be replaced with a franchise pizzeria that will operate at its own risk, and all guided group activities in the park will be dispensed with. The park will lose its unique identity and people will lose their jobs. The park will be bled dry and eventually run into the ground.

I do not plan to sign anything or sell or give up anything either. I plan to keep my park, and I plan to save my employees' jobs.

Ultimately, there's only one obstacle in my path.

And that's Juhani.

Who right now is munching on Sachertorte and explaining, perhaps drunk from the combined effects of the sugar and the apparent success of his scheming, how easy it will be to expand our activities first throughout the Nordic countries, then further into Europe and eventually to North America. Of course.

Juhani leans forwards a fraction, waves his dessert spoon first at me, then in Kuisma Lohi's direction.

'Disneyland is dead,' he says.

11

My head aches. I'm sitting in my office, the door is shut, and the sounds from the hall seem muted, as though the screams and squeals are coming from underwater. Lunch, however, has left a nasty taste in my mouth. Naturally, I have no idea what Juhani and Kuisma Lohi talked about after I left, but I can make a number of educated guesses. I left at the point when Juhani began speculating about the kind of share options that might be available to the new owners. I declined Lohi's offer of a ride; instead I walked to the metro station at Itäkeskus, and after arriving back at the park I came straight to my office, where waiting for me was the most recent report on our customer numbers. And there is a direct correlation between the data and my burgeoning headache.

We are losing customers.

On a day-to-day basis, the loss isn't very dramatic, but the direction of travel is clear. I can see where the downward trend started: the same week as our competitors revealed their new acquisitions and announced that the extension to their facility was ready to be opened. They are taking our customers. We have to fight back, but that isn't going to be possible in the current circumstances, with Juhani trying to sell the park off to Kuisma Lohi and with Toy of Finland sending us old-fashioned equipment for which we're expected to pay through the nose. On top of that, we need something that will turn the tide and bring the customers flocking back to us.

We need the Moose Chute.

Either we get the Moose Chute or we—

There's a knock at the door.

I do a mental roll call of all the potential door-knockers and their probable reasons for doing so. Minttu K wants more money for marketing, advertising and sponsorship agreements. Samppa wants to expand his therapy sessions and thereby increase the provision of spiritual wellbeing at the park. By this point, we can assume that Esa would like the park to acquire its own Space Force Unit to patrol the park from the skies. Johanna might well want us to hire a fisherman from Normandy for her own personal use. And, depending on the time of day, Kristian wants a whole variety of things from becoming CEO to new mint-flavoured protein bars, and his whims all have one feature in common: without exception, they come at the worst possible time.

Once I am ready, I beckon the door-knocker inside. The door opens, and my headache becomes suddenly more acute.

Pentti Osmala remains standing in the doorway for a good while. At first I wonder if this is his attempt to make his entrance all the more dramatic, but then I realise he has stopped because he has noticed the name on the sign by the door. It still bears Juhani's name. I don't know why that sign is still there. Osmala stops scrutinising the sign and steps into the office. He bids me good afternoon and says he hopes he's not interrupting anything important. Continuing my strategy of telling him half-truths, I say, 'Of course not,' and show him to the chair opposite me. Osmala sits down in the office chair, which looks like it belongs in a doll's house compared to the detective inspector. He spends the next thirty seconds adjusting his jacket, his trousers, shirt and shoes – those shiny brown ballet shoes – then tugs his jacket again before finally reaching a comfortable position. He looks at me with those blue eyes, his rugged face like a chunk of hewn rock.

'I'll get straight to the point,' he says, and I think to myself that this is hardly the case because he's already been in my office or standing in the doorway for over a minute without getting anywhere near the point. 'It's to do with the guy we found in the pond in the forest, the one with a ticket to your park in his pocket.'

I tell him I remember the case.

'There were other things in his pockets too,' says Osmala, and starts rummaging in his own pockets. 'Lots of things that we couldn't immediately link to anything in particular. But over time, things started to make sense.'

Osmala pulls his hand from his pocket.

'This,' he says, holding up his hand. The serrated edge of a key is pointing towards the ceiling, but that's the only thing I can say about it. It looks like any other key. 'First you have to work out what kind of lock it fits, then where that lock might be. The latter can take some time.'

I'm not sure whether I am supposed to offer some suggestions as to where that lock might be located. I say nothing. Osmala looks at the key, and when he finally speaks again, it seems as though he is speaking to the key in his hand.

'This key fits the kind of lock you find in only one place,' he says. 'Caravan doors. And not just any kind of caravan. First we had to establish where this type of caravan might be, then think what might be the most probable location for a guy operating in and around the Helsinki metropolitan area. You work with probabilities, isn't that right?'

'Yes,' I say, then for some reason I add: 'And risk management.'

Osmala moves his eyes from the key to me. 'Really,' he says, and nothing about his intonation suggests this is meant as a question. 'That's convenient. In many ways, I mean. Well, eventually, we found the caravan in question. In Helsinki, just as I suspected we would. In Rastila.'

I've already had a few seconds to prepare myself for the revelation that I know is coming. I'm familiar with Osmala's way of presenting information now. And yet, when he says it, it's like a bomb going off; its shockwaves run through me, and I have to command them to stay there. Eventually, I don't think there is any discernible change in my demeanour. What's more, Osmala can't see the back of my shirt, which is soaked with sweat and glued to my skin.

'We didn't find much in the caravan,' Osmala continues. 'A few guns, knives, a can of pepper spray. The usual for these guys. There was a phone, too, but it was clean, as they call it. The cleanliness of the caravan, however, left a lot to be desired.'

He pauses. I'm certain he expects me to ask something. The only question that comes to mind isn't the most ingenious question ever posed in the history of humanity, and it isn't even really a question I want to ask, but asking it feels inevitable.

'And?'

'Not so much *and*, more *but*,' he says and in doing so seems to accept my attempt to move the conversation onwards. 'Or better still, *however*. Let's look at the matter from another angle for a moment. Our man leaves his most hardcore tools in his caravan – he even leaves his phone, so his movements can't be traced – then carefully locks the door behind him. What does that sound like to you? Exactly, me too: he's going to work. This is an easy gig: a little pressure, a little intimidation, maybe some fisticuffs, a spot of wrestling, boxing, strangulation – and the message is loud and clear. But something goes wrong. Or, if we look at it from the perspective of this guy's target, things might have gone very right.'

Osmala looks at me – we stare at each other. Then he clenches the key in his hand, slips his hand into his jacket and, I assume, drops the key into his pocket.

'Well, this is just me thinking out loud about different probabilities,' he says. 'And maybe a spot of risk management too.'

'Absolutely,' I say, though I'm not sure I wholly agree with his mathematical categorisations. But that's a conversation for another time. During my time at the adventure park, I've learnt not to get involved in disputes and inaccuracies like this that appear from time to time, no matter how much they bother me.

'How is the artist doing?'

Osmala's question affects such a different world, a different dimension, that it takes me an extra second to understand what he means. I realise he is referring to Laura Helanto.

'As far as I know,' I say, 'she's doing very well.'

'You told me last time she was planning to create something new here.'

'She is planning...' I begin, then realise I'm not sure quite how to describe what she is planning '...some additions to the murals.'

'Contemporary sculptures, you mean? I like that sort of thing very much. Especially the kind that turns old junk into something new and surprising, something moving. Kari Cavén is a personal favourite.'

I haven't counted how many times Osmala has taken me by surprise during the course of this conversation, but it's a lot.

'That would explain the pieces of tape on the floor,' he continues, and he looks as though he has been giving the matter a great deal of thought. 'And the other markings too. It all sounds very promising.'

Of course. He's already walked around the park.

'Give her my best, won't you,' says Osmala, and starts getting up from his dollhouse chair. Watching him stand up is like watching a giant tower being built up to roof height in seconds. 'I'm really happy for her success. A fresh start. It's rare, you know.'

I say nothing. Osmala gives his jacket another tug. Eventually he gets it into a position he approves of and looks like he is ready to take his leave. I'm ready to sigh with relief.

'Perhaps you could walk me to the front door,' he says.

I follow him out into the corridor, and from there into the hall.

Osmala doesn't take the most direct route to the entrance hall but sets off behind the Komodo Locomotive and around the Strawberry Maze. We try to avoid the customers, and Osmala appears to refrain from talking, perhaps because our voices might not necessarily be heard above the din. Then we pass the Crocodile Canyon, which Kristian seems to have almost completely dismantled. Osmala glances at the canoes piled one on top of the other, then looks at me. It's possible that I have a tendency to connect things that aren't necessarily connected, but as for probabilities, they are always either greater or smaller. Osmala knows the three men from Toy of Finland, he already told me he's very interested in them, so he may well know the origins of the Crocodile Canyon. And now he wants to show me that all roads lead not only to the heavy, badly designed plastic fangs of the crocodiles but back to him too.

We arrive in the entrance hall, and we have taken a few steps out into the darkening evening when a curious little scene plays out around fifty metres in front of us.

An expensive, exotic car comes to a halt. The driver, who seems to walk on air and looks as though this is something he does effortlessly, gets out of the driver's seat, walks around the car, opens the back door. Juhani gets out of the car, adjusts the position of his sunglasses – which, given the weather, are wholly redundant – then starts walking towards the staff entrance. The car pulls out almost silently, then glides serenely away. Juhani disappears inside the building.

Osmala and I stand for a moment in silence.

'Looks like the adventure-park business is a better money-spinner than I'd thought,' he says and walks off towards his car.

12

Schopenhauer is still angry the following morning. He hasn't said a word to me since I came home yesterday evening, though I gave him a lengthy apology for being away and made him a lovely dinner. He looks right past me, he sleeps longer than usual and doesn't seem to listen when I tell him about what's been happening recently or explain the conclusions I've reached. Even now, he's sitting on the balcony chair keeping an eye on a group of four men in hi-vis jackets mending an electrical distribution box at the other side of the park. I know that while Schopenhauer is keeping note of everything that goes on in the neighbourhood, he is also showing an example.

I drink my tea at the kitchen table and again try both to think and not to think. And over and over again, I find myself thinking about things I shouldn't or don't want to think about, and trying to avoid the problems that need to be resolved most acutely. On the other hand, these things all overlap upon one another.

I don't particularly want to think of how and how much Juhani and Laura Helanto have been in touch with each other. Perhaps arranging to pick me up yesterday was the one and only time since Juhani's reappearance, but even that feels unlikely. Especially taking into consideration that Juhani lied to me when he said he'd tried to call me first. Then there was the enthusiasm with which Laura Helanto told me about it. Because now, looking back on the events of yesterday morning from a suitable distance, I can see that she was keen to give me the message and just as keen to send me off with Juhani, though she didn't know where I was being taken. Unless she *did* know after all and realised there was nothing to worry about. Which, naturally, leads to a series of follow-up questions, such as: why would she do such a thing in the first place, and what else does she know?

Another matter I have been avoiding, but which has been brewing in my mind, is the question of Juhani himself. How far is he really willing to go?

I know how excited he gets about things and how, once he is excited, he works himself up into a frenzy and doesn't know when to stop until, time and time again, he comes crashing into truth, facts, reality.

All this might still be controllable if only he hadn't somehow changed since his return. He seems even more desperate than before and, paradoxically, all the more capable of concrete action. The fact that this action is undesirable and even dangerous to me and the park doesn't seem to slow him down in the least. If I had to define the boundary that Juhani is no longer prepared to cross, I simply wouldn't know where to draw it. And yet, right now, knowing exactly where that line runs is more important than ever.

I've finished my tea, but my thoughts aren't any the clearer. I get up, put the dishes in the dishwasher and wipe the table and kitchen counter. I fill Schopenhauer's dry-food bowl and his water cup and call him in from the balcony. Then I brush my teeth, choose an appropriate tie and set off for the adventure park.

Kristian has almost completely dismantled the Crocodile Canyon. I can tell he is taking his new, secret title very seriously indeed. When I look at the orderly pile of canoes and other parts of the canyon, such as the spear-like oars and the blue, spiky brush heads, I can't help thinking that he really has earned some kind of bonus

– as soon as we can afford bonuses again. I continue on my way, and I'm almost at my office when I hear a gruff voice to my side.

'If I were you,' says Minttu K, 'I'd be careful.'

I stand in the doorway for a second then step inside. Even at this hour of the morning, Minttu K's office is like a night club. There is no natural light, instead the ambiance is like a discotheque, and the air is heavy with perfume, tobacco and alcohol.

'Careful of what?' I ask, and try to see where the voice is coming from. At first I can't make her out in the dimness of the room, but the burning end of her cigarette and the trail of smoke help me locate her. The smell is strongest closer to her. She is sitting on a sofa at the far end of the room.

'Kuisma Lohi once bought up a business where one of my mates was working,' she says, and shifts position on the sofa, swinging her left leg over her right. 'That business is long gone now. Well, it exists, just not for the people that used to work there.'

'I'm not selling—'

'I didn't say you were,' says Minttu K with a flick of the hand, either to waft tobacco smoke around the room or to dismiss my comment. 'And that's not Kuisma Lohi's tactic either. The way he works, he'll get you to ask his permission to sell him your park, because by that time it'll be the only option you have left. If he says he wants to buy your park, that means he's buying a whole lot of stuff around it too. Why look for a needle in a haystack when you can just take the whole damn haystack, then squeeze it dry?'

It comes as no surprise that Minttu K knows Juhani and I have been talking to Kuisma Lohi. We were sitting in the Curly Cake Café; counting all the customers and their parents, there must have been at least seventy witnesses. And Juhani could easily have mentioned it to the other members of staff. And I'm not really surprised that Minttu K has this kind of insider information either. In the past she has demonstrated she knows very well what's going on, and I know for a fact that her network of contacts stretches at least across the country, if not further afield. The only complication in our recent cooperation has been her strong opinions and her occasional complete inability to compromise, a quality that gets stronger as the evening progresses. She sips whatever is in her coffee mug.

'I'll be on my guard,' I say. 'Thanks for the warning.'

Minttu K doesn't answer. The end of her cigarette glows in the dark. I imagine I should leave before I get high simply from breathing the air in her room. I turn.

'Oi.'

I stop and look back towards Minttu K.

'About the karate sensei I mentioned,' she says in such a low, gravelly voice that it could strip paint. 'I folded him over like a sheet of paper. He wouldn't have been a good look for us. Just so you know.'

I ponder what to say for a moment, but can't think of anything. Eventually, I thank her and leave the room.

Once in my own office, I boot up my computer and get to work. Dealing with the standard matters in the daily running of an adventure park feels like a holiday right now. I have to think all the more clearly about the order things should be booked in and paid for, but these are simple, straightforward mathematical calculations compared to, say, choosing the broadband provider least likely to kill me. And because I do most of the park's accounts myself, I manage to concentrate quite effectively. The same applies to the passing of time. The hours seem to fly past.

That afternoon I eat quickly at the Curly Cake – at Johanna's brusque suggestion I take Popeye's Spinach Soup and three thick slices of Long-Jumper's Loaf – and return to my desk.

I exchange more text messages with Laura Helanto. She tells

me she will be starting work at the park after closing time. She also tells me she has managed to book the babysitter for this evening and all through the night, so later on we can do something besides measuring and installing her works. I'm not quite sure what she's referring to, but I'm happy that she is coming. But I'm still a little on guard, as I can't help thinking about the potential contact between her and Juhani. I do my best to push the black cloud from my mind, without much success. The unpleasant thought takes root inside me like an icy rock.

I get the bookkeeping up to date just after closing time. I put the paperwork in the relevant folders and make sure the folders are all in the right places on the shelf. The row of folders is neat and ordered both chronologically and by content. With everything else going on, I can safely say that I still manage to keep this part of the park in good order. When I first stepped into this office, there were unpaid bills everywhere, on the desk, the chairs, the floor – 318 of them, to be precise – and the bookkeeping hadn't been taken care of in a very long time. Today, all those bills have been categorised, paid and archived.

I do a walk around the park. Everything seems to be in order, the staff all appear to have left for the night, the lights are mostly switched off. I stroll alongside the Strawberry Maze, behind Caper Castle and the Big Dipper, past the Komodo Locomotive, and finally walk around the Doughnut. I stop in the middle of the main hall and check my phone again. This is futile; it won't make Laura Helanto get here any quicker.

I'm about to set off again when I hear a dull thud somewhere up ahead, perhaps somewhere at the back of the park, near the dismantled Crocodile Canyon. I head in that direction and conclude that the thud must have come from even further away. I recognise the sound: the door to Esa's monitor room. Just then I hear footsteps. They are getting closer, and it sounds like Esa, so

I'm expecting him to step out from behind the Strawberry Maze. Which only adds to my confusion when I see Otto Härkä from Toy of Finland instead.

'Well, well,' he says. 'Working late? Needs must, I suppose.'

'The park is closed,' I say.

'Surely not?' says Otto Härkä. 'I was just thinking I'd love to have a little row in those canoes everybody's talking about.'

'The Crocodile Canyon has been dismantled,' I say, then add, 'almost entirely.'

Otto Härkä has slightly changed direction, and now he's walking right towards me.

'Poor crocs,' he says and sounds genuinely disappointed. 'Who would do a thing like that?'

'Where is Esa?' I ask.

Otto Härkä stops approximately four and a half metres away from me. His moustache is bushier than at our last meeting – if such a thing is possible. Or perhaps the light is exaggerating this part of his face – that and the fact that he is a slender man with a tight, rounded belly testing the strength of the buttons on his blue shirt.

'Where's the payment for the goods we delivered?'

'I don't think it's reasonable to—'

'The deadline was very clearly printed on the invoice.'

'The Crocodile Canyon is not—'

'And we threw in the installation as a sign of good will.'

'I did not order—'

'I'm sure we can sort this out here and now,' says Otto Härkä with a clap of the hands. As if we have been engaged in some kind of negotiation and come to a mutual understanding.

Again, he sets off, takes one step, another. I start to back away. He takes more steps forwards, towards me. Our speed increases. I walk backwards faster and faster, we shuffle like this right past the Strawberry Maze, then arrive at the area where, only a few hours ago, the Crocodile Canyon was fully installed. Now we are walking across the bare concrete floor, and we'll soon arrive at the last bit of the Crocodile Canyon to be taken down – the widest stretch of the river. I have just decided to turn and start running when Otto Härkä slips a hand into his jacket pocket, and I realise that he must have some kind of weapon. Of course. Now turning my back on him doesn't feel like such a good idea...

'Perhaps I might suggest another round of negotiations...'

'Perhaps we'll negotiate with your brother instead,' says Otto Härkä, and though his choice of words is the same as always, now he doesn't sound nearly as jovial or chatty as before. 'And if I'm perfectly honest, I'm getting – how should I put this politely? – a bit cheesed off with...'

I've changed my mind. I'm going to run for it. But I'm going to do it backwards, and very carefully. I hope Otto Härkä hasn't acquainted himself too closely with the ins and outs of the Crocodile Canyon. I don't imagine he has. He and his business associates don't seem like the kind of men with a passion and dedication for the delivery and installation of adventure-park equipment. I have almost arrived at the river. I quickly glance over my shoulder before trying to cross it.

The blue brush heads gleam like a tight, thick carpet. At this point the river is around three metres wide, and I don't think Otto Härkä will be able to jump across it in his ankle-high winter boots. Right in the middle of the river, Kristian has left one of the Crocodile Canyon's steel stepping stones, presumably so that he can easily step back and forth across the river while taking it apart and so that his shoes won't become stuck in the sea of brushes and he won't waste time trying to extricate himself. And therein lies the crux of my plan.

I plan to reverse myself across the river by stepping on the steel platform, then remove the plinth, thus leaving Otto Härkä on the other side with only two options: either step into the ferocious current of brush heads or walk around them. Both options will buy me a few precious extra seconds of time. More to the point, I would be on the side of the river where Kristian has piled up the dangerously spiked oars. I doubt Otto Härkä has anything this long in his pocket.

My backwards leap is a success, the steel platform remains in place. My second leap is successful too. The platform is closer to my side of the river, and I grab it, I pull it towards me, lift it up with both hands and realise...

My plan wasn't so ingenious after all.

Otto Härkä has taken his hand out of his pocket, and I can see he is holding a small black pistol. He stands at the other side of the river and points the gun at me.

'Nice moves,' he says. 'Now there's a man who knows his amusement parks.'

I decide not to put Otto Härkä right and explain this is an adventure park and the difference is plain: in an amusement park people get whirled around, in an adventure park they whirl themselves around. But this is no time for semantics. This is no time for anything.

'Now you and I,' Otto Härkä begins, 'are going to get the hell out of this park and go for a little walk.'

I realise that going for a little walk with him under these circumstances would be extremely unwise. And I also realise that if I were to start running, the probability of Otto Härkä's pulling the trigger would increase dramatically. We are standing three metres apart, a river of brushes between us. I don't know how good a shot he is, but I conclude that missing me at such close proximity would require a unique level of clumsiness.

'Very well,' I say.

'Let's go then,' he nods, and his moustache flashes as the light hits it. The secret to its bushiness must lie in the fact that he has waxed it.

'I'm prepared to enter another round of negotiations...'

'Christ alive,' shouts Otto Härkä, and at that moment we both act instinctively, governed by the power of our most fundamental impulses.

Otto Härkä shoots. I raise the steel platform to protect myself.

Otto Härkä seems to have lost his cool, and I'm simply trying to protect myself from his hot-headedness. There are several shots. They sound the way I've always thought gunshots must sound: like loud bangs. All except the last one. That one makes two sounds: a loud bang, then immediately afterwards a higher, clearly angrier thump, leaving a long, tense sound echoing through the air. At the same time, I realise I can feel that second sound in my hands. I've managed to protect myself. The bullet must have struck the steel platform, ricocheted off and...

...hit Otto Härkä square in the forehead.

He is still standing. His eyes have turned, and from what I can see, he is trying to look up at his own forehead. For some reason, the situation is prolonged. His standing position doesn't look entirely natural; he seems to be standing straight with his knees locked. A dark spot in the middle of his forehead gleams, just like the moustache slightly lower down his face. And he still looks absolutely livid, but because his eyes aren't focussed on me anymore, it looks as though he is angry at his forehead. He slowly starts toppling forwards, and the river's brush heads cushion his fall. Otto Härkä slumps into the soft blue current and lies there, motionless.

My phone rings.

🦌

Laura Helanto sounds happy and a little impatient. She has just got off the bus and is walking towards the park. She tells me she is weighing up her options after all: she can't make up her mind where to start, she's still trying to decide between Frankenthaler and Krasner. She asks my opinion.

I look around.

I can see half of the Frankenthaler mural, I can't see the Krasner at all, though I remember it very well. I like them both, a lot. Meanwhile, I can also see Otto Härkä, and little by little I start to understand what has happened and what the immediate repercussions of these events will be. Furthermore, I know what I absolutely must do before Laura Helanto gets here. I can hear in my voice that I'm out of breath as I say we can look at things together once she gets here and explain that before that there are a few matters to do with the park's storage and logistics that need tidying up. Laura pauses for a moment – I can hear her steps, carrying her inexorably closer to the park – then she says we'll see each other in a few minutes anyway, and we can talk about a few other things too. I don't know what she means, but right now prolonging this conversation is out of the question. We say goodbye and I hang up.

As I run to the storeroom, I think of actuarial mathematics. This branch of mathematics is all about assessing risks and probabilities. Naturally, it doesn't provide any direct solutions to multifaceted problems like the one facing me right now, but it helps when you have to approach something analytically, taking all contributing factors into account, and it keeps the solutions as practical as possible. I try to make this my guiding principle through the course of the following minutes. The principle itself won't make these minutes any less unpleasant. As I have been forced to accept several times already, even actuarial mathematics doesn't have an answer for everything.

I gather the pieces of equipment I need and return to the Crocodile Canyon and Otto Härkä. With some difficulty, I wrap him in a length of disused carpet taken from the Doughnut. One of the many benefits of this carpet is the layer of Velcro underneath it, which helps keep the parcel tightly wrapped. I realise Laura Helanto will knock on the front door any minute now, and that I only have at most thirty seconds to transport Otto Härkä somewhere out of sight, and at the same time I realise I don't have enough time to take him anywhere at all.

I disassemble one of Kristian's neat piles of canoes, roll Otto Härkä next to the lowest canoe, lift him and – by this point I'm already covered in sweat and my muscles are cramping – try to slide him inside the canoe. Eventually the roll of carpet slips neatly to the bottom of the canoe, and from the side it's almost invisible. To see it, you would have to crouch down and peer inside the canoe specifically, and you can't do that if the canoes are all piled on top of one another. I build up the pile again, and I'm just lifting the final green canoe to the top of the pile when I hear a knock. I wipe the sweat from my brow, adjust my tie and realise I had plenty of time after all. Then I look around: Otto Härkä's black pistol is shining on the concrete floor. I pull on my blazer, though I'm far too hot and bothered to need it, pick up the pistol and slip it into my pocket. Then I walk to the door, trying to steady my breathing as I go. Laura Helanto waves at me from behind the door. Once I get closer, I hear what she is trying to say.

Krasner.

13

I'm on top of Laura Helanto and trying to make sure my actions are as efficient as possible. She is breathing heavily, we are in my apartment, in my bed. I try to focus as much as I can on what is happening right now because this is undoubtedly a unique moment. We started the evening by shaping a work of art together, then we drove to my place, ate dinner together, then took off our clothes in very quick succession before getting down to the business of finding the kind of positions and movements to produce optimal amounts of sensory pleasure. However, I don't think I'm really in the moment, which I understand is an expression meaning the state of mind whereby one is doing one thing but thinking about three others all at once.

Laura Helanto is making the kind of noises that I think must be a good sign both in the short and long term. We are both covered in sweat, our skin is slippery, sticky to the touch, the air in the room seems to have turned thick and damp, the smell is a mixture of something sour, salty and sweet, something I've never smelt anywhere else. I know that at any other moment, on any other night, I would experience all this in a different way. In fact, I hazard to suggest that I would be swept away by the course of events with nothing left to hold me back.

But right now, all I can think of is Otto Härkä's moustache.

In fact, Otto Härkä's moustache isn't the only thing I can think of; I'm thinking about Otto Härkä himself, and thereby also Toy of Finland, and thereby also Juhani and Kuisma Lohi, then Juhani again, and that brings me back to Laura Helanto – whose voice is now high and piercing yet still indistinct as she repeats a number of strictly vernacular nouns and verbs. I'm being careful to increase the rate and pace of events evenly and try to heighten the effect with variations in depth and length while keeping their respective frequency as regular as clockwork. I think it's important to keep my actions cumulative and their effect on an upward trajectory, just like the value of good shares and investments over a long period: there can be small dips along the way, even a crash here and there, but when we look at the progression over a ten-year period, the curve leads inexorably upwards. A few minutes later, I begin to sense we are soon approaching the peak and a very generous pay-out. Laura Helanto shouts and grips my arms.

Fifteen seconds later, I conclude that there are certain matters I simply must bring up with her. I roll onto my back, see the sharp boundary between light and shadow dancing across the ceiling and prepare myself for my first question, when I hear Laura's voice.

'Have you ever thought about what it might be like if you moved in with us? You and Schopenhauer?'

I turn my head. The light is coming into the room from the kitchen on the other side of the apartment, and the streetlamps filter through the curtains in a variety of colours. Laura Helanto's face is so close that everything looks distinctly enlarged. Most noticeable of all are her eyes. They are staring at me while at the same time looking somewhere deeper, somewhere further away, and suddenly I'm not thinking about Otto Härkä's moustache anymore or anything else I was thinking about only a moment ago. What Laura has just said takes me completely by surprise. She is smiling at me in a way that's hard to interpret, then I notice I am smiling too.

'Based on what I know and feel right now,' I begin, 'I'd say I feel very positive about the idea. Drawing up a suitable timetable and making a public announcement about it is another matter. But I'm prepared to give a rough estimate right now, if we agree that doing so might be mutually beneficial.'

'That must be the most romantic thing anyone has ever heard in these circumstances.'

'I'd say it's virtually impossible to assess that in any objective—'

'Henri,' says Laura Helanto and brings her face closer to mine. 'Sometimes, a simple yes or no will do.'

'As a general rule I—'

'Yes or no?'

I realise something crucial. Laura Helanto has skipped a stage in the process, she has put analysis and the overall assessment of the situation to one side. She's no longer asking about these things on a theoretical basis. Now she means business, real decisions, real actions.

At the same time, I feel as though every part of my life has intensified of its own accord, as though time itself were constantly becoming thicker and denser, as though a giant remote control were speeding everything up. There are places in the universe where this happens. At the edge of a black hole, even time itself changes form.

Naturally, I don't imagine I'm literally about to be sucked into a black hole. Laura's apartment isn't that far away.

But in general I can safely say that my life is undergoing a powerful condensing and acceleration, a process it's about as easy to control as the universe itself, black holes and everything. Every day is like the adventure park: ups, down, rollercoaster rides, collisions, sweat, surprises ... so many surprises. So maybe Laura Helanto is right. Maybe I can simply say...

'Yes.'

Laura's hand touches my cheek.

'It feels so good,' she says, 'to know that I can trust you.'

14

The following morning is both very pleasant and very difficult.

It's still quite dark beyond the windows while we are having breakfast. Laid out for breakfast are the things we bought together; we went to the supermarket the previous evening, together, for the first time. This was a turning point, in a financial sense too. We bought bread that was much more expensive than I would normally buy. We bought two kinds of cheese, yoghurt with different layers in it, organic eggs. I was taken aback at how little impact the sum total of our shopping – which, at a quick calculation, revealed that the average price of my breakfast was about to rise by one hundred and thirty-five percent – made on me.

I can tell that Schopenhauer is quite torn by the situation: he is clearly interested in Laura Helanto, though he is perplexed that someone else is spending so much time in his territory. The balcony door is ajar, and from time to time Schopenhauer goes outside to check on events in the yard, then inspects all the spaces inside the apartment, yet doesn't seem happy with any of them. I understand him. My sentiments are quite similar. I don't enjoy being in anybody's company as much as I do with Laura Helanto, but I can't stop thinking about the crocodile canoe that I filled only a few hours ago. I look at the clock on the kitchen wall. I want to get to the park before the others arrive. I don't know what I'm going to do with the stuffed canoe, but whatever it is, it'll have to be done during the quiet time of day. I glance up at the clock again and think that if I were to leave now...

'You'll be the first one in,' says Laura.

I recall moments in the recent past when I've had the distinct impression that Laura Helanto can read my thoughts. Of course, this isn't factually possible, but still: there are many times she seems to know what I'm about to say or do next. I don't know how she does it. I don't think I'm giving off any signals or any other indication of my intentions. On the contrary, I try to base all my decisions on careful, thorough planning, and I only speak or act once I am sure of what I am about to say or do.

'I know how important it is for you to be on time,' she says with a smile. This is a different smile from the one I saw the night before. 'But you mustn't forget that everybody at the park knows what they're doing. Everything's fine, right?'

I don't want to lie to her.

'A few problems with a device being taken out of use,' I say. 'I want to get everything wrapped up. No need to burden the others with it.'

This is all true: the Crocodile Canyon has been taken out of service and, as unpalatable as it is to admit, so has Otto Härkä. I must take care of the matter, and for very obvious and acute reasons, clearing up the mess is my responsibility. Laura looks at me.

'That's the cutest thing about you,' she says.

'What is?'

'On top of everything else, you're so ... nice.'

I drive Laura Helanto to her studio, then I do something I've never done before: I exceed the speed limit. The park's van isn't designed for great speed. The brisk November wind shakes it about in exposed places, and the acceleration leaves much to be desired. I have always considered speeding a rather pointless thing.

In built-up areas, the amount of time saved can be counted in seconds, minutes at most. But right now I need every minute I can get, every second. To my bewilderment, I note that my excessive speed still isn't enough to overtake people driving even faster. It's hard to imagine that they might have something more pressing to deal with and even harder to imagine what that something might be. Several men, several crocodiles? How many of these Audi drivers – because speeding seems to be a particular feature of this expensive German vehicle – are worried about what to do with an attacker hurriedly wrapped in a length of carpet? My thoughts are speeding too, and my eyes nervously flit between the clock and the speed dial.

I steer the car into the car park, which is still empty. I drive around YouMeFun and arrive at the staff car park – and sigh with relief. No cars, no bicycles, no vehicles of any description. I leave the car in my space, take the stairs up to the loading bay, stride across the steel platform to the door and open it. I go through the staff areas, noting that they too are empty and there is no one else in sight, then I open the door into the park itself and listen. Silence.

The situation is favourable, given the circumstances. I now only have one problem to solve instead of many. And sometimes a single problem, no matter how big, is actually preferable.

I pass the Trombone Cannons, turn the corner, then arrive at the Strawberry Maze, and just behind it I see...

Precisely nothing.

I have to hold on to the Strawberry Maze for support.

I manage to stay upright, though the room around me is swirling and my stomach is churning. The dizziness lasts only a few seconds, but it is followed by a clamorous rush, a mixture of fright and disbelief that fills my body. Even breathing normally requires the utmost concentration. Very cautiously, I release my grip on the Strawberry Maze and continue looking ahead, as illogical as everything feels right now.

The Crocodile Canyon has disappeared.

Not just dismantled and piled up. It's completely gone.

There isn't a single piece of it to be seen, neither the river nor the brushes, the oars nor the steel structure. And more crucially, I can't see any of the canoes. Not one. Everything has gone. I force myself into motion and walk to the spot in the hall where I crossed the river only yesterday, where I deflected a bullet and adjusted the piles of canoes. But there is nothing there except for the cool indoor air of the adventure park. I know this because I even run my hand along the place on the floor where the piles of canoes once stood, where only a moment ago the river was flowing. I sniff the air, and my sense of smell confirms what my sense of sight told me earlier.

'Boss,' I hear behind me. 'The leading operational manager has taken care of it.'

I spin around, and Kristian is right there. He looks the same as always: he is wearing a very tight-fitting, brightly coloured adventure-park T-shirt which enhances his defined pectoral muscles and his washboard stomach, and his expression is the usual mix of eagerness and excitement.

'What?' I ask, before I've had the chance to formulate the question in greater detail.

'This morning,' he nods. 'I ordered the van for quarter to six; that way we got a twenty-percent discount. I got to work at half past three to take down what was left. This is a good system.'

'What?' I ask, again without any more specific formulation.

'See, I've been reading this book,' he says. He has appeared right next to me, his usual chirpy, strongly deodorised self, and he's standing almost exactly where Otto Härkä fell face first into the river for the last time. 'It's about the five o'clock club. The trick is to get up at five in the morning, so you can get everything done before the people who only wake up at six, not to mention the ones that wake up at seven or eight or nine or ... you get the picture. But then I realised something even better. I decided to get up at four. Then I read online that someone else had had exactly the same idea and started waking up at four. So I decided to get up at three instead. And here's the result.'

Kristian raises his bulging arms. I realise he's not actually trying to show off his muscles but simply to draw my attention to the empty space around us.

'You appointed me to run this operation,' he continues. 'In secret. I haven't breathed a word about it to anyone. Not even you.'

I'm still suffering from mild dizziness, and I'm still in some degree of shock. The process of putting the pieces together in my mind is painfully slow. Nonetheless, I can feel the next tidal wave of nausea building inside me and gathering strength, and the crest of the wave looks a lot like a certain thick, dark, shiny moustache. I hesitate before asking my next question, but ask it I must.

'Where...' I begin, and this time I try to be more specific '...did you send everything?'

By now Kristian looks unbearably pleased with himself.

'Back where it came from, obviously,' he says. 'To Toy of Finland.'

15

I don't know if there is any official guidance on how to run an adventure park, but I know that if there were, it wouldn't recommend sending the body of a criminal subcontractor back to his accomplices. I try to think of possible ways of approaching the subject once they realise what has happened, but I can't come up with a single way of making it all go away. Otto Härkä didn't crawl inside that canoe by himself. And the final result doesn't reflect what actually took place: that it was a work accident, a mishap, an unforeseen turn of events. There's a hole in his forehead and he's wrapped in a carpet. It doesn't look like an accident; it looks more like something out of *The Godfather*.

I sit in my office as the morning daylight grows behind the window.

I have lots of park-related work on my desk and computer, but right now it's hard to decide where to start: how can I put things in order of urgency or importance in a situation with so many moving parts – some of which are probably armed? Right now, the sugar invoice for the Curly Cake Café feels a little less ... consequential. As does the matter of putting all my problems in a timeline to find the optimal way of resolving them. What use is there in knowing where the line ends, if right at the start I'm next in line to be wrapped up in carpet?

As I am about to get up from my chair – I'm not entirely sure what I am doing or where I am going – I hear footsteps in the corridor. I wonder whether the delivery has reached its destination and whether the remaining owners of Toy of Finland could have got here already. I don't think it's likely, but it's possible.

I move instinctively to the side, away from my chair, to where there is a direct sightline to the door, and grab a metallic miniature slide from on top of a pile of folders. I don't know what I'm planning to do with it, especially if Otto Härkä's undoubtedly armed accomplices have decided to attack me. And I'm not at all sure whether an attacker armed with a handgun would back away if faced with a man brandishing a miniature slide. Irrespective, I instinctively raise my hand in readiness.

Kuisma Lohi doesn't knock or announce himself in any way. He simply walks right into my office, with Juhani following behind him. Lohi sees the slide in my hand.

'Self-defence,' he says. 'I perfectly understand. I'd want to protect myself too if the customers were to attack. And I wouldn't spare my wrath either. Those sticky, messy little creatures shouldn't be allowed anywhere near your office.'

I lower my hand and glance at Juhani. He looks both extremely nervous and as though he has just woken up. Something has happened, that much is obvious.

'This will only take a moment,' says Lohi. 'Number one: the validity of my offer has been shortened since our previous conversation, and that was a shortened offer too. Number two: Toy of Finland.'

Again, I glance at Juhani. He looks like he wants to say something but can find neither the right words nor an appropriate moment. This isn't typical of Juhani. In fact, it's very out of character.

'I believe I made it quite clear that I want to buy an adventure park,' Kuisma Lohi continues. 'One that operates as seamlessly and as cost-effectively as yours. But it's come to my attention that this might not be the case after all.'

I say nothing. I genuinely don't know what we're talking about, and I think my best option is to keep hold of the model slide and listen.

'I realise your park has an exclusive deal with Toy of Finland,' says Kuisma Lohi. 'And I'd like to hear how you think that collaboration is going.'

I quickly go through everything I can already see and conclude. Kuisma Lohi is not Pentti Osmala, he's not investigating a suspicious death. The next thought that comes to mind is, I believe, the most likely scenario: he is protecting his future investment. At the same time, I note that Juhani doesn't need to know any more than is necessary: it seems as though everything he finds out can and will be used against me, one way or another.

'The new owners' understanding of the general price of things is rather different from what we're used to,' I say, then add: 'Considerably different.'

Kuisma Lohi's light-blue eyes don't give any hint of what is going on inside him. But for some reason, he doesn't look at all upset about what I've said.

'Sounds perfectly normal. It's to be expected after a change of ownership,' he says. 'What exactly has taken you by surprise?'

The threats, the blackmail, the gun (which I have hidden in the park's tool cupboard). Returning a body to its sender, I think to myself.

'Their reluctance to compromise,' I say quite honestly. 'It'll take some getting used to.'

Kuisma Lohi remains silent. Eventually he looks over his left shoulder at Juhani, then at me again.

'When I mentioned the matter to your brother just now,' he says, 'he thought he might be the right man to handle the negotiations.'

There it is – one of the reasons Juhani seems so confused and agitated. Not only has he been operating behind my back, but he's been promising the impossible. Again. Of course, there's nothing new about this, but there's something about his body language that tells me there's more to come. Normally he would butt into the conversation and, in his usual manner, talk a whole lot of gibberish. Now he's just standing by the wall, seemingly at a loss.

But another matter altogether is what Kuisma Lohi is talking about. He is behaving as though he already owns the park, which is most emphatically not the case. I'd like to ask him to leave by the most direct route, but I won't, I can't. I'm unsure how much he knows about the state of affairs between me and Toy of Finland. Furthermore, I don't know what he knows about the state of affairs between me and Juhani either, not to mention our recent activities. Juhani is tugging his shirt sleeves and looks like a man who could well have let something slip.

'I'll discuss that with my brother,' I say.

Kuisma Lohi turns to look at Juhani again. He stops fidgeting, takes his fingers from his jacket pocket. He nods.

'Yeah, that's what I meant. We'll talk about it, then we'll decide – what's best.'

That's all Juhani says on the matter. I notice that Kuisma Lohi and I both seem to have expected him to say more. Lohi and I look at each other again.

'In that case,' says Lohi, and for the first time I see an inkling of a smile on his lips, 'I will consider this little bump in the road with the suppliers resolved. I'll leave you to discuss the particulars.'

Once Kuisma Lohi has left, Juhani and I find ourselves alone in the office, and I realise I am wondering yet again quite how well I know my brother. Or rather, how badly I know him. He glances at me and shrugs. I think of Osmala's story about the man who floated to the surface of the pond, the man who was completely coincidentally staying at the same campsite as Juhani.

Of course, there are a number of reasons I can't start grilling Juhani directly. Firstly, he wouldn't answer my questions honestly or in full, because he seems pathologically incapable of doing so. Secondly, a barrage of questions might put me in jeopardy too, and Juhani must not come across any information that he might use against me in his own shady dealings.

Juhani still hasn't sat down. He is standing in the middle of the room, his arms swaying almost imperceptibly. I sit in my chair and wait.

'As I see it, there are only good outcomes here,' he says eventually. 'And it's not just because I always think positively. Either we take his offer of quick cash or we start up a long-term partnership with him. Both excellent options – brilliant ones, if I'm honest. I might even say fantastic, but...'

'But?'

'I'm glad you asked that,' says Juhani, and I can hear he is trying to muster that jovial style of his, but now the tone is wrong and forced. 'That's exactly the way I think we should approach this too. By asking questions. But we need to answer them too. And the answer, my friend, that's something that requires real bravery...'

Juhani continues talking, but I've already understood the gist.

'You need money,' I say, interrupting him. 'And you need it quickly.'

Juhani's arms stop swaying. He sighs.

'As you know, I was dead,' he says, and I don't have the energy or inclination to correct his limping logic. 'And before my death, I took out a substantial life-insurance policy, and on that policy I named the person who, shall we say, funded my dead lifestyle in eastern Finland.'

He pulls a chair from under the desk and sits down.

'The insurance money hasn't come through yet,' he says, and it sounds as though he is genuinely shocked and affronted at this turn of events. 'And now this guy wants his money back. With interest. A bit quicker than I'd been planning, actually.'

'You've promised too much,' I say, 'and you believed it when someone did the same to you too.'

Juhani looks at me. He looks expectant.

'Is that it?' he asks.

'What do you mean?'

'I'm in the biggest jam for ... a while. And all you can offer me is hindsight. Of course, after the fact you can always say so-and-so wasn't such a great idea after all and you should have done such-and-such instead. But at the very moment you've got to make a decision, it's impossible to weigh up all the pros and cons. You can't predict the future.'

Juhani is both right and completely and utterly wrong.

'I suggest we take Lohi's offer,' he continues. 'The quicker one. It's the best outcome all round.'

'And by all round, I suppose you mean...'

'You, me, the park's employees.'

'How will it benefit me?'

One minute, Juhani is looking me right in the eyes, the next he has turned away.

'You'll finally be able to get rid of the park and all its troubles,' he says. 'And all it needs is a bit of quick decision-making.'

I am about to ask a follow-up question when I notice something. Juhani is doing his best to hide it, but the fact is he looks genuinely desperate. I realise two things at once. These two assumptions are based on probabilities, on what I know and what I've seen and experienced. If Juhani can't pay off his debts, sooner or later someone will turn up asking me to pay them. After all, it wouldn't be the first time such a thing had happened. If, on the other hand – hypothetically speaking – I were to sell the park, I won't be able to put the park's business behind me, because in all probability I will still be blackmailed by Toy of Finland once they locate Otto Härkä in his canoe. And more probable still: first they will blackmail me, then they will provide me with a canoe of my own. The only option is to continue and to find another solution altogether. And for that I need time. Naturally, the idea of time goes against the general lay of the land right now.

'We still need to—'

'I knew it,' says Juhani. 'No matter what I suggest or what I do, you'll always find an excuse to oppose it.'

'This is about—'

'It's about me,' he says and looks me in the eyes. 'I get it.'

He stands up, straightens his blazer once more, and walks out.

The very idea of picking up a screwdriver or a wrench or hammer feels absurd in so many ways right now. What's the use in fixing a single pedal on the Komodo Locomotive when floating somewhere around the city is a moustachioed body packed inside a plastic crocodile, heading inexorably towards its final resting place, and my own brother is prepared to resort to even more desperate measures with every passing day?

At first glance, one might say there is no use to it at all. And yet, mathematics tells us that the matter is quite the opposite of what we might reactively and spontaneously think. We can illustrate this with a measurement that is only a millimetre out. In three years' time, that millimetre, which today feels quite insignificant, will have grown into a discrepancy of over a metre. This is the main reason that so many plans and projects grind to a halt or fall apart altogether. Today there would be nothing easier than to give a millimetre. With the whole project in mind, it feels like nothing, and with the naked eye it looks as though it won't cause any significant damage. However, mathematics tells us quite clearly and unequivocally that the distance from our original point has grown.

Every millimetre counts.

I finish replacing the pedal, which I have put together from a variety of different parts, and attach it to the Komodo Locomotive. I push the carriage onto the track and watch what happens. There are quite a few customers in the park, and everything looks as it should. The carriage soon has a driver, and it seems to work perfectly well.

I haven't forgotten the next item on my to-do list. I head to Esa's monitor room.

I don't know why I still haven't learnt to prepare myself for the change of air pressure in the room. Again, I think I should have remembered to fill my lungs out in the corridor and step inside the monitor room while exhaling. It's too late for that now. The smell is like wading up to my neck through an old-school cellulose factory filled with rotten eggs. A new symptom I notice is a distinct change in my intraocular pressure. I aim for maximum efficiency. I tell Esa that one evening I noticed the door to his monitor room was left unlocked. I'm referring, of course, to the moment when Otto Härkä appeared from the room, but naturally I don't tell Esa this. Contrary to what I had expected, Esa tells me this was a deliberate plan.

'To be honest, I'm making a few other changes round here too,' he says. 'My new demob diet is a lot richer in fibre than before. Keeping the park's response units at the ready is fundamentally important, so I will be starting this new diet next week.'

'Right,' I say, and try once again to urge him towards the point. 'The door was—'

'Open, yes,' he says with a firm nod. 'I suspect a few of our customers are operating as double agents. They visit both us and our competitors, and sell their services to the highest bidder. I've gathered a number of alien juice cartons and sweet wrappers that point to this conclusion. I intend to feed these agents with false intel and see where it leads us.'

'Yes,' I say, though I don't really understand what Esa is saying. I thank him and reverse out of the room.

'Lots more peas and beans,' I hear him say, 'and onions, celery and leek too. Tough and sinewy.'

Laura Helanto and Tuuli arrive at the adventure park later that afternoon. Tuuli asks me to perform more multiplications in my head; it always tickles her when I give her the right answer. Then she disappears into the park and I start helping Laura. I realise quite quickly that my thoughts are a long way from art, and even from my role as artist's assistant. I think through the conversations I had that morning with Juhani and Kuisma Lohi. I go through everything that has happened and try to form an overall picture of the current state of play. It seems impossible, but all I can do is try to come up with a solution. Maybe Laura Helanto is reading my thoughts again – either this or she simply notices me about to bend the length of plywood differently from her instructions. I apologise for my absent-mindedness.

'It's okay,' she says, then gives me a light kiss on the lips. 'You've got a lot on your mind.'

I imagine she must be referring to the adventure park in general, and I'm about to say something to that effect when she asks:

'Is Juhani still here?'

I haven't seen Juhani since our conversation this morning. But that isn't the reason I am once again filled with a sense of something cold and unpleasant. I tell her I haven't seen Juhani for some time.

'Why do you ask?' I ask, trying to sound as neutral as possible.

'He promised me some materials.'

'When was that?' I ask before I even notice it.

'A while ago. Last week.'

I say nothing.

'Well,' she sighs, and turns away and looks at her unfinished piece. 'I don't need them today. But if you see him, you can tell him where to find me.'

16

Is that what I'm doing here? Is this my reason for sitting in the adventure park's Renault on this dark November evening: taking my greetings to the campsite in Rastila?

I step out of the car and start walking. The evening is cool – cold in fact. Late November has so many different faces: it can still sometimes be crisp and autumnal during the daytime, but the evenings already feel like winter. I wrap my scarf tighter to protect my bare neck and zip up my jacket. I walk through the campsite gates and turn left. The campsite actually looks quite homely. Warm light glows in the caravan windows, and the air carries the smell of sauna and barbecue. The seagulls have fallen silent, I can hear the distant rumble of traffic, and a little closer the rush of the sea wind.

I arrive at the penultimate crossing in the wide pathway, and I'm about to turn right onto a smaller path. But before I even realise it myself, I walk right past the crossing and continue straight ahead, without turning.

Once I am out of sight behind the caravan at the plot on the corner, I quicken my pace.

I walk briskly, and this time I do turn when I reach the final intersection and set off along a smaller path running parallel to the one where Juhani keeps his caravan. A moment later, I slow down again and keep my eyes fixed on the now-familiar caravan. I see flickers and glimmers; the lights are on. And what I see next tells me I was right to continue at the crossing and take the roundabout route to the caravan.

I would recognise the man anywhere, anytime.

I can hear my heart thumping like a pounding bass in the

distance, but not from exertion. If I hadn't turned off the path when I did, just a few fractions of a second later I would quite literally have stepped on the heels of those small, brown leather shoes. I get a sense of what the encounter might have felt like in a series of rapid, fragmented images that come together to form some kind of warning sign: the largest blazer I've ever seen, the small shoes (given the size of the man in question), the slow, heavy but purposeful gait, the sloth that somehow always follows him around and that is either real or part of a deliberately cultivated image. Either way, I knew what I was seeing before I actually registered it. Juhani's caravan shudders as though an earthquake were underway as Osmala climbs inside it.

Then Osmala sits down.

This I can tell from the way the caravan wobbles, then seems to settle into place again. And for twenty-two minutes, the caravan looks like any other run-of-the-mill caravan: miniature in size, but normal all the same. The cold wind whips in across the sea, but I barely notice it. Luckily, the caravan next to me is dark, so I won't need to explain what I'm doing on their plot, lurking behind a tree, blowing on my hands to keep warm and craning my neck to see into the next row of caravans. I think of a lot in twenty-two minutes. Some of my thoughts are a result of agitation, some are genuine questions.

The caravan starts shuddering again. Either the earth is trembling or Osmala is on the move again.

The door opens, and Osmala steps down into the garden. And he wouldn't be Osmala if he didn't turn again and address whoever is inside the caravan. I can hear their voices but can't make out the words. I assume this is all part of Osmala's regular strategy, his final roll of the die, designed to throw his opponent off balance and perhaps to leave him as confused as possible. But then something happens, something that isn't part of the script. Juhani appears in the doorway, steps out of the caravan and walks up to Osmala. I hear Osmala's voice again, then Juhani's. Then they courteously shake hands.

I wait a further eight minutes before making my move.

My first steps are brisk and agitated, then my speed steadies and I start to regain the sense of why I came here in the first place. And in this light, as the wind chills my thoughts all the more, I start to see alternative theories for everything that has happened. Maybe Osmala was here making further enquiries. The man who attacked me lived right here. Juhani works at the adventure park. Osmala is interested in both of them. But none of these scenarios explains that respectful handshake, the agreeable voices.

I've almost reached Juhani's caravan when I realise that one small detail might solve the whole equation. The crucial question is: will Juhani mention Osmala's visit? If he doesn't, that handshake will obviously take on new significance; I can safely assume something has passed between them.

In a matter of moments, I have walked along the row of caravans and arrived at Juhani's place. I walk right up to the door and can't hear any other voices from inside. I knock and wait. The door opens, and I can see from Juhani's expression that he wasn't expecting to see me. It's only a brief moment, then he quickly manages to wipe the confusion from his face.

'I'm still not ready for a mathematical lecture,' he says. 'And I don't want to hear how I should have done things differently.'

Warm indoor air wafts out into the garden. It feels somehow inviting as I stand there in the November evening. But Juhani doesn't look like he is about to ask me in.

'I'm not here to lecture you—'

'And I don't want to hear any more of your ten- or hundred-year plans for the park,' he continues, 'or how in the year 3151 we can conclude that the entrance tickets have grown enough interest that we can buy some extra lemonade from the sales.'

Juhani is holding on to the doorframe as though he were in danger of toppling out of the caravan.

'I've come to talk...'

'Talk,' he scoffs.

'I don't have a simple solution to our many and varied problems, Juhani. Perhaps there isn't one. We need to—'

'*We* don't need to do anything,' says Juhani. 'As you know, I don't make the decisions. And you're not interested in anybody else's suggestions.'

It's obvious that Juhani is in no mood to negotiate. But in what he has said, I see the possibility of moving forwards.

'What kind of suggestions do you have?'

Juhani looks at me. 'You know,' he says.

'Kuisma Lohi has made a proposal, but who else? You said "suggestions" in the plural.'

'I meant in general,' he says. 'Toy of Finland, for instance. They've made a proposal as well, but you've said no to them too.'

The moment feels longer than is factually possible. Right now, I don't plan on going into the details of the relationship between me and Toy of Finland. In fact, it doesn't really have anything to do with this conversation. I remind myself of what I came here to do this evening: to try and forge unity, to give Juhani one last chance. To give myself one too.

'I've been busy and a little preoccupied,' I tell him, honestly. 'I might have missed something important. Is there something else I should know? Have you received any other proposals or spoken about the park's business with anyone else?'

Juhani pauses before answering.

'No,' he says eventually. 'Not since we met Kuisma Lohi this morning. I spent the afternoon walking around the park thinking about things, then I came back here. Quiet evening in.'

17

My phone beeps. It's a message from Laura Helanto. I quickly formulate an answer, try to punctuate it with appropriate emojis – three of them, just like in Laura's message – send it and slip my phone into my pocket. Then almost immediately I take it out again and double-check what I've written. I sigh with relief; at least I kept on topic. I must admit, my powers of concentration aren't at their best right now.

It is a dim and drizzly morning. I walk to the car, and something about this perfectly ordinary action reminds me of what a veritable swamp of conflict and confusion I am wading through. I like using public transport. Of course, it's the most sensible option, but it's also liberating, it is freedom and movement all in one. It feels as though each occasion I have used the park's van has either caused me considerable problems or had something to do with clearing up those problems. Which, in turn, has only led to a sense of more constraint and less freedom. Is this what using a private car is all about, and is this the reason I soon find myself sitting in the morning traffic jam: I have got myself into problems spiralling further and further out of control, and now I am trying to survive them by myself in a constant cycle of driving, delivering, visiting and managing.

I switch on the windscreen wipers.

I've been thinking about my evening meeting in Rastila, going over what happened, trying to remember every word. I've tried to combine times, places, events and people, but I haven't been able to find anything I might call clarity. Moreover, I don't know what to think of Juhani. I was surprised at myself too, at the calm with which I said good night to him after our short conversation last night. Maybe this is all like a simple division and multiplication exercise that always gives the same answer. Maybe.

Twenty minutes later I am in the staff car park behind the adventure park. I switch off the engine but stay in the van.

I can't hear the rain, but I can see it. As though the world were filling up with thin water, the kind of water that doesn't weigh the same as normal water but that still drenches everything, soaks the earth, trickles along every furrow and fissure, forming ponds both large and small in every fold, every dip and knoll. I don't have the energy to correct myself, to remind myself of the density of water, the nature of matter and constants. And I don't know whether this temporary disturbance is the greatest of my problems. I don't know precisely what this temporary disturbance is, so I can't assess whether one of my big problems is bigger than another big problem, or a third one. I don't even know what order I should try and resolve them in, if I were to embark upon such a project. I'm about to grip the door handle when a conclusion about all my restless thoughts appears in my mind with dazzling clarity.

Perhaps things really are as bad as they can possibly be.

The Duck Tunnel, however, proves me wrong. Things are in fact much worse. The bright-yellow construction is standing exactly where only a while ago Kristian disassembled the Crocodile Canyon. The Duck Tunnel is a long tube about two metres in diameter; the aim is to proceed along it while trying to avoid soft ducks that jump, dive, fly, fall and try to hinder the runner in all possible ways. In theory, that is. The fact of the matter is that not a single child has ever come out of the Duck Tunnel without crying. The ducks are hard and rough, some have even knocked a child out.

The Duck Tunnel is an even older apparatus than the Crocodile Canyon. It's more dangerous too, and therefore even more shunned by the customers. The Duck Tunnel is a reminder of how everything that can possibly go wrong in the design and manufacturing of a piece of equipment can sometimes go wrong all at once.

But the Duck Tunnel itself isn't the end of my woes.

Kari Liitokangas and Jeppe Sauvonen from Toy of Finland are standing next to the Duck Tunnel talking to Kristian. There's no mistaking them. The fifty-something Kari Liitokangas looks like he has been assembled from several different men. He has a large chest, but skinny arms and legs. He has a strong, Hollywood jawline, but a small red nose indicative of a fairly close relationship with the bottle. Jeppe Sauvonen is standing next to him like a short, stumpy bollard, his dark monobrow slithering like an adder above his eyes, and this time he is wearing a T-shirt bearing the words *FOLLOW ME*. I'm not quite sure what this text is trying to suggest or who it's appealing to, who it's supposed to impress.

By now they have all noticed my arrival, so I walk right towards them. I reach the group and glance briefly at Kristian. He looks perhaps a little tired. I assume this means he's discovered that waking up at three o'clock in the morning isn't a sustainable solution after all. As I get closer, I see that Liitokangas and Sauvonen appear to be in rather a bad mood. At the same time, however, I reach an important conclusion: the men would not be behaving like this if Otto Härkä had been found. Of this, I am relatively certain. They wouldn't just be in a bad mood, they wouldn't have forcibly sent us the Duck Tunnel and forced Kristian to construct it. And they wouldn't be standing next to a bright-yellow plastic tube, waiting for me.

'Here it is,' says Liitokangas without any pleasantries as he points at the yellow side of the Duck Tunnel. 'And here it's going to stay.'

'It's not moving an inch,' adds Sauvonen.

'We have the order form right here,' says Liitokangas, and takes some folded sheets of A4 from his jacket pocket. 'And the invoice, of course.'

'And the payment deadline is, like, today,' says Sauvonen.

I take the documents from Liitokangas's hand and unfold them. I look at the invoice and the price at the bottom of the page. It is utterly ludicrous. The order forms haven't been filled out with the same care as last time. I can tell at a glance that it's a forgery. I fold the papers again and slip them into my pocket.

'We will try this out,' I say, 'and return it if we can't find any use for it.'

'Just shove the kids inside,' says Jeppe Sauvonen, 'and *voilà*, it's in use.'

'From what I've heard about the Duck Tunnel—'

'People hear all kinds of things,' says Liitokangas. 'You shouldn't believe everything you read online. Before you know it, the world will be flat again.'

'Just pay the fucking bill, all right?' says Sauvonen. 'I mean, how difficult can it be?'

'Paying a bill like this is very difficult indeed,' I say.

'Why?' asks Sauvonen.

I look him in his brown eyes. The black adder wriggling above them highlights the intensity of his stare.

'Because the sum is so big,' I say. 'And the product so unfit for purpose.'

Sauvonen takes a step closer to me. 'We haven't even been able to unload your little delivery yet,' he says. 'Because it stinks. Smells like you've been screwing those crocodiles yourself.'

'I've never done such a thing in my life,' I say, and it's the truth.

Sauvonen and I stare fixedly at each other. My suspicions have been confirmed. Otto Härkä is still in his canoe.

'What Jeppe means is that sending the product back is no longer an option,' says Liitokangas. 'And that we will take action if the payment isn't in our account by the end of the week.'

I don't think it's a good thing that Kristian is listening to this conversation, and because he is within earshot I can't speak freely. Sauvonen seems to have said everything that's on his mind. He steps back, and he and Liitokangas begin to take their leave. I decide to give it one last try.

'The Moose Chute,' I say.

Liitokangas and Sauvonen both turn and look at me.

'What about it?' asks Liitokangas.

'I want to buy it.'

'It's not for sale,' he says.

'I will pay this invoice,' I say, 'and I will pay for the Moose Chute. If I can get it.'

What I have just said, what I have just promised, is only theoretically possible. But, as I see it, I don't have any other options; all I can do is try. I have a very real feeling that I am like an astronaut whose cord connecting him to the mother ship has long since been severed. I realise I've seen this image in many a film, but that doesn't change the fact that I really am running out of oxygen and that the only spot of warmth is on a tiny blue sphere all too far away.

Sauvonen is about to say something, he is about to lunge towards me again when Liitokangas holds an arm out in front of him.

'The Moose Chute is not for sale,' he says once again, then adds: 'Not to you anyway. Ever.'

18

I tell Laura Helanto I need some fresh air and leave her working on a tall, wave-like construction rising out of the de Lempicka mural.

It is evening, and the park will be open for another hour and a half.

I do the thing I always do these days whenever I step outside: I look around before moving in any direction. And as I don't see any potential attackers or anything else life-threatening, I start walking. In one respect, I can trust Toy of Finland: if Jeppe Sauvonen is going to attack me, I will surely notice him before he even reaches me. I walk along the wall of the building, breathe the cold, light air, in, out.

The car park is about a third full.

The number of cars parked outside only gives a subtle indication of our footfall, but when converted into raw data the direction of travel is clear. Every day we have several dozen fewer customers. You can tell this right now by the fact that the edges of the car park are practically empty. This development isn't unclear in the least. It's only a matter of time before the car park is completely empty.

I arrive at the corner of the building and decide to turn back again. The November wind gives me goose bumps. The shivers might also have something to do with the expensive, exotic car slowly gliding towards me. It pulls up next to me, and before I have properly registered what is happening, the driver has stepped out of the car and opened the back door.

'Mr Lohi wishes to have a few words with you.'

The driver's fitted and doubtless exorbitantly priced suit is immaculate, with not a single crease, which seems strange given he must have been sitting in the car for some time.

'And what if I don't want to have a word with him?' I ask, but there's no conviction in my voice. At least, not the kind of conviction I try to give it, and maybe this is why the driver doesn't answer. In fact, I don't hear anything at all; the driver simply stands at the door, his hand on the upper edge. The wind is buffeting my clothes and hair but, most bewilderingly, whereas my tie is slapping against my chest and messing up my parting, nothing about the driver moves in the least. We stand there a moment longer, staring at each other, then I sigh, walk to the car and climb in. The door closes softly behind me, and we are on the move.

In the darkening evening light, Kuisma Lohi's home in Marjaniemi looks like a giant light-yellow collection of surfaces and annexes without forming anything resembling a house. A few outdoor lights flicker into life as the car takes the short driveway up to the entrance. The car stops and we repeat the same silent piece of theatre whereby the driver magically moves round to the other side of the car and the door opens. I get out of the car, follow the driver up to the front door and step inside, then into the hallway, then on to Kuisma Lohi's office situated at the end of a long corridor to the left.

At least, I assume this is his office. The room is like a pared-back version of an operating theatre: the blinding lights bouncing like radiation off the white walls, the white-washed parquet floor and the few items of glass-and-chrome furniture. Kuisma Lohi stands up but remains behind his desk and gestures that I should take a seat in an angular-looking chair, made of steel and white leather, on the other side of the desk.

'Lauri will take you back to the park in a few moments.'

I glance over my shoulder.

The driver has disappeared, the door has closed behind him. I didn't hear anything. Contrastingly, I can hear my own footsteps as I walk over to the chair and the creak of the leather as I sit down. Kuisma Lohi sits down too. His slight face with its small features and light-blue eyes is even harder to read than usual. Behind him is a large, dark window where I can see recursive reflections of the interior and the two of us sitting there, and everything looks somehow fake, unreal.

'There are going to be a few changes to the order of events,' Kuisma Lohi begins, 'and their speed. I'm bringing our negotiations to an end. Which is a relief, I might add. I'm perturbed by how difficult everything is, the constant arguing, the fact that you and your brother seem rather ... out of sync. We can also dispense with the various options I've offered. We'll be moving from offers directly to the signing of the contract. And the price will be cut in half.'

Kuisma Lohi says the last sentence as if this were the most trivial point of all. This is not at all the case. Right from the outset, my biggest problem when it comes to Kuisma Lohi has been that I don't know how much he knows. Now, with a degree of certainty, I reach the conclusion that he knows far too much. But because I don't know exactly how much he knows, I need to continue behaving as though I'm in a much better negotiating position than I probably am. From the perspective of game theory, this could be an interesting scenario, but when we take into consideration the resurfacing of a violent criminal in a remote pond and the armed adventure-park supplier who died by his own hand with the intervention of a steel platform, and whose body is currently hidden inside a plastic crocodile, the situation could be lethal.

'What if I don't—'

'Sign the kind of contract I suggest?' Kuisma Lohi finishes my question, then answers it himself. 'Then Detective Inspector Osmala will come into the possession of some information that will eventually force you to give up the park another way. That's fine by me too, but it's a slower and messier path to take, and it isn't a very attractive strategy with a view to sustained financial benefit.'

Of course, Kuisma Lohi doesn't say it out loud, but he has just moved from the realm of hostile takeover to out-and-out extortion.

'Why now?' I ask.

Kuisma Lohi gives what looks like a smile, a tiny twitch of the lips. 'I have some fresh information, and you should thank your brother for that,' he says. 'He's easily excited. But the person who deserves most thanks is you. Without you, I wouldn't have realised quite how much the adventure park depends on suppliers like Toy of Finland and their, shall we say, delivery methods, or how we can make the adventure-park business more efficient and cut costs. And when you bring the two together in a happy marriage like this...'

At first, I don't know how it can possibly have taken me this long to understand what's going on, then it dawns on me. This has been going on for some time. I haven't been at my best; I haven't been able to put two and two together as effectively and accurately as I should.

'But of course,' I say. 'You're going to buy out Toy of Finland too.'

Now Kuisma Lohi smiles enough that it genuinely looks like a smile. The lower half of his face broadens out, but his eyes remain impassive.

'Not for the amount they're asking right now,' he says. 'But the price will change. Negotiations seem to be moving in the same direction as ours. There's lots of commonality, lots of shared interest. Your brother has been a great help there too. I'm not sure he knows it himself.'

Kuisma Lohi's attempt at a smile ends abruptly.

'As for the timetable,' he continues, 'I want to be crystal clear.'

I don't see what can be achieved by continuing this conversation. I already know the essentials. The reflections in the window look even more contorted.

'Two weeks,' he says. 'That's how long it will take to draw up the contract with my lawyers. Once the contract is ready, we will sign it. Lauri will drive you back to the park now. Thank you for your time.'

We have been driving for about fifteen minutes when I hear Lauri's soft, pleasant voice.

'Are you aware someone is following us?'

I look behind me, but that doesn't tell me anything. All I can see are the headlights of the car behind us, but I don't know how long they have been there.

'No, I wasn't.'

'An electric car,' says Lauri. 'A Volkswagen. The driver is heavyset. The car is slightly tilted towards the driver's side. Unless I'm mistaken, he's wearing a light-blue or grey blazer. His face is exceptionally angular.'

Lauri says nothing more; he doesn't need to. It starts to rain. There's a low humming sound inside the car.

I stand under the awning at the main entrance and wait. I watch as the Volkswagen glides slowly and precisely into a parking space right in front of the door. The door opens and the small, delicate brown leather shoes pace carefully to avoid the puddles. By the time the man reaches the awning, his blazer is dappled with rain. He takes a small packet of tissues from his pocket, then with admirable dexterity takes out a single tissue and wipes his face.

Osmala is a bewildering combination of, on the one hand, the proportions of a blue whale and, on the other, a ballet dancer with the precision and delicacy of an experienced stamp collector. Of course, I only know him in passing – though still far better than I would like to – but I can already say that he deploys these various qualities quite deliberately. Every move is aimed at putting his opponent in even greater uncertainty.

'I was on my way home,' he says, 'because that Fellini film's on TV tonight. I've seen it before, of course, but I really like it. And it's a suitable topic for today, don't you think? Then I looked around and thought – look who's coming?'

I say nothing. It's no accident that Osmala found me in a car with Kuisma Lohi's driver and decided to follow us. And I doubt he wants to start a film club together either, so I wait for him to get to the point.

'Some new information has come to light,' he says, 'about the guy who visited your park then ended up in the pond. Links to the trio running Toy of Finland. One in particular, whom I'd very much like to talk to. But I can't find him anywhere. The two I did find aren't talking. They seem like the kind of people who like to solve their problems by themselves. What do you think?'

I'm standing outdoors without a jacket on. It's cold, and the wind is thrashing me with my own tie.

'Well,' Osmala says eventually. He must have noticed that I'm not really in the mood for conversation. 'I don't know either. But

I don't understand why you won't just tell me everything you know.'

Osmala has turned, and now he's looking right at me.

'You just had a meeting with Kuisma Lohi. Nobody has a meeting with Kuisma Lohi unless they're desperate. I'm not suggesting such a person is necessarily acting illegally, but on the other hand I've never met anyone who's had dealings with him and come out happier at the other end. I don't know what's going on between you and Toy of Finland, but I can see something's up. They send you equipment, and you send it back. And this I've worked out using just my eyes. Now your park has a bright-yellow duck contraption that's out of service, it's cordoned off with ropes, tapes and warning signs. When I asked your park's security manager about it, he told me that people have even disappeared inside that tunnel over the years. That doesn't sound like an acquisition that's been properly thought through. Would you like to comment?'

I ought to comment that my park's security manager has a tendency to use somewhat overblown language when talking about things and that one should take his words with more than a smidgeon of salt, or at the very least try to filter the wheat from the chaff, as it were. But I don't. I say absolutely nothing. I realise I have been standing in the cold evening air while Osmala has given a fairly comprehensive assessment of the situation. And at the same time, I understand exactly why I've done this. I don't have the strength to do anything else. I'm quite simply exhausted, I'm finished. It is a revelation of sorts, but not the kind of revelation that brings relief, that opens up new horizons. This one doesn't open any new doors. It is simply ... the truth.

'Very well,' says Osmala. 'I've tried to reach out a helping hand. I've done so for many reasons, and one of the biggest of those reasons is inside finishing her latest work of art. Which I have every intention of seeing.'

We are still standing opposite each other, the wind whipping us both in equal measure.

'Here's how this is going to go. From now on, I'll be watching you a little more closely,' says Osmala. 'If you think we've been running into each other a lot lately, you can forget it. Starting this evening, we're going to be seeing a lot more of each other. And not all of our meetings are going to be nice little chats like this. I might as well tell you, you're the focus of our investigation now. Everything seems to come back to you, one way or another. This isn't exactly a secret.'

Osmala pauses briefly, then continues:

'And I'm sure you know that you're in a great deal of danger right now. I don't want to sugar-coat this. From experience, I can tell you that these chains of events have a tendency to speed up before reaching their conclusion. If I'm not wrong, and I don't think I am, right this minute you're in the middle of a pretty intense – how should I put this? – event horizon.'

Osmala has been speaking in the same moderate, contemplative, friendly voice as always. He turns and appears to be looking out into the car park and the rain. Then I hear a sound that is either a stocky man's sigh or a particularly strong gust of wind and rain.

'Fearless,' says Osmala. 'That's what she is. That artist in there. She brings things together in a way you could never imagine.'

We stand under the awning a moment longer, then Osmala turns without saying anything and walks back to his car. This time he doesn't bother trying to avoid the puddles.

19

The Strawberry Maze shudders, the Turtle Trucks spin round and round on their track, the Komodo Locomotive trundles onwards, powered by its little peddlers. Children come careering down the Big Dipper, sliding and screaming. Someone stamps on the horn at the Trombone Cannons, sending little balls shooting into the air. The Curly Cake Café is still giving off the aroma of the day's menu: Trapeze Tortellini, Magician's Mash, Apple Bombs and Whoopsie Buns.

All this, I think to myself.

I walk through the park and try to concentrate on keeping my balance, making sure my feet carry me forwards and don't, for instance, sink through the concrete floor into the depths of the earth or get blown away from underneath me, like ash, and cease to exist.

Laura Helanto is working on the crest of a giant wave at the de Lempicka mural.

There is about twenty metres between us.

At this moment.

I can feel some dark power pulling me away from her. The distance grows, first by only a few metres, then hundreds of metres, then an unquantifiable number of kilometres.

I'm going to lose her. I'm going to lose everything. Laura and the park are the last bolts holding everything together, and now they too have come loose.

I hurtle downwards, almost in freefall. That's what it feels like. I remain on my feet, but something vital, some essential part of me collapses and continues falling down a bottomless abyss.

Our customer numbers are down, the park is about to be forcibly sold off for next to nothing, Toy of Finland is trying to extort me and threatening my life, Juhani is working for Osmala, it's only a matter of time until Otto Härkä is found and the gangster from the pond is connected to me, until Osmala comes to the park and takes me away for the last time. If I'm lucky, I'll just end up in prison. If I'm less lucky … And to crown off all my countless failures, there's the burning question of what will happen to the park and its employees and Laura Helanto's art project once I'm gone.

All the calculations, I think, all the probabilities I built this on, the promises I have given. The sense and mathematics I have always trusted. It seems it was all just ideals and abstractions after all, and nothing will ever come of that.

I watch Laura Helanto at work, I see her joy, her focus.

Laura notices me approaching her. She greets me warmly, then – at least, this is how I read it – she sees my expression, which I can't seem to make even a millimetre happier, a single decimal more hopeful. I can see her face becoming more serious, her eyes more quizzical, and (this might just be my imagination) more concerned.

She doesn't need to feel concerned for me, I tell her. I was wrong, I say, and I take responsibility for my actions, and first of all I plan to hand myself in to Detective Inspector Osmala and take what is coming to me. I tell her I'm sorry and that I've done everything I can.

Laura Helanto brushes a lock of hair from the side of her glasses, looks at me and asks:

'Everything?'

I finish my story in Herttoniemi, just after midnight, once Tuuli is asleep and Laura Helanto and I are sitting at the kitchen table. She is quiet and serious, as she has been the whole time I've been talking. Naturally, I've left out any bits that might put her in an awkward position, not to mention the fact that telling her certain things could make her an accomplice. For this reason, I don't speculate about the loose knots around the legs of the Banana Mirror or my fortunate positioning of the steel platform, and neither do I tell her where the body is buried, after a fashion. But I do give her a good overview of the situation, and I'm sure that she will be able to draw a number of conclusions from my story.

An hour ago, Laura dimmed the lamp hanging above the dining table. The light is soft now and spreads out from under the dome of the lampshade like something warm and tactile, though of course this isn't the case. I have the evening's third cup of tea in front of me.

'I'm glad you told me this,' she says. 'There's something I should tell you too.'

I flinch a little, and Laura notices.

'Nothing like that,' she smiles. 'I just mean, I guessed things weren't quite right. The Crocodile Canyon and the Duck Tunnel were pretty big red flags. It says a lot about the new owners of Toy of Finland and how our collaboration with them is going. Osmala has been to see what I'm working on, but I can't imagine he was visiting the park just to see my artwork. Then there's Juhani. I've known him for a long time, and to be honest I did a lot of the work around the park that he was supposed to do. I'm not exactly surprised that he's gone and got himself into trouble or that he's got you into trouble in the process.'

'But if you knew about—'

'A while ago, I said I can trust you,' she continues. 'And that feels wonderful. It's different from what I'm used to. You're

different. You're reliable, even now, in a situation like this. It feels
… every bit as good as I thought it would. That's why I asked if
you'd like to move in with us. That's why I've started to let Tuuli
get to know you. That's why we're sitting here now. I can trust you.
Now there isn't a single doubt in my mind.'

What Laura Helanto says is obviously very pleasant; as she says,
it feels good. But it doesn't sound at all logical, in light of
everything I've just told her.

'I don't understand,' I say quite honestly. 'You sound as though
simply talking has resolved all our problems, but—'

'Do you remember what you said to me on our first date?' she
asks, props her elbows on the table and leans closer to me. Her
blue-green eyes glisten, her wild, bushy hair looks almost golden
in the dimmed light of the lamp. 'When we went for a beer after
the exhibition. You told me about how you approach very
complicated questions. You used a mathematical problem as an
example, but then you said the same can apply to all kinds of
questions. You said that first you break the problem into its
constituent parts, see if you can solve one of the parts separately
and whether that will help you move forwards.'

'That only works when—'

'You need the Moose Chute,' says Laura. 'You need a lot of
other things too, that much is obvious, but to me it looks like
those are problems for a later date.'

'Later?'

Laura Helanto nods. 'I think you need to go back to doing what
you do best: counting. And go back to the beginning, find out
where all this started.'

'Everything started when Juhani came back,' I say.

'And what does Juhani want?'

Laura Helanto is right. When a problem is split into pieces, it
often reveals its true nature. This time the effect is manifold.

Something moves aside, part of my fatigue evaporates right away. I start to see the possibilities. And once again I start … to count. I look at Laura, her sparkling eyes. I know I don't have to say anything for her sake, but I want to say it, because this is a simple calculation, yet until now it felt all-too complex. I have to hear it for myself.

'He wants the park,' I say.

20

Johanna, Samppa, Kristian, Esa, Minttu K.

Everybody arrives at the Curly Cake shortly before ten. Juhani came to the park a little earlier, we had a short negotiation, and he signed the papers I'd drawn up for him. And now he's having difficulty staying in his chair. Johanna has been working in the kitchen since eight o'clock and came into the café's seating area a moment ago. Minttu K's cup of morning coffee smells like she's had a recent visit to a vodka distillery, and she is holding two unlit cigarettes in her hands, one in her right and one in her left, while adjusting the position of her peroxide hair. In his camouflage jacket and with his aviators lifted onto his forehead, Esa looks like he is awaiting deployment to the front, and Samppa has already made several suggestions about how we could make this meeting more interactive, more conversational, regardless of what we are planning to discuss.

I haven't taken him up on these suggestions, and besides I haven't revealed to anybody why we have gathered in the café this morning. I suspect Juhani's body language might give them a good idea: his cheeks are bright red, and he is clearly trying to find a position in his chair that gives him a little more authority. I thank everyone for attending and get straight to the point.

I tell them the truth.

The park finds itself in a difficult situation. Our customer numbers are dropping. There is less money coming in. Our whole survival is on a knife-edge. I have cut back our costs and tightened the budget in every department. I haven't paid myself any salary at all. I have tried my utmost to make good investments at a reasonable price, all while maintaining a period of financial austerity. All this I have tried to do, so that the park and its jobs will thrive and still exist in five or ten years' time.

My words hang in the air for a moment. If I'm reading the room correctly, people seem to have been listening, I think they have heard me. All except Juhani, that is. He looks like he is about to burst with anticipation.

'It's time to try something new,' I continue. 'And so, today we are going to change manager at the park. I'm going to step aside and help during the transition period. Juhani will be taking over the park again. Juhani, please.'

Juhani no longer has to hold himself back. He jumps to his feet, smiles and spreads out his hands as though he were sending beams of sunlight out in all directions.

He speaks.

At length.

What's most important isn't that Juhani is being a little economical with the truth. Most important are people's faces. They are listening to him. And they seem excited. To an extent. But unless I'm mistaken, their enthusiasm isn't the same as when Juhani first came back, when he first painted these images of a glorious, fantastic future. This time their reactions are more subdued, more reserved.

Naturally, this doesn't apply to Juhani, who has always had a knack of making himself the most excited person of all.

Which leads, either accidentally or on purpose (for a variety of reasons, I suspect the former), to the bit in Juhani's speech that I've been waiting for most of all.

He promises Johanna a bistro, Samppa a therapy centre, Esa a minesweeper unit, Kristian a seat on the board of directors, and Minttu K collaboration with a world-renowned influencer to help with marketing. I watch their expressions as each promise appears, flies into the air and lands at their feet.

Their expressions are different from what they were only a short time ago.

My new office will be in the storeroom. Behind the tall piles of plywood, I set up a small desk with enough room for a computer and pull up an old bouncy seat originally taken from Caper Castle. The seat was supposed to work like an ejection seat in an aeroplane, but setting it up properly proved impossible: the seat sent our young customers flying far too fast, and after one final bounce that knocked out two milk teeth, the seat was moved to the storeroom. It's a very nice chair and perfectly supports my back.

I work for several hours. Juhani has asked me to take care of the park's finances and bookkeeping until he has – in his own words – got the park's balls rolling. I manage to finish several matters I haven't had time to concentrate on. At the same time, I start another project that I simply haven't been able to pay any attention. Or rather, I didn't realise I needed to pay it any attention. Now I can see and think more clearly than for quite some time.

At some point I hear the storeroom door open and close, but there's no rattling, no sounds of dragging or lifting or placing anything on the floor. From this, I conclude that whoever has come down here isn't on normal storeroom business. The footsteps get closer. Samppa peers from behind the wall of plywood.

'Five?' he asks.

Nowadays I know that this monosyllabic question means, do I have time for a short conversation?

'By all means,' I say, and close the lid of my laptop.

'That was a brave speech,' he says. 'You looked deep inside. You really took off the mask, made yourself vulnerable. You came out of the shadows and demonstrated that you really want to put yourself out there, you want to show us your true self, live your best life. There's a quiet power in vulnerability. Weakness is still a taboo, but when love makes some cracks in it, it bursts like a dam. Bravo, man. Respect.'

I'm not entirely sure what Samppa is talking about, so I wait for him to say something I can latch on to a little more easily. Samppa checks the tension in his ponytail, then shakes his copious bracelets into place.

'I can talk openly, right,' he either says or asks. I'm unsure which.

'It's probably for the best,' I agree.

'You probably don't think about things like this,' he continues. 'You're focussed on leadership, and you're more of a behind-the-scenes kind of guy. But I'm out there in the field, as it were; I engage with people face to face. So, you and I have quite a different approach to things. You look at everything from your ivory tower – and I don't mean that in a bad way – while I'm right at the coalface getting my hands dirty. Esa might say you're the general far away in his headquarters, and I'm the cadet thrust into the line of duty.'

'I think I understand what you're saying,' I nod. I don't plan on telling Samppa that in the course of my adventure-park career I have been shot at, stabbed, chased, almost run over, beaten up, threatened, blackmailed and very nearly dropped into a pond wearing a pair of concrete boots while he was holding fairy-tale rhythmic gymnastics classes and processing his break-up in animal fables – the orphaned zebra and the bloodthirsty lion, the fragile butterfly and the clumsy donkey – with which he entertains our younger customers.

'So, you know better than most that I'm not afraid of confrontation,' Samppa continues. 'Anyway, I made it clear my days of spying on people are over.'

I don't think my face gives anything away. I've learnt that Samppa likes to talk, especially when he feels he can talk on his own terms, his own turf.

'It was brave of you to step up like that,' I say, channelling his own jargon.

Samppa nods and looks perhaps a little agitated. 'I came out,' he says. 'As myself.'

'Exactly.'

'I am what I am.'

'This is true.'

'Once was enough,' he says.

I don't know what Samppa is referring to, but I have to keep this conversation going.

'You defended your lived experience,' I say, grasping for all the buzzwords in the lexicon. 'You embraced your vulnerability.'

'See, from what you said back there, I knew you'd get it,' he says. 'It was a few weeks ago. I was supposed to hide in front of the park while you were working late, then make a call when you switched the lights off in your office. I was hiding in the bushes over by the car park, the lights went out, I made the call, then cycled home.'

Samppa's words bring back vivid images of the night I was attacked by the loading bay. I remember thinking about the bicycle left at the edge of the car park, the one I'd seen from the window. The same bicycle that had disappeared by the time I walked past the very same spot a moment later. And how, another moment later, my forehead was being battered against the steel steps. And how...

'Juhani asked you to spy on me. Is that right?' I ask in as neutral a voice as possible.

Samppa nods. 'I thought, what harm could it possibly do?' he says. 'And, of course, in the end there wasn't any harm done, right? But when I listened to you today, and because this has been bothering me, then I thought I could share it with you in a spirit of friendship, and we could deconstruct it together.'

'Consider it ... deconstructed.'

Samppa pauses for a moment. He is watching me carefully, and I can see he is thinking things through.

'Burnout?' he asks.

'Excuse me?'

'Burnout. That's why you're taking a back seat, right?'

I feel I should be honest with him, because he has been honest with me. 'Sometimes business life can be full of ... rough and tumble,' I say.

'If you ever need to talk,' he says, raises his hands, gives me the thumbs up, then points his thumbs at himself.

It takes a moment before I understand what he is saying. I'm about to thank him for the offer when I remember something else.

'Samppa, one more thing. Don't tell Juhani that you and I have ... deconstructed this together.'

'Everything is in absolute confidence,' he says, then taps the left side of his chest. 'It's all in here.'

21

Schopenhauer is purring, murmuring like a small, old car, looking for a comfortable position on the sofa. I've told him all about recent events, and I even tried my best to bring up the subject of possibly moving house. Schopenhauer dealt with this the way he deals with everything: he is trying to find his place, a perspective that will allow him to observe matters over a longer period rather than running in headfirst. I've told him I would like to do the same, but it seems as though sustained, thorough consideration isn't always possible. It feels odd to hear myself say something like this. But if there's one thing I have learnt in my adventure-park career then it's the simple truth that nothing is predictable. All you can do is count. However, these two things aren't as mutually incompatible as I once thought. Schopenhauer finds a suitable place in the corner of the sofa, rolls onto his side and starts washing his face.

I reach across to the coffee table and put down my cup of tea. Outside it is dark, save for the illuminated windows of the building opposite, which seem to be floating in mid-air. Golden, multicoloured, dim, bright floating squares in a sea of black, or in an endless universe, all set in soothing, regular formation.

I get up and think to myself that of today's remaining chores there only remains brushing my teeth (four and a half minutes) and sending Laura Helanto a text message (anywhere between ten and fifteen minutes), then I will try to sleep. Five seconds later, I think rather differently.

The sound of the doorbell is both loud and unexpected. I can't imagine who is visiting me at this hour. I walk into the hallway,

think for a moment, then lift the entryphone handset and hear a
familiar voice.

Juhani barges his way inside before I've even had a chance to say
good evening, let alone ask him what he's doing here. He leaves
his shoes in the hallway but keeps his coat on as he marches
straight into the living room. Then he stops and sits down in the
armchair in front of the bookcase, though he doesn't look like he
is about to examine the extensive, mostly mathematical, library
on his right. He is just as ruddy-cheeked as he was earlier this
morning, but now he looks nowhere near as happy, enthusiastic
or carefree in that quintessentially Juhani-esque fashion. I see that
Schopenhauer is keeping an eye on him too.

'I don't understand what's happened,' says Juhani. 'Kuisma Lohi
contacted me again. I thought we'd agreed on the timetable and
when we were going to sign the agreement. But now he says he's
lowering his offer. The new offer is only a tenth of the previous one.'

I sit down on the sofa, where I was a moment ago. Juhani is
sitting across the coffee table. My reading lamp, a tall floor lamp
behind him on his right, makes his hair and cheeks shine all the
more and casts shadows under his eyes. He looks suddenly much
older. I think of my calculations and of what I know he has done.

'A tenth won't even cover the life insurance, which I really need,
like, yesterday,' Juhani says and shakes his head. 'A tenth won't even
… You're going to have to work out how we get the old offer back.'

'Me?'

'You're still in charge of the park's finances and the
bookkeeping, the raw numbers.'

'Only pertaining to my time as CEO. And I don't think the
current problem has anything to do with the numbers.'

Juhani looks over at Gauss's handwritten equation on the wall. Again I am reminded of the pleasure it has brought me over the years. If I look closely enough, I can always find something new in it. Normally I don't look for anything in particular, I simply admire it, follow the familiar markings that always lead to the same beauty and clarity.

'Henri, I just can't sell the park for that little,' he says eventually.

We sit in my living room for a long while. In the building opposite, some of the windows turn dark. Juhani talks, going round and round, always coming back to where he started. Which, of course, is no surprise: in this situation, it would be impossible to end up anywhere else. And I can't offer him what he is asking for – a solution to a problem that doesn't take all the variables into account. And as I listen and watch my brother, I conclude that my calculations thus far have been correct in all but one respect: the speed of events. Of course, I should have taken the laws of physics into account. Juhani is a force of nature. He is potent, untamed and unpredictable – except that he always, with tireless regularity, ends up working against his own interests.

Juhani leaves shortly before eleven. I walk from the hallway back into the living room. Schopenhauer gives me a knowing look, then he stretches, rests his head on the sofa and closes his eyes.

The following morning, I wake up before my phone's alarm clock, and it's hardly surprising. In all probability, I'm going to be busier in the next few days than at any other point in my adventure-park career, and this naturally has an impact on the quality of my sleep.

I shave, get dressed, give Schopenhauer some food then open the balcony door for him, eat the same good and healthy breakfast that, with a number of carefully considered variations, I have been eating for a few decades now, give the newspapers and the business pages a quick look, knot my tie, pull on my outdoor clothes and leave.

With one change of train, I arrive in Tapanila thirty-six minutes later.

Tapanila is a leafy district full of detached houses, and even in mid-November it is beautiful and idyllic, like a little village all of its own. Some of the buildings are clearly older wooden houses, well-kept properties whose value has doubled many times over the last hundred years. Some of the gardens are large, and the black, twisting branches of the abundant old apple trees are like something straight out of the pages of a fairy tale. I notice the quiet, which seems to increase and thicken the further I walk from the train station. Six degrees above freezing feels warmer than the figure suggests, thanks to the still air. The sun peers from between the clouds and guides my steps.

It takes nine minutes to find the address I'm looking for. I ring the bell on the wall of the brick house. When nothing happens, I ring it again, with the same result. I take a few steps back. The house looks like it was built in the 1970s: it is on two floors with a flat roof, and is in clear need of some renovation. I suspect the owner must have thought he would get enough money from the sale of his company to cover the renovation costs. And now that the sale isn't going quite as planned...

I recognise the sound almost immediately. A chainsaw, behind the house. That must be why nobody heard the doorbell. The path leads through the front garden, turns the corner, then continues along the side of the house and winds its way round the back. I can't hear the chainsaw anymore, but I can see where the trunk of a spruce tree has been chopped and split into logs. I walk towards the spruce. The back garden is square and large. Flowerbeds, berry bushes, a cherry tree, apple trees and...

A chainsaw.

Which I can hear again, and which is now hurtling towards me. The saw wails – and so does the man brandishing it.

In an instant the world is awash with the noise of thousands of tiny, razor-sharp teeth.

The man is wearing a lumberjack's helmet and visor. He raises the screaming saw and brings it crashing downwards. I dive to my right and land on my side. The blade sinks into the lawn, sending mud, earth and brown grass flying in all directions. The man raises the saw again. I roll across the ground, again the saw cuts into the grass. I manage to stand up, the man is already coming after me but trips on a loose clump of soil. The chainsaw flies from his hands, he spins around, fumbling for the saw, and falls flat on his back. The saw cuts out, and the man groans in pain. Then everything is as quiet as it was a moment ago.

'Hannes Tolkki?' I ask. 'Former CEO of Toy of Finland?'

'That's me,' says the man lying on his back. 'Who's asking?'

'I'm Henri Koskinen,' I say, 'from the YouMeFun adventure park. We've spoken on the phone, but we've never met in person.'

'Right, yes, I remember it well. Sorry about that. I thought you were ... someone else. Back's playing up again. Can you give me a hand?'

I walk over to Hannes Tolkki and crouch down, and he grips my arm. Standing up is hard for him, he has to be careful of his back and I have to support him under the armpits. Eventually he is on his feet, but even this looks like quite an ordeal.

'You thought I was one of Toy of Finland's new owners,' I say.

Tolkki looks at me. He is a man in his sixties, fair-haired, and in his grey eyes I can see that my guess wasn't too wide of the mark.

'I thought, enough's enough,' he says. 'I'm not giving an inch more.'

By and large, Tolkki's account is as I expected. A quick debt, taken out in an emergency and strictly off the books, grew over time into a monster, and eventually paying it back became simply impossible. In addition to this, there came the physical reminders and other forms of blackmail, culminating in the forced sell-off to Liitokangas and his associates. And even that wasn't enough. According to Tolkki, two of them visited him yesterday, demanding money. I decide not to tell him why there are only two of them left, but I give him some choice examples of my dealings with the new owners of Toy of Finland, particularly my problems with the new equipment. And the longer we discuss this, the more it seems we have in common. Finally, the only unclear question appears to be how to get Hannes Tolkki out of his garden, indoors, and lying down on his massage table.

22

Kristian comes bounding up to my desk in the storeroom and, in his own way, answers my questions about time and place. Questions I have asked only myself, silently, over the two days since my visit to Tapanila.

'They're twisting Juhani's leg out the back,' says Kristian. 'They've driven a car up against the loading bay, and Juhani's leg is trapped between the bumper and the grille. He says not to call the police. That's the way to conduct negotiations these days, he says, to gently take your opponent out of his comfort zone. But I'm not so sure. I've done plenty of business courses, and I've never...'

Kristian looks confused, but also a little disappointed, if I'm reading him right. It's generally quite easy to read him, and many times I've had the distinct impression that he always says what he is thinking – even when it might be wise to consider other options instead. He is wearing the park's T-shirt, as always, regardless of the temperature inside the hall, which has been lowered several times now. He looks muscular and out of sorts.

'Toy of Finland?' I ask.

Kristian nods. Then neither of us says anything for a moment. I go through my calculations mentally one more time. With every passing moment, Kristian looks more eager to hear what I have to say. I decide that the time is right.

'Kristian,' I begin. 'This park means a lot to you, yes?'

'I like everything about it,' he says bluntly. 'And the career opportunities are endless, as you've shown me. I've lost count of all the different titles I've had.'

'That's true,' I agree. 'And now you've got plenty of experience at building up the equipment and taking it down again.'

'I don't know anybody quicker,' he says.

'Neither do I,' I say honestly. 'That's why I'm soon going to ask for your help again. This is about the park. About building and taking down equipment. In record time.'

Kristian clearly thinks about this for a minute; I can see it with the naked eye. And he no longer seems as disappointed or discontented as a moment ago.

'People think I'm all brawn and no brains,' he says. 'But I can think too, you know.'

'I can see that.'

'What's my new title going to be?'

I quickly think over the task at hand and what it will require, not forgetting the direction our last conversation about titles took.

'Leading construction and dismantling manager?'

Kristian seems to shed the last vestiges of disappointment. That doesn't mean he isn't thinking. He's thinking so hard I can almost hear it.

'I think leading construction and dismantling managerial manager would be clearer,' he says, after a moment's consideration.

'Then that's agreed,' I say. 'One more thing. Like the last one, this task is top secret. Not a word to anybody.'

Kristian confirms that he understands and seems content at the outcome of our conversation. Then he remembers something.

'Juhani's leg,' he says. 'It's still jammed between the bumper and the loading bay.'

'I haven't forgotten Juhani,' I reply in all honesty. 'I'll take care of it. Thank you for bringing it to my attention, Kristian.'

🦌

Liitokangas is standing next to the car, and Sauvonen is sitting behind the wheel. The car door is open and the engine is running. Liitokangas shows Sauvonen a tiny gap between his thumb and index finger, and Sauvonen slowly releases the clutch. I don't see the car move, but I assume it must have edged a few millimetres closer to the loading bay because Juhani's panting and low-pitched growls intensify. He is in a tight spot, quite literally a jam, and in what looks like a particularly awkward position. His left leg is stuck between the car and the loading bay, his right leg is trying to climb up onto the bay, and the rest of him is lying quite uncomfortably across the car's bonnet. Liitokangas is the first to notice my arrival.

'We're not really getting anywhere with your new CEO,' he says.

I've walked along the bridge to where Juhani is stuck, and Sauvonen sees me from the car. He slams on the hand brake, switches off the engine and jumps out.

'He's about as useless as you,' says Sauvonen, pointing at Juhani.

'I wouldn't go that far...' Juhani gasps.

'So, what exactly is the problem?' I ask.

Sauvonen looks at me as though I have said something to offend him personally. Liitokangas slowly shakes that giant chin of his.

'The problem,' he begins, 'is that this so-called CEO claims he can't afford to pay for the equipment we've delivered.'

'Same shit, different arsehole,' Sauvonen confirms.

Sauvonen's words prove in part what I've suspected all along – they affirm my calculations, and at the same time they give me the chance to proceed a little more quickly than I'd been planning.

'That doesn't sound right,' I say. 'Our financial situation is about to change.'

Sauvonen and Liitokangas exchange glances, while Juhani's eyes widen and he shakes his head, really wobbles it back and forth, but only at me. His expression tells me he wants me to keep quiet. But I'm only just getting started.

'We are slightly modifying our business structure,' I say, 'selling off part of the park, maybe all of it. We've already been in negotiations, and we've had an offer.'

Sauvonen turns to Juhani, who stops shaking his head as though he has run into a wall – which is, after all, literally the case.

'That means there *will* be money coming your way,' says Sauvonen. 'Why did you say there's no money?'

I know Juhani. He's pretending he hasn't heard the question. Sauvonen takes a step closer, leans over him.

'You get money from selling a business, right?' he asks, stressing each word individually.

'Yes,' says Juhani. 'You get money from selling a business.'

Sauvonen remains leaning over Juhani for a few seconds more, then stands up straight and turns to Liitokangas. 'Can I release the hand brake?'

Liitokangas looks at me. 'How do we know you'll pay up once the park is sold?'

'We'll have a binding contract,' I say. 'And we'll sign it.'

'And when will this happen?' he asks.

It is a bleak, grey day. Maybe this is why I think of the warmth of the Curly Cake Café and the fragrant, oven-hot pastries. The Blueberry Whirl and the Hot-Chocolate Hiccups. They come to mind without even trying. Naturally, I'm not especially enjoying seeing my brother pinned between a car and the adventure park – even though he got himself stuck in this predicament all by himself – and I don't like having to use my mathematical and contractual expertise for arrangements like this, but right now I can't see any other options. I want to save my life, I want to save the park – and I want to save Juhani too, whether he realises it or not.

'The paperwork is all ready,' I say. 'Shall we sit down?'

As they leave, Liitokangas and Sauvonen threaten us both once more for good measure. Most of the threats are aimed at Juhani, which is understandable: before ending up crushed by the car, Juhani had made it clear to Toy of Finland that he runs the park now and he's the one who makes the decisions, so the buck stops with him. Sauvonen glowers at us from the door of the Curly Cake, the dark monorail of his eyebrows accentuating his expression, then the two men disappear.

The sound world in the café is the usual: the steady din is punctuated with higher shrieks and squeals, and at times with loud cries. Dishes clatter, chair legs rattle and scrape across the floor. Juhani and I sit next to each other. The men from Toy of Finland had been sitting across the table from us, both enjoying their Bandit's Butterscotch Buns and glasses of Raspberry Hiss. Finally, Juhani breaks the silence.

'My own brother,' he says, stands up and walks out of the café.

23

In the last two and a half days, Laura Helanto has worked harder and more quickly than I've seen anyone work before. I count myself here too, even during the period when I was able to dedicate myself solely to conundrums of the actuarial variety.

Now she is working on all of her new pieces at once. They are growing in size and their exterior and appearance are gradually starting to take shape, and once again I have to admit that I very much like what I see, though I don't necessarily understand why. Laura Helanto gives me a carefree smile and says that's what art is all about, that's its nature. I'm still not entirely convinced by this argument. I am sure there must be a rational, logical explanation for this. The gigantic steel petal built alongside the O'Keeffe mural is a startling, violet optical illusion, which is at its best when seen from two different perspectives: the viewer can see his friend disappearing inside the O'Keeffe mural then reappearing as the petal turns. The whole structure is so beautiful that it almost forces me to stand there looking at it. And I do, until Laura asks if I could help her for a moment. I follow her from the Georgia O'Keeffe to the Tove Jansson.

Laura's reimagining of Jansson's seaside landscapes has a melancholy beauty of its own, but the cosy-looking fisherman's hut now standing next to it, complete with fishing nets hung along the walls, makes its somehow more real and alive, though the entire hut and everything around it is merely a three-dimensional extension of the mural itself.

I hold on to the fishing nets and admire the hut. Laura Helanto is working with her back to me, so she can't see what is happening behind my back either. Both of us hear Osmala's voice at the same time.

'I think I can say these are going to be even greater than I'd imagined.'

I turn my head.

'These have the same kind of skill, optical illusion, the element of revelation, and that certain serious playfulness you find in the works of, say, Markus Kåhre,' says Osmala, and I notice both from the angle of his face and his tone of voice that he is directing his words exclusively at Laura. 'And I say this with the utmost respect for both of you.'

'Thank you,' says Laura, and smiles.

They both smile. I'm still clutching the fishing nets. Then Osmala turns his attention to me. He's not smiling anymore.

'I hear you're taking a back seat,' he says. 'Stepping back from the front line, as it were.'

I confirm this is the case, but I say nothing else.

'Everything going to plan?' he asks.

The question takes me by surprise. It is said in the kind of only half-interested voice you might use to ask about the weather.

'Overall, yes,' I say, honestly.

Osmala looks as though he is trying to say something but doesn't say it. This is a rare occurrence; one might say, unique. Osmala has never hesitated before. The moment passes quickly, then he returns his attention to Laura and Tove Jansson.

'Best not stand here admiring your unfinished work,' he says. 'I'll be back when it's all done and dusted.' Then he glances at me, and adds: 'I want the surprise to be perfect.'

He wishes Laura good luck with the rest of her tasks and looks as though he really has come to the park for no other reason but to admire this work in progress. But given my calculations and past experiences, I find that hard to believe. Once Osmala has disappeared behind the Trombone Cannons, Laura tugs one end of the net.

'Let's bring up the nets,' she says. 'Then we can have a break. Looks like you could do with a little walk.'

Laura Helanto is, of course, absolutely right. Except in thinking I want to walk. It took us several minutes to attach the nets to the walls of the fisherman's hut, and now all I want to do is run. But I don't. I walk briskly through the park, trying to avoid a group of oncoming customers moving in a most unpredictable fashion. I slow my step as I approach the start of the corridor, at the other end of which is what is now Juhani's office. The corridor is empty. I step silently. The door to Minttu K's office stands open; I can't hear any sounds coming from inside, but I'll have to walk past that door. There are no points for artistic merit here; what's most important is getting to within earshot of Juhani's office. Whatever Juhani and Osmala are talking about, and very possibly agreeing between themselves, will have direct consequences both for my timetable and my future plans. I make sure to place my feet very softly and carefully on the floor, ensuring that my steps are as long as possible, which will shorten the number of steps I need to take, thereby reducing the risk of being caught. I'm just approaching the last bend in the corridor when...

'Honey,' I hear a rough voice from my side. 'Hey, Batman, triple-jumper...'

I look to the side. I've just placed a long step past Minttu K's doorway, but from her sofa she has a direct sightline into the corridor.

'There's no one there,' she says and takes a drag on her cigarette. 'Hasn't been for ages. They just had a little chat.'

'Chat?' I ask and straighten myself up. Once I have reached my normal position and height again, my physical wellbeing improves by a factor of around one hundred percent. 'Did you hear what they were talking about?'

'No, but when they left I heard what Juhani said to the tall, stiff guy,' Minttu K croaks. 'That this is the last time.'

'The last time?'

'Yeah, like in the movies,' she says, takes a long sip from her can of *lonkero* then wipes the corner of her mouth. 'Which always means it isn't really. The last time, I mean.'

Minttu K's common sense and clarity of thought have left an impression on me in the past. Which obviously stands in stark contrast to what I can see with my own eyes and smell with my own nostrils here in the low-lit room. I decide to dismiss the most acute of my sensory observations and tell myself that, right now, every single crumb of information is a tool I can use to solve the equation.

'What makes you think this isn't really the last time?'

Minttu K looks at me from across the room, crosses her right leg over her left, drags on her cigarette and blows the smoke right out in front of her.

'This morning, Juhani suggested I sell my apartment and invest the money in the adventure park,' she says after a beat. 'According to him, in a year's time I'll have enough money to buy two apartments, or one that's twice as big. He insisted that in only twelve months my investment would increase by over a hundred percent. Of course, he admitted there's a certain amount of risk to this kind of investment and maybe the amount of appreciation won't be quite that high, but in all probability that's the general direction of travel, if we all invest, and that we all need to think of the bigger picture. I told him that's exactly what I'm doing and that's why I won't be selling my flat or investing my money in the adventure park. Juhani asked why I even need a flat when I sleep here on the sofa or spend my nights elsewhere. I threw the question back at him and asked why he needs an adventure park if he doesn't know how to run it. Then he asked what's wrong with all the staff round here, as only a moment ago we were all gunning for French bistros, warships and therapy groups. I asked whether he'd already asked everybody else, and he said yes, and apparently everybody said no. He came to me last because he assumed I'd have drunk all my money anyway. That really offended me. I'm a moderate drinker, I have way less than thirty-six units a day.'

I'm standing in the doorway, thinking several thoughts all at once. Juhani has likely reached the end of the road. He's used up all his opportunities, pulled every string. Osmala has him in his grip. And, paradoxically, Minttu K has just admitted to having a drinking problem: I remember reading that the definition of a heavy drinker is thirty-six units *per week*.

'So,' Minttu K continues before I have the chance to thank her or do anything else, 'I think it looks like Juhani has got himself in a situation where he's going to find it really difficult to say no to someone who might be blackmailing him.'

Yet again, the clarity of Minttu K's thought is bewildering. All this she deduced from overhearing a single sentence. She knocks back the rest of whatever is in her can.

'And I know all this,' she says as she lights another cigarette, 'because the tall, stiff guy told Juhani he has twenty-four hours to sort it out.'

24

I am an actuary.

And I feel acutely aware of this fact right now, sitting in a chilled car in Rastila for three hours on the trot. It is a cold and dark night. The landscape has been stripped of all life: leaves from the trees, people from the streets, lights from the windows. I think of actuarial mathematics and how much it has taught me over the years about the stochastic nature of human behaviour. When carefully defined, insurance mathematics is simply an application of mathematics and data analysis whereby the mathematician assesses the probability – the risk – of any given event, in order to define an insurance policy that will be economically viable for the insurer. When we exclude the final insurance payment from the equation, we are left with a highly functional method of approaching any matter or event. Including – and in particular – tonight's events.

I have parked the car around one hundred and thirty metres from the entrance. The gates leading into the campsite and the area immediately around them are very well lit, so distance shouldn't be a problem. And it won't be easy to identify me sitting in my car, which is partly hidden behind the lorry parked in front. My problems are more internal; they are the culmination of conflicting wishes and expectations. Even in this respect, mathematics can help us. It doesn't care about our wishes and ex-pectations. It doesn't approach my problems emotionally or by in any way colouring reality. It tells us the truth, unflinchingly and unequivocally. And right now it doesn't even take forty minutes.

It happens in the early hours, at twenty-one minutes past one.

I recognise the car from the bonnet. A red Toyota Avensis. The car glides forwards, slowly and surely. Bumper, bonnet, front tyres – and the driver sitting behind the wheel. The car continues inching its way forwards, then comes fully into view – towing a caravan behind it. The red car pulls the yellow-striped caravan right out into the road, the short convoy straightens itself up and starts making its way towards me. The sections of the road are at a diagonal to each other and there's a crossroads in between. The car and the caravan slowly take the slight incline, arrive at the crossroads then turn left, or from my perspective, right. Towards the end of the curve, the car is only about twenty metres from me. The streetlamps are bright, and I can see the driver's profile, clear and photogenic and shaded like a silhouette.

My own brother, Juhani.

Running away.

And taking all the variables into account, it's all too logical.

Strictly speaking, the moment is only brief, but it feels distinctly longer, as if all the hours I've spent waiting were in fact part of this same, inevitable event.

An insurance company knows that, among all the people it insures, there will always be someone who enjoys mountain climbing, motocross, jumping from tall buildings or swallowing burning torches, but a good insurance company will even insure a person like that. This person's risks are taken into account in all the other policies, where the greatest risk is falling asleep on top of the remote control. Probability does its job, the risks are all accounted for. All we have to do is recognise this fact.

And, when all is said and done, who do I know better than my own brother?

In his own way, he's like a Swiss clock. And right now, as I see his pale features and his hunched, slightly agitated driving position, it makes me sad. I calculated everything, and I knew what he would do. There's nothing new about this. Nothing about him has changed. The equation gives the same answer every time. This time, my only uncertainty was about the order in which everything would happen, and in this respect the help of Pentti Osmala – via Minttu K – was crucial. Right now, the thought that I am doing this in Juhani's best interests and to save the park doesn't soothe me as I watch his lonely nocturnal flight and think of him ending up somewhere in the woods, in a faraway campsite where he will...

...soon get himself into new and as yet unknown difficulties.

And there's something about this thought, as the car pulls out into the road, that's almost a little comforting, hopeful even. Juhani will continue being Juhani. I wish I could flash my lights at him, wish I could make him stop. I wish we could talk things through, that I could make him understand what I'm trying to do. And that as a result of this conversation he might change his ways and together we could look for a way out of our current predicaments.

But mathematics and the laws of probability don't care about what I want. Juhani, the car and the caravan have turned all they need to. The convoy straightens itself and disappears into the night.

Instinctively I am about to bid him farewell, but I can't seem to make any sounds at all. There's something caught in my throat, something filling it up.

25

But I don't have time to think about Juhani anymore. Not tonight. I make two quick phone calls, start the car and drive off.

I arrive in Konala at one minute to two in the morning.

The offices and warehouse belonging to Toy of Finland are dark. Liitokangas and Sauvonen left the premises at eight o'clock this evening, and there hasn't been any sign of them since. I know this because Hannes Tolkki has been monitoring his former business all afternoon. I find Tolkki in his old van and climb inside. Tolkki complains about his back but says, other than that, he's ready. I believe it. The streetlamps cast only a faint glow, but I can see Tolkki's face clearly. There's that same stoic determination as when he tried to cut me in half with a chainsaw.

We wait another fifteen minutes.

Then a lorry approaches from the opposite direction. The trailer behind it is long. The lorry slowly pulls up in front of us. At first it passes the gates to the Toy of Finland warehouse, then it slows down, steers the cab to the other side of the road and comes to a stop.

Tolkki and I pull the balaclavas over our heads, step out of the van and start walking towards the gates. We advance as quickly as Tolkki's back will permit. Our speed isn't great, but there's a sense of purpose in his steps. We arrive at the gate, Tolkki types in the security code. The code is correct, but on top of that we need a key. He has one of those too. He has kept all the keys to the business that was stolen from him. I never knew why I kept them, he told me in Tapanila, but now I know. Once the lock is released, I push the gate open and hear the lorry's engine roar into life.

The lorry starts reversing, and Tolkki waves his hands to guide it through the gates. This is unnecessary because the plan includes detailed drawings of the warehouse and the forecourt and the secluded spot where the lorry will stand parked for the next hour and a half. I close the gates behind us. The lorry comes to a stop, the engine falls silent, the lights are switched off. The lorry doors open, and Esa and Kristian – both in balaclavas – jump out of the cab. We congregate at the warehouse door, which Tolkki opens with another one of his keys. Then he keys in the security code to disable the alarm system, and returns to his van to keep watch. Kristian, Esa and I go inside, but we don't switch on the main lights. We plan to complete our task using only flashlights and in record time.

We have come to catch a moose.

Luckily, our intelligence was correct. The current owners of Toy of Finland have only partially constructed the Moose Chute. We only have to dismantle a small part of this massive machine, which will considerably help our operation.

Esa and Kristian work silently and efficiently. I leave the warehouse door open and notice that both Kristian and I are trying our best to work, as it were, upwind from Esa. But though from time to time I have to move to keep myself on the right side of the breeze, I don't consider Esa's navy-seal diet a bad thing; it seems to raise everybody's productivity levels.

Esa was my last recruit for tonight's mission. He agreed immediately because, as he sees it, this is a diplomatic way of maintaining the park's inalienable right to self-determination. And, as he freely admits, this is a timely reminder that the monitor room is his and his alone, and that he has not forgotten Otto Härkä's unauthorised incursion into his territory. I don't know how Esa knows about the visit, and I haven't asked.

I haven't forgotten Otto Härkä either, and that's part of

tonight's plan too. Once the situation with the Moose Chute starts to look promising, I take a walk around the warehouse – and find everything except the Crocodile Canyon. Whenever I shine my torch, I see bright colours, yellows, reds, blues, but I can't see any bright-green crocodiles or canoes, and by extension I cannot see Otto Härkä either. Eventually I have to conclude that the crocodiles have disappeared, taking Otto Härkä with them. I return from my walk and stop at the dismembered Moose Chute.

An hour and a half was a good estimate.

We open the warehouse's large folding door and start loading parts into the back of the lorry.

Kristian is sitting in the forklift truck, as though it were a race car, and Esa is using the lift platform at the back as though it were an extension of his own body, and in every other respect is moving as though he really has been trained by special forces. The back of the lorry quickly starts to fill up.

We close the doors at the back, then glance at one another.

Now for our final tasks.

Kristian and Esa open the sports bag they brought with them and take out the necessary tools, while I return to the warehouse. I run the flashlight around the tall, empty space. Everything is exactly as it was when we arrived; the only things missing are the Moose Chute and, along with it, Toy of Finland's future. I take out Kuisma Lohi's leather gloves, which I slipped into my pocket while sitting on the back seat of his expensive car. I don't know why I did it, but somehow I knew that one day they would come in handy. I place the gloves on a counter by the wall, making sure to leave their embroidered initials facing upwards.

I return to the door, switch the alarm system back on and close the door behind me. Esa is walking back from the gates, where he has smashed the lock to make it look like a break-in. He climbs up into the cab while Kristian batters the folding door until the alarm goes off, then prises the alarm system from the wall with a crowbar. After this, he jumps into the lorry, and I run to my car. I give Hannes Tolkki the okay, the van does a U-turn and disappears around the corner. The lorry glides out of the gate, turns back in the direction it came from and pulls into the distance.

I start the car and leave Konala behind me.

26

I send the email as soon as I get home. Sitting at the kitchen table, it takes time to find the correct phraseology, because Otto Härkä had a rather florid way of expressing himself. I recall the conversations we've had, I hear his voice and his long-winded negotiating style with its undercurrent of total obduracy. Forty-five minutes later, I've drawn up an email in which Otto Härkä explains how he has come to find himself in a pretty precarious position: his business associates want to make a deal with Kuisma Lohi, and he objects to the deal. According to Härkä, the situation is potentially life-threatening. I end the email there and schedule its release for a few hours hence, adding a sentence in which Härkä explains that the message will be sent, unless he is able to deactivate it within the next twenty-four hours. I don't think it's too much of a stretch to say that Otto Härkä will not deactivate the message. And thus, Detective Inspector Pentti Osmala of the Helsinki organised-crime and fraud units will receive the message before long.

I operate the way Juhani once taught me and send the message via the dark web. This way, the sender and IP address remain anonymous.

This is the most speculative part of my plan, I must admit. Not just because, right now, Otto Härkä has rowed his canoe into uncharted waters, but because the message must lead to direct action. In this regard, with a probability of almost one hundred percent, I can rely on the remaining owners of Toy of Finland for help. In this equation, Sauvonen and Liitokangas are the variables whose values I know to the greatest degree of certainty; in their case, x can only be the multiplier.

Hannes Tolkki calls at eight a.m. and wakes me in my armchair.

All night, Tolkki has been changing cars and lookout positions, and he tells me his back is feeling much better too. But none of this is the main news item. The headline is that Sauvonen and Liitokangas have arrived in Konala. The men went into the warehouse building, then came out again, looking visibly agitated. But they did not call the police.

I call Esa.

He gives me a detailed update of the night's events, carefully and chronologically, then tells me that both Kristian and the lorry are now in the designated location and that Kristian is still working at the same pace and with the same intensity as earlier that night, explaining that now he's even ahead of all the people who wake up at three. Esa informs me that the terrain allowed us to conduct reconnaissance operations 'in all forms'. He stresses these last three words. Then he tells me that Kuisma Lohi is alone at his mansion in Marjaniemi, that he has just come out of the shower, where he used copious amounts of expensive shower gel, then prepared himself a breakfast of eggs Benedict on brioche with crispy bacon and hollandaise sauce. I don't ask Esa how he knows all this, but I thank him for his excellent work.

I sit down at the computer again. This time the message is from Kuisma Lohi to Toy of Finland. Lohi informs them that the offer is now only a tenth of what it was before. Kuisma Lohi speaks down to Toy of Finland like a manager to a subordinate. I have first-hand experience of this, I remember our conversation word for word. I write the message quickly and press send. Then I wait for Hannes Tolkki's next phone call. This happens seventeen minutes later.

Sauvonen and Liitokangas have left Konala.

Until now, all communications have gone through a phone that I will soon dispose of. And now, I pick up my own phone and call Osmala.

What happens next, I learn from Esa. Liitokangas and Sauvonen arrive at Marjaniemi. They gain entry to the property. A struggle ensues. Before long, Kuisma Lohi is being dangled by his feet from the balcony facing out towards the sea. They ask him where the Moose Chute has gone. Kuisma Lohi hurls insults at them, even though he is hanging upside down in the bracing morning breeze. Meanwhile, Osmala arrives at the property. The door is open. Osmala walks in through the front door, the noises are coming from the back of the property. Sauvonen notices Osmala, leaves Liitokangas holding Lohi by the ankles, dashes into the living room and grabs a large southern-European steel sculpture (the piece is called 'The Scabbard'), holds it aloft and charges right at Osmala. Osmala raises his weapon and fires. Neither man hits his intended target. Sauvonen trips on the leg of an armchair, Osmala's bullet hits a painting depicting a Finnish rural idyll. Still carrying 'The Scabbard', Sauvonen falls to the floor on his stomach, regrettably sticking the tapered point of the sculpture right into a power socket as he does so. All the lights in the house go off at once. Osmala sees both Sauvonen, thrashing on the floor, and Liitokangas, who is still dangling Lohi from the balcony, and reads Liitokangas's intentions. Liitokangas lets go of Kuisma Lohi. Kuisma Lohi calls Liitokangas an imbecile, then disappears from view. Osmala points his weapon at Liitokangas.

Esa retreats from his lookout point.

27

Osmala suggests we meet somewhere other than the adventure park. The reason, he says, is that he doesn't want to see Laura Helanto's new works before they are ready. This may well be true, I think, though at the same time I expect that 'somewhere else' might very quickly turn into the police station. For a moment there is perfect silence at the other end of the phone. Then Osmala suggests a place, and I note that it is suitably far away from the police station in Pasila.

In the six days that have passed since I called Osmala and alerted him to the situation in Marjaniemi, winter has arrived.

In that phone call almost a week ago, I told him – honestly – that the owners of Toy of Finland have been threatening me and are most likely threatening Kuisma Lohi too. Osmala was particularly brief in that phone call but said he would go to Marjaniemi to take a look.

Now he's waiting for me on the shores of a certain small pond.

The daylight and the thin, pure-white layer of the first snow make the landscape look rather different from how I'm used to seeing it. There are three vehicles on the shore, one of them an unmarked van belonging to the police. I pull up at the end of the line in the adventure park's Renault and step out of the van. It is a cold, bright, windless day. The first snow won't last long; in places, it has already melted into puddles, making the ground black and shining. My shoes are wholly inappropriate for the shore, but on the other hand their very inappropriateness is essential. I don't want to give the impression that I know this area or how muddy the banks and pathways are around here, how cold and wet everything is. I squelch my way over to Osmala, who is standing almost at the waterline, and I notice that, as he greets me, he very quickly glances down at my feet. I know what I have to ask.

'Is there a reason we're meeting out here?'

Osmala looks as though he is weighing things up. I've learnt a lot about the ways in which he tries to create an imbalance between himself and his interlocutor, and this is one of them. It's as though he were suddenly embarking upon an exceptionally strenuous bout of thinking and pondering, the kind he's never tried before.

'Perhaps you remember I told you about the guy we fished out of here,' he says with a nod towards the pond. 'The one with a ticket to your park in his pocket.'

I do indeed remember.

'Though, of course, you don't have anything to do with the matter,' he continues, 'but it suddenly occurred to me that because there's a connection between this pond and your park, you and I could come out here and brainstorm a little.'

Osmala looks at me, and I look back and consider that it was only six days ago that he fired his weapon at a Finnish pastoral landscape and I abducted the largest moose in Europe, and that these two events are linked in a not insignificant way. Still, I don't see the need for any mutual brainstorming. For a variety of reasons.

'Let me tell you a bit about what we're doing here today.' Osmala nods once again, then points towards the cottage. The same cottage whose pontoon bridge Juhani and I borrowed a short while ago. 'We're conducting a little investigation over by that cottage. We're not going to get anything definitive, DNA or anything like that, but we've concluded that the guy that ended up at the bottom of the pond must have been transported from that jetty over there. We're trying to reconstruct the storyline, you'll appreciate. Maybe that will help us make some progress.'

'Quite,' I say, keen to change the subject. This is only natural; given the connection between the victim and my park, it would be strange if I weren't at least at little interested in the matter. 'What about Marjaniemi? I gather there was some kind of ... altercation.'

Osmala doesn't seem at all perturbed by my change of direction. He takes a deep breath, gazes out across the pond.

'You were right. Toy of Finland were in no mood for playing silly buggers. We've got two men in intensive care. One fell from the balcony, the other stuck a piece of contemporary artwork into the power socket. A very nice piece, I might add. The former is in an induced coma, the latter ended up unconscious all by himself. Doctors suspect both will end up with lasting brain damage. There was a third man there too, but he's not talking. And one of the men from Toy of Finland seems to have disappeared into thin air.'

Osmala returns his grey eyes to me. The pond behind him gleams a dark blue.

'And when I say all this out loud,' he continues, 'and think for a moment and look at it from different angles, it's hard to avoid the thought that behind the apparent chaos there must be something planned, something more logical. People sometimes talk about the domino effect, one piece knocks the next piece over, and so on. What if everything that's happened wasn't a coincidence after all? What if, perhaps, there's a little mathematical thinking involved?'

I say nothing.

'Well, this is just me semi-officially thinking out loud,' says Osmala. 'Fishing, if you will. Unless there's something you'd like to tell me.'

I shake my head. 'I don't know what I could possibly add,' I say, perfectly honestly.

Osmala remains silent for a moment.

'Don't suppose you've seen your brother in the last few days?'

'No, I have not.'

'And you don't know where he is?'

'No.'

All this is true. I have not seen Juhani, I have not heard from him and I don't know where he is.

'Pity,' says Osmala after a beat. 'I was really looking forward to our next meeting.'

Again I say nothing. I recall the story Minttu K told me. And I get the distinct impression our conversation is reaching an end. I start to turn, the wet ground spatters under my feet.

'This was just my little way of helping to jog your memory,' says Osmala halfway through my turn. 'In case you remember anything or notice anything. Just in case this place has some particular significance for you. But we'll have plenty of opportunities to return to this subject. I'll be seeing you again very soon.'

Osmala looks me right in the eyes.

'As soon as that artist of yours finishes her new project,' he adds.

THREE WEEKS LATER

The opening of Laura Helanto's exhibition is a great success. I'm happy to reach this conclusion barely half an hour after the doors are opened. I walk among the assembled guests (at a quick glance I count seventy-three) with my tray, listening to people's enthralled comments, and I find myself filling up with a feather-light yet steely strong sensation. It's almost like being drunk. I soon realise that this is what pride feels like. My tray is laden with the Christmassy treats that Johanna has conjured up, and I have to remind myself not to eat them myself. I think to myself that Johanna has clearly raised her game a notch or two, as they say, as the tray is suddenly empty again and I have to fill it up. I deliberately take the longer route to the kitchen so I can admire our latest acquisition. In all honesty, I could probably see part or parts of it from any location in the park, but I'm so happy with it that every day since its arrival I have visited it simply to make sure it is real.

The Moose Chute is real.

It arrived at the park from Tapanila, and Kristian and Esa assembled it. It stands tall and dominates this part of the park, its antlers almost touching the ceiling. What's more, the park has signed a new, long-term payment agreement with the current owner of Toy of Finland, Hannes Tolkki. This, in turn, was only possible because of the agreement that I had already signed with Juhani, Kari Liitokangas and Jeppe Sauvonen. That agreement gave the owner of the Duck Tunnel the opportunity to return the item in the event that either Toy of Finland or its owners are found to have broken contractual law – or any other law, for that matter – and to select a replacement item from the catalogue. The same principle applied to the repurchasing clause regarding the entire company, and using this clause I managed to return ownership of Toy of Finland, via the adventure park, to its rightful owner, Hannes Tolkki. Osmala was right: everything has been a combination of domino effect and following a carefully laid plan. To my great satisfaction, I can say that our customer numbers are once again on the up.

But even more than the Moose Chute, I am fascinated by Laura's artworks. Their ingenuity, their forms, shapes, colours and different dimensions offer something new and pleasing every time I look at them. I no longer even try to think of a rational explanation for why they captivate me so profoundly that I could stand there examining them for hours. I like them, that's all, and I let them awaken exactly the kind of thoughts and emotions they want to. This is a new experience for me, and, naturally, it too comes from Laura Helanto.

I continue on my way towards the Curly Cake Café. Again I see the part of the park where most of the guests are milling around, talking feverishly and pointing at the works. I see a few of the park's employees among them. Esa is taking care of security, Johanna is in charge of the catering, Samppa is keeping the conversation going and offering support to anyone who needs it, Kristian is the general technical manager, making sure everything is running smoothly, and Minttu K is mingling voraciously, striking up marketing deals not only for the park but for Laura Helanto's artwork too.

I head straight for the kitchen. I leave the empty tray in the sink and step towards the fridge to choose one of the many full ones. One of the trays instantly catches my attention. Some of the treats have already been nibbled, and there are teeth marks in them.

I know of only one person who would do something like this. Only one person who thinks (probably sincerely) that nobody will notice little nibbles like this, that nobody will notice his little incursions because they are only small, harmless and barely even visible. I return to the hall and gaze out across the crowds but can't find what I'm looking for. Then I think back to where all this began. I sigh, then walk to my office and stop at the door.

Juhani is standing with his back to me, going through some papers on the desk. He lifts them, turns them, gives them a cursory glance, then puts them back at random. He is doing this so feverishly, with such concentration, that he doesn't hear my arrival. I let him examine the desk a moment longer, then say:

'Looking for something in particular?'

Juhani spins around.

'Henri!' He only seems confused and surprised for a fleeting moment. Then he's back to being Juhani again. 'Great to see you. You've got a party going on, I didn't want to disturb. I see you've finally got the Moose Chute. So, everything was cleared up in the end.'

He smiles, as though everything being cleared up was his doing. And that's quite possibly what he thinks too, I imagine. I realise that though I'm still filled with joy and happiness, that feeling is in danger of fading and disappearing, sliding into something altogether different. And so, I must be as quick as possible.

'As I said,' I begin, 'if you're looking for something in particular, it'll be faster if you ask me. The opening party is—'

'A roaring success, of course it is!' Juhani interrupts me. 'Listen, Henri, there's no need to worry.'

I say nothing. Throughout my entire life, every time Juhani says there's nothing to worry about, it always means the exact opposite.

'Anyway, it's not this adventure park I've come back for,' he says. 'I just came to see ... if I've forgotten anything.'

It takes a moment to fully grasp what I've just heard. And I don't mean Juhani's last sentence.

'*This* adventure park?' I say. 'Which adventure park have you come back for then?'

I can see from Juhani's expression that, once again, he realises he has said something he shouldn't have.

'I just mean I'm not, I mean, I don't want to ... run or ... be ... I don't want what I used to want. That's what you wanted to hear. So now you've heard it. The park's yours. All of it. Good news, right? Your evening just keeps getting better...'

Words gush from his mouth. I watch him. Something about him has changed. He isn't as desperate as the last time we saw each other. I can see it in his body language, hear it in the levity of his voice. He's regained a certain ... certainty. I'm beginning to think I know the reason why.

'You just said you're not interested in the park. And you haven't even mentioned money. What's happened?'

Now Juhani shifts position, he seems to stand more sturdily, and his expression turns serious.

'Right, yeah,' he says. 'In fact, you and I might have some shared interests there. Given my new job and who I'm working for.'

'Really?'

Juhani nods firmly.

'I'm a consultant,' he says.

'Good for you,' I say sincerely. 'Congratulations on your new job. And who are you ... consulting?'

'Right now, Somersault City in Espoo,' he says. 'But I'm still a free agent...'

I raise a hand, my palm facing Juhani, to stop him in his tracks. 'Our competitor?' I ask.

'They really value my expertise in the field and they're looking to increase footfall in a big way,' he says. 'And they're aiming to shore up their position as market leader in the adventure-park scene in and around the capital...'

'I know what their aims are,' I say. 'I'd be careful with them. They're not members of the Association of Finnish Adventure Parks. There's something not quite right about their ownership structure. And I don't know how they've got enough money for the constant expansion and acquisitions. Their customer numbers can't grow that fast, though we temporarily lost a few customers in their direction. But that's not even the crux of the matter. The bottom line is, you cannot work for me and them at the same time.'

'I'm a freelance consultant.'

'Maybe, but if you work for two adventure parks at the same time, you might be a freelance industrial spy too. I'll have to ask you to leave.'

Juhani looks as though I've just slapped him round the face. He's offended.

'After everything I've done for you.'

I didn't plan to say what I say next, but I realise at some point I have to tell him I know what happened.

'I was almost murdered because of you,' I say. 'Round the back of the park.'

Juhani doesn't seem nearly as perturbed that I know what I know as he does about the accusation itself.

'I saved you,' he says.

'From a situation that you created.'

Juhani shakes his head. Now he is both offended and agitated.

'Henri,' he says. And I can hear the anger in his voice. 'Without my help, they're going to crush you.'

The room is suddenly silent. I imagine it must be down to several simultaneous factors. We have both said what we've been meaning to say, what we've wanted to get off our chests. Juhani has done what he came here to do: to look for something without finding it, to try to sell something nobody wants to buy. And I have let him know what I know and learnt what I feared. Juhani straightens his blazer. He looks at me, his expression tense but perhaps a little apologetic.

'This is war,' he says. 'Adventure-park war.'

I say nothing. Juhani stares at me a moment longer, then sets off. I hear his footsteps disappear along the corridor, then I watch him from the window as he walks through the Christmas lights in the car park towards his Toyota, sits down and drives away.

I return to the exhibition and the opening gala via the Curly Cake Café. Carrying my tray, I walk with determination – I have a clear goal and destination. Once I reach it, the tray is empty and I hand it to Kristian, who takes it back to the café like a runner who has grabbed a relay baton.

This is my goal, my destination: Laura Helanto. She notices me, thanks the couple standing in front of her, then turns towards me. She is holding a bunch of roses, her cheeks are almost as dark red as the petals, there is a glimmer of happiness and emotion in her eyes, and she kisses me on the lips.

We place an arm around each other, and during the course of our kiss I calculate what I have to do in order to keep all this, to keep our happiness.

Now I know where to start.

ACKNOWLEDGEMENTS

I would like to thank the one and only Karen Sullivan at Orenda Books for publishing this book in the English-speaking world, and for her support and kindness over the years. It's a true privilege to work with you. Warmest thank you and much admiration for the English translation to David Hackston, who makes translating Finnish seem like an easy, natural thing to do (which it is not, I assure you). Thank you to West Camel for the precise editing and continuous support. Thank you, the talented Mark Swan, for yet another killer cover. Thank you to Cole Sullivan for working hard on behalf of my books in the UK and elsewhere. A huge thank you to my agent, Federico Ambrosini, and everybody else at Salomonsson Agency. I'm so grateful for the work you do. Thank you to the bloggers, festival organisers and literary helpers of every kind – you are so much appreciated. Thank you, Anu, I love you so much. Finally, thank you, dear Reader. I hope we meet again.

Antti Tuomainen
Helsinki, 2022